NO REFUGE

Thea M Hartley

Copyright © 2013 Thea M Hartley
All rights reserved.

ISBN: 1492867845
ISBN 13: 9781492867845

CHAPTER ONE

"Jodie"

I didn't scream. I just stood there in a state of shock, transfixed at the scene before me. I could see a leg poking out of the skip, where I was just about to deposit two black plastic bags. Next to the leg was a longish object which resembled a chewed up bone with bits of red meat still attached.

Queasily I realised it was the other leg. I dropped the bags and turned away from the skip to vomit.

My stomach retched until there was no more food left to expel. I could feel the perspiration running down my face and my heart beating so fast it was pounding in my eardrums. I managed to get my mobile phone out of the back pocket of my jeans and dialled 999. "Police and Ambulance" I said firmly, surprised at how steady my voice sounded " there's something in a skip ...I think it's a body ". "Where? ....at the side of Doctor Harrison's surgery in North Street.....yes, that's right, opposite the Church. Yes, I'll stay here. Jodie, Jodie Harrison," I rang off and proceeded to wait for the authorities to arrive.

A flurry of action started to evolve around the skip. I saw two paramedics arrive in their fluorescent jackets, weighed down by various lives - saving equipment. It was far too late for the life in the skip. I thought. Reluctantly they moved back from the scene as the Forensic Pathologist's team got its hands on the body after the initial police inspection of the corpse.

I stood in the shadows, still slightly nauseous, but deeply inquisitive. Who was this person dumped in with the rubbish and recycling bags? How did it get there? And more importantly who had disposed of a lover, relative, friend or stranger?

I really craved a cigarette despite my New Year's Resolution to abstain. I promised Josh no more fags, not if we were going to try for the baby we both wanted. My hands scrabbled around in my pocket in case some forlorn Benson and Hedges had somehow made its way into the depth of the lining. No such luck. I took some deep breaths instead, realising they were no substitute for the satisfying feeling of smooth smoke filling my throat and lungs and calming my jangled nerves.

A police officer sought me out. I was still half hidden in the shadows away from the site of the skip on the opposite side of the lane. "Excuse me madam " he said in that tone which coppers all seem to replicate " Can you tell me exactly what happened this evening ? " " It's pretty obvious officer " I said , shrugging my shoulders " I came out to the skip, which is ours by the way, and was just going to throw in two more black bags of rubbish, when I saw a limb...a human leg. I thought I was seeing things, so looked more closely and noticed what looked like a meat bone ...but I quickly realised it was the other leg . I'm afraid I felt really sick, turned away from the skip and I was sick...over there "I pointed to a large puddle of green and yellow vomit. The policeman took a cursory glance and looked quickly away. "Then I rang you ".

" What do you mean by it's your skip madam? "He asked "Just that. We hired it whilst we are renovating the premises. My husband is the late Dr Harrison's son and he has taken over the practice. We decided the house and surgery needed a complete overall, so we have been working on it for the past three months. It's almost nearing completion now. " " Just you and the doctor live here? " he asked " You make him sound like Doctor Who" I said , smiling, with an attempt at levity, which the police officer didn't seem to appreciate. "yes, " I sighed " just me and my husband " " Have you any idea who the person found in your skip is? " he asked solemnly " None whatsoever " I replied " I do not even know if the body is male or female , let alone their identity " "

"The body belongs to a dark haired Caucasian female, aged around 35 to 40 , slim build, around five foot four, with a tattoo on her left shoulder of a Celtic dragon and the name 'Chris' " he informed me, adhering strictly to his formal "police speak". "No idea then, "I shrugged "I know no one by that description and I would certainly remember a tattoo like that." " Would you

No Refuge

care to look at the body? "He asked" umm no thanks "I replied with a shiver. This was my husband's area, not mine. I was a college lecturer, not a medic. "OK " acknowledged the "friendly " policeman." Where is your husband? " " in a conference in London " I told him " Due back around 9 pm " " Well alright then Mrs Harrison " he gave a polite nod, " I'll say goodnight. One of my colleagues will be around to see you sometime tomorrow. "

I could see I was being dismissed, so I turned back into the house through the back garden. I opened the old wooden back door with its rusty latch. Made a mental note: "we'll have to replace that" and searched through the pockets of my old Barbour jacket which was hung on a hook in the small tiled porch. . I was just emptying out the fourth pocket when I struck gold! An old packet of Lambert and Butler, worse for wear, but containing two fags, albeit a bit bent.

I took the large box of kitchen matches from the high shelf above the door, and lit one of the elicit cigarettes. The hit was immediate. I felt my throat fill with soft smoke and the tang of tobacco and inhaled it down into my lungs, immediately calming all sensation. I stood by the back door and blew out the wisps of smoke which glided into the evening air, making patterns in the sky, before dispersing. Feeling better, I took another long, satisfying drag, and considered the events of the night, not yet knowing how they would impact on our lives and change my perceptions forever.

CHAPTER TWO

"Jodie"

"Hi, I'm home "it was Josh's voice. He called out as he arrived back from London " I'm in here love" I shouted from the half- finished living room , where I was curled up in an armchair , near the old, two bar electric fire. The house would be lovely when it was finished but at the moment it was like living in a building site.

He came into the room, looking ruffled, yet tired. I noticed purple shadows beneath his eyes, and his lower lip was slightly askew as he chewed at the side of it. "What's wrong?" I asked, immediately aware that something was bothering him.

"What's that yellow crime tape doing around our skip?" he demanded, obviously concerned "I found a body in it "I replied.

He looked at me with a strange expression in his eyes; I could have sworn it was suspicion. Did he think I bumped off strangers for fun when he was away? Immediately I became irritable "What are you looking at me like that for?" I snapped "I FOUND a body, I didn't bloody put it there" "I never thought you did "he insisted " but I did find a used cigarette butt by the back door ". I had the grace to blush, but said nothing.

"I called the police. All I saw was two legs....one was all chewed up ...like a dog's bone" I shuddered, pulling the conversation back to the body. He smiled wryly, but kept his eyes narrowed. "It's really upset me Josh. I haven't been able to eat or anything. Sitting alone here I've felt really vulnerable " " The dead can't hurt you " he replied dismissively " No, " I agreed . " but the person who made them dead can. " my voice was quivering and I could feel tears springing to my eyes. "Why would you think it has anything to do with you? "Josh enquired "I don't.... but it scared me. I'm not like you, I'm not used to dead bodies....I was sick, vomited all over the place. ". I tried to explain how I upset I felt to Josh, I wanted his sympathy.

"You shouldn't let yourself get in such a state "he replied "Why can't you understand? "I cried "For normal people this is a very upsetting experience "the tears had started to flow now. I kept imagining the chewed up leg sticking out of the skip. The dark, decaying flesh that was once a live human being. Josh handed me a handkerchief in an awkward attempt at kindness. I wiped my eyes and took a few gulps of air, trying to regain my composure. "Who was it?" asked Josh. "No idea" I said" a woman about 35 to 40 apparently. "

"So what happens now?" "The police said we have to leave the skip alone and they'll be back to see us, sometime tomorrow." Josh pulled a face which indicated annoyance. He was probably worrying about the renovations which were taking longer than expected already, I thought. Never mind someone's dead, and we could be in danger.

The surgery was just about completed, and was state of the art, with individual examination rooms, haematology, and nurse's clinics and well equipped consulting rooms. Josh had been seeing patients for the last three weeks. We moved in six weeks ago, leaving our old friends in Cardiff and Liverpool. We were making a new start in this valley practice.

The adjoining house, which we were now occupying, was, however, only half finished. The bedroom had a temporary wall. The bathroom consisted of one wobbly toilet, and the living room had a sheet hanging from the ceiling separating the plastered walls from the broken ones. The skip out of action and policemen milling around could only add to the general chaos and delay the building work even further. I could partially understand Josh's frustration.

"I'm starving "declared Josh "anything to eat?" " There's ham in the fridge and I bought some fresh bread and cheeses this afternoon. If you like I'll make you some sandwiches or we could order a takeaway. ". " I'll have some sandwiches then "he said, slumping into the other armchair in the room and loosening his tie.

He slumped back in the seat, and closed his eyes, kicking off his shoes and wriggling his toes. I got up and went into the tiny area known as the

No Refuge

'kitchen.' It was a small room, originally a scullery, at the back of the 19th century four bedroom house and was eventually going to become the utility room. At the moment however, it housed a small hob, microwave and a fridge with an old welsh bosh served by a loose tap on the end of a copper pipe which swayed as you tried to turn it. There was no boiler or hot water, so any we needed had to be boiled in a saucepan on the rickety gas camping stove. I took the ham and cheese from the fridge and the bread from a cupboard. On an old Formica table, I cut Josh a variety of sandwiches.

I returned to the living room to find him dozing in front of the electric fire. Gently, I shook him and gave him his snack. He looked confused for a moment, then shook his head and glanced at the plate. He picked up a ham sandwich and bit in with real hunger. I left the room and returned with two mugs of tea. We both sat in silence whilst Josh chewed and drank until all the sandwiches were demolished.

"I sent off some job applications today "I said hesitantly, looking at my feet, not at my husband." WHAT!" He shouted, as I had half expected. "I told you I want you here. To supervise the house renovations and to help with my practice. ". " I'm not a builder or a practice manager "I replied, feeling the tension knotting in my stomach as it so often did when we broached this subject. " I'm a college lecturer. I teach. That's what I do. I studied for years to qualify, I was one of the youngest women in the college to make senior lecturer, I need to work "." No you don't. I need you here "he insisted" and what about the baby? You agreed we'd try for a baby "I sighed deeply. I wanted a baby, yes, but sometimes they didn't come along that easily. Anyhow, I could work until I had one, and I could take maternity leave. I tried to explain this to Josh, but he didn't listen, he never did. All he would do was scowl at me and accuse me of wanting to get away from him and have a separate life. This was a load of nonsense of course, but there was no reasoning with him in this mood. I just picked up an old magazine off the floor and pretended to read it, holding my anger inside, hoping it would fade away. I was too tired to argue, especially after the events earlier in the evening. Josh dozed off again, and I left him to it.

By eleven o' clock I was fed up of sitting in silence and decided to go to bed. I called to Josh and he moved his head slightly, still asleep, so I roused him by shaking his arm " c'mon time for bed " I cajoled " Ummm...ok s'coming " he mumbled " I put out the sitting room light and put on the one in the hall.

Josh shook himself and ran his fingers through his thick, blonde hair. 'He's a good looking bugger ' I thought to myself, ' even tired and irritable, he still looks handsome and boyish, with an indefinable charisma. . I do wish he would relax at times and let things just happen '. It so infuriated me his constant planning. For the practice, the house, us. As if it all had to happen in distinct stages and at precise times. He lived to an internal timetable.

We made our way up to bed. I had filled a large bowl with hot water in the temporary 'bathroom', so that we could both have a quick wash. The bedroom was freezing. Our large kingside bed was set up away from the window, with a makeshift wardrobe (a rail) and mismatching bedside tables. I had piled two duvets on the top for warmth and usually went to bed in pyjamas, a cardigan and socks. Josh also donned jogging bottoms, a tee shirt and old jumper. This bedroom did not encourage intimacy.

Tonight, however, Josh pulled me towards him. He put his hands under my layers of clothing and on to my bare skin. His lips searched eagerly and met mine. To be honest, I was surprised at first, this was an unexpected turn of events, but soon, I responded to his kiss.

Our kisses became more passionate, we began to seek each other's tongues and chew each other's lips. I found his bare skin under his tee shirt, and he helped me pull the garment over his head, and took off my pyjama top and cardigan. We pressed our bodies together, reaching for each other, desire growing. Josh linked his thumbs over the elasticated waist of my pyjama bottoms and pulled them down, I shook my legs to free myself, whilst kissing and biting his bare chest on my way to his jogging pants. I pushed them down with my nose, as if rutting towards his cock and Josh gave a low, deep chuckle. He held my head downwards in one hand and unclothed him with the other. I continued my path, teasing him with my tongue. He took my face in his hands, pulling me upwards and kissed me long and deep, then licked my body down to my pubis. His tongue darted in and out, licking my clitoris. I could feel desire overwhelming me as an orgasm built up and my back arched. He touched me roughly, impatiently, teasing

No Refuge

me with his fingers. I caught hold of his cock, hard and engorged and led him towards me, opening my legs wider to allow access. He entered me from above, penetrating deeply. I could feel his hardness grow inside me, as he began to move, with slow, tantalising strokes, making me beg him to go harder...harder ...faster...faster. He picked up pace and we moved to the same rhythm pushing and plunging, rolling on to one side, then the other , finding him back on top of me ...and then...a glorious orgasm which released my desire and enveloped my whole body. Josh shuddered and stopped, collapsed upon me, his weight holding me down.

I was warm, for the first time in this bloody bed I felt warm! A laugh escaped my lips. Josh asked me what I was laughing at. I explained, and he joined in until we were both rolling about with mirth. I felt so close to him at times like this. Why couldn't we always be so happy, so carefree...so together?

Josh held me tightly to him. I snuggled into his warm body, feeling the perspiration on his chest. He caressed my hair with his fingers. I enjoyed the feeling of my long locks as they spread over my shoulders. I breathed in the musky smell of him, smiling to myself.

Josh began to talk. He always enjoyed conversation in bed, in the enveloping dark, after love making. It was more intimate he explained, more inclusive. I just loved to luxuriate in our closeness, pulling the two duvets over our cooling bodies.

" Tell me more about this body in the skip " said Josh, leaning his chin on my shoulder " there's nothing more to tell " I replied , sleepily . " Did they give you her name? A description? Anything?" He pressed "They didn't know who she was" I replied "dark haired, about five foot four they said" I snuggled my feet around his legs " oh yes, she had a strange tattoo. A Celtic dragon with the name Chris inscribed under it. "

Josh sat up as if I had struck him "What did you say?" He cried. I described the tattoo once more "Why the fucking hell didn't you tell me?" he shouted. , his voice loud and harsh "I did" I replied "I just told you" " Why didn't you tell me before ...you stupid cow" he roared. All signs of intimacy were gone now; the atmosphere had smashed to smithereens.

"Don't swear at me" I shouted back "I didn't swear" he replied "I called you a stupid cow...and you are. Why the fuck didn't you tell me about the tattoo when I got in? " " I forgot...I didn't think ...it's not that important anyway "I stuttered, picking up my discarded clothing and putting it back on, for protection against the freezing night air." Of course it's fucking important "he screamed once more at me as if I were miles away, instead of right next to him "Why?" I asked? "Why is it so important?"

"Because I fucking know who she is "he replied, pulling on his clothes now, and searching for slippers or any footwear." I've got to get in touch with someone "he continued, putting on the light and searching through the bedroom.

"What the fuck...I never thought this would happen" Josh muttered, his eyes wide, his face alarmed "Why? What does this mean? "I asked him" Confidential information "he stated " My god ...my god.....can't believe it "Josh muttered to himself " Who is she Josh. Tell me, I'm getting worried "I pleaded "I can't tell you anything. Don't ask me again "he said in a voice which made me shiver, so I pulled the duvets closer around me.

He came towards me ...... his face almost touched mine and I thought he was going to kiss me "Don't ask anything. Don't tell anyone about this. Keep your mouth shut" he warned me in a cold, steely voice, his eyes like ice. I felt my insides contract with fear. Where was the Josh of ten minutes ago? Who was this cold stranger who threatened me?

Before I could do or say any more, he turned around and exited the room. All that was left were the sound of his footsteps echoing down the stairs and out of the house.

CHAPTER THREE

"Josh"

Josh walked around the side of the house, opposite the cordoned off skip. He got in his silver Audi, finding his hand shaking as he tried to start the ignition. "What the fuck has happened?" he thought as he turned the key, the ignition sparked and he eased it into gear, driving slowly from the alleyway and onto the main road. His eyes were wide as he tried to shake off tiredness and to concentrate on where he was going.

Josh was badly shaken; he knew who she was alright. There could be only one woman who answered that description. Candice Roberts. He wondered idly, not for the first time, if Candice was her real name. 'How the hell did she end up dead, in a skip outside my house? 'He pondered, thinking of the first time he saw her, in the surgery with her husband, Chris.

He drove through the lanes, swiftly and confidently. He was brought up in this small valley town; he knew every nook and cranny, every short cut and main road. These were the places he played in during his youth. Everyone knew him; "Doctor Harrison's son". He could never get away with any mischief or schoolboy pranks. He never tasted true freedom until he left to study in London, and later to work in the University Hospital in Cardiff. Even his GP training had been in Manchester. In truth, he had enjoyed the anonymity. But it was time to come home, take over the practice and raise a family. Now this had happened. He was not going to let the death of one old scrubber ruin everything.

His mouth was set with determination as he pulled into Glassier Road, where Candice lived. Lights were blazing in the house, despite the lateness of the hour. Yellow police tape cordoned off the garden and the front door. A copper was standing by the gate, on guard. It was obvious she had been identified and the house was being regarded as a crime scene. He drove past. There was nothing he could do. He began to regret his decision to drive here in the first place. Hopefully, no-one had noticed him he thought, as he pulled away in the direction of the town.

Josh pulled up outside the local police station. He locked his car, and walked up the steps to the main entrance. There was a dim light in the foyer, and a hatch on the right which was closed, but a notice read: "please press bell". There was a large bell on the small ledge beneath the hatch, which Josh immediately pressed.

He waited a few minutes, then the hatch was pulled back to reveal a grey haired male police officer in his fifties. He appeared distracted, as if his mind was elsewhere. Josh wondered if the excitement of a murder in the vicinity had stirred up the whole force.

"Hello "Josh said with a perfunctory smile." I'm Doctor Josh Harrison. The body you found this evening was in my skip. I was away at a conference, and when I returned my wife told me what had happened and I realise I know the identity of the corpse "

The officer looked indifferently at Josh. "Thank you, sir. I shall fetch one of the Officers involved in this incident to see you. If you would care to take a seat in the waiting area, they should be along shortly. " he informed him , in a distinctly underwhelmed tone. The Officer indicated the grey plastic chairs lined up against the wall in the small vestibule in which Josh was standing. "Thanks " replied Josh, having no other option, and sat in the chair nearest the hatch.

I hope they don't keep me too long thought Josh, looking around the small seated area. There were police posters on the wall warning civilians against crimes such as car theft, and instructing them on the best means of prevention. A peeling poster gave the number of the towns drug addiction centre, and there was a list of various other organisations which may be able to assist the occupants of this waiting room, including, incongruously, the address and opening times of the local library.

He yawned, feeling the fatigue creeping through every inch of his body. He wished he was back in the king size bed with Jodie, enjoying the welcoming

No Refuge

heat from her body as she wrapped herself around him. He regretted his reaction to her description of Candice's tattoo. He had to think of an explanation that Jodie would accept, whilst hoping that the whole thing would be sorted out without his involvement coming to light.

The thought of the possible repercussions made him break out in a cold sweat and caused his hands to develop a slight tremor. 'Calm down' he told himself, perhaps when he knew more about the circumstances, he would be reassured.

A young police officer opened a door on Josh's right, and called "Doctor Harrison? ". Josh answered "Yes" and stood up. "Would you follow me please? "He said, starting to walk down a narrow corridor with doors on either side. Josh followed him, and was ushered into a small room on the left, which consisted of a desk and two chairs - one on either side. The policeman sat on one of the chairs, indicating for Josh to be seated on the other.

"I am police sergeant Mark Dawson, and I am one of the COS officers allocated to this investigation. " the policeman introduced himself, "Doctor Harrison, I believe you have some information regarding the body found today in the rubbish skip adjacent to your property?" . "Yes, I do" said Josh "I believe the victim was a woman named Candice Roberts, although I am not certain that Candice is her legal Christian name. She was a patient of mine, aged 39, I saw her in my surgery some weeks ago, and noticed her tattoo"

" The body was found by your wife at 5pm this afternoon I believe " said Sergeant Dawson " She had no idea who the victim was. How has it taken you so long to inform us, sir? It's now gone 1.30am " "I was in a conference in London." replied Josh "I had no idea about it until I returned home." " What time would that be, sir? ". Dawson was writing on a notepad he had placed in front of him. "Around 9pm ". Answered Josh "Why did you wait until now? ". "My wife was extremely distressed over the discovery as you can imagine. She was quite distraught when I returned, and all she could tell me was that the body was that of a woman. I comforted her, and persuaded her to go to bed. It was not until about an hour ago, at the most, that she started to tell me any details. It was then she described the tattoo, and immediately I realised I recognised it. I thought that I had better let you know as soon as possible in case you needed to make identification. ". " I see" nodded the police officer.

"Why didn't you simply phone, rather than drive down to the station?" he asked "Well, I thought I might have to sign a statement or something. You may have wanted me to look at the body...I'm quite used to cadavers in my profession ". Mark Dawson looked at him quizzically.

"You'll be glad to know Doctor Harrison, that we identified her as Candice Roberts almost immediately, as she was carrying some ID. Her husband has also seen the body and confirmed it was her. However, I should like to thank you very much for your concern, and swift action. One of the team may be calling round to see you and your wife in the next day or two, depending on developments. "

Dawson stood up, obviously dismissing Josh" Is there anything you can tell me about her death or the circumstances?" "Josh asked" I am so sorry sir "Dawson replied" But I can give no further information at the moment as this is an on- going enquiry. . I will contact you in the near future. "He walked to the door, and Josh had no option but to follow.

Sitting back in his car outside, Josh felt anxious. 'That was a waste of bloody time 'he thought. 'What's more I've got a policeman wondering why I drove there in the middle of the night instead of making a phone call. The last thing I want is drawing attention to me '

He drove off, making his way back to North Street, and back to bed. He was hoping that Jodie would be fast asleep. There was no way he could face a cross examination off her at this hour. He needed to sleep before morning surgery, he was absolutely knackered.

His thoughts turned to Candice and the last time he saw her. There was no way he was mentioning that to the police. He could only hope that they would find a simple solution to her death and that the case would be quickly solved. The last thing he wanted was for a nosy plod to do some digging and find out what had been going on......

CHAPTER FOUR

"Jodie"

*I decided to leave them all to it the following morning. The builders were taking down more parts of the house, plastering and redesigning. Josh had morning surgery in his beautiful, comfortable surgery and the police and auxiliary staffs were buzzing about the skip like a swarm of bluebottles.

I wanted to go to the local library. I could go on the 'net' and search for more job vacancies and I also wanted to look into societies or groups where I could go to meet people.

It was ok for Josh, he came from this town. Old friends had got in touch with him - he even had buddies to go for a boy's night out with....and had done so already on several occasions. But me? I knew no one. My friends mostly lived in Cardiff, and although it wasn't too far away, it took an effort to arrange to meet. You couldn't just drop in and have a cup of tea on the off chance, or a quick mooch around the shops.

Searching the rail for a pair of jeans and a suitable top, I turned on the portable telly we were using at the moment. The local news was on. A newscaster with shoulder length dark hair, immaculately styled and lacquered to within an inch of its life, was reporting on the murder: " The body found locally , in a rubbish skip yesterday, has been identified as that of Candice Roberts, a 39 year old mother of two. A 45 year old man has been arrested in connection with the murder and is helping police with their enquiries ".

'Thank goodness for that 'I thought. It had really upset me finding the body, and after Josh's extreme reaction last night, I hadn't slept a wink. When he returned around 3am I pretended to be asleep because I didn't want any more arguments with him. He had got up early this morning and rushed off to the surgery before we had a chance to talk. I wish I knew what the hell was bugging him...he was like a bear with a sore head, and his moods could change within seconds.

Putting these concerns to the back of my mind, I set off for the library. I browsed the 'net' for a while, made a note of any possible job vacancies, ordered a couple of books from Amazon and did a search on ' groups and activities in your local area'.

There were the usual W.I meetings and exercise classes. There was a Historical Society which sounded interesting and I thought I might investigate, so I jotted down the contact phone number. Nothing else appealed to me and there was no mention of a book club. I decided I would ask the librarian if she knew of one.

The computer suite was located on the first floor, so I walked down the impressive solid wood staircase to the main library area. It abuilding, with many period features, high ceilings and a great deal of solid oak fixtures and fittings. It had so much more atmosphere than the modern square glass buildings which local authorities tended to build. I could imagine people, over a century ago, browsing for books in this regal setting and sitting in high backed chairs whilst perusing the daily papers or chronicles of the time.

There was a queue to speak to the librarian, so I
passed the time looking through pamphlets and flyers for various literary events. Another woman was doing the same thing and we laughed as we went to pick up the same pamphlet. "Sorry" I said as I gave it to her, whilst she said "sorry" almost simultaneously.

Finally, the librarian was available and I asked about a book club "Alison has been trying to get one off the ground" she said "so far she's only got six names. She intends to start it as soon as the numbers reach eight. "Well I'm interested, so there's another name "I declared "Hey...and me " said the woman from the pamphlet display. She was a friendly looking brunette in her

No Refuge

50s and I instantly warmed to her. "Ok then ladies " said the librarian can I have your names and telephone numbers please? "." Jodie Harrison" I said, giving my phone number "Anita Cox " said the brunette and handed over a card with her details on it." Thank you very much ladies "said the Librarian" I'm pleased to welcome new members to the library, and hope you enjoy all our facilities "She handed us both our new cards and a booklet. We thanked her and made our way to the main doors

Anita turned to me and said "I'm new here. Only arrived in this town with my partner six weeks ago He's been given the job of manager in the new Job Action Centre. How about you? ""I'm new as well. My husband's taken over his father's doctor's practice in North Street. He was brought up here. But I'm a complete stranger and know no one or anywhere "I said with a chuckle. Anita took hold of my arm "Well then, let us two strangers explore this town together. Let's find a cafe and get better acquainted over a cup of coffee. "With that we strode down the street arm in arm.

After spending an hour or so with Anita in a lovely little cafe we discovered in the high street, we found out that we had a lot in common despite our age differences. Anita was divorced with two grown up children, a boy and girl. Her son was living in Carmarthen, where Anita had originally hailed from. Her daughter however, had moved with her partner to a house near her mother. Anita appeared concerned about her, but tried to hide it. Perhaps she felt she didn't know me well enough to confide in me as yet.

I told Anita about our renovations, my job applications and finding the body in our skip. "That must have been terrible!" she declared, with a horrified look on her face. I told her that it was. I described how I had been sick, and even smoked a cigarette, after giving them up. "I felt so vulnerable" I confided "I didn't know who she was or why the killer had chosen our skip. I thought it might have been mistaken identity and the killer really targeted me! ""Oh how awful " empathised Anita "you were in a dreadful state." " Yes "I agreed "I couldn't sleep. When I told my husband about it, he was quite dismissive. All he cared about was whether it would hold up the building work!" " Pooh..... Men!" she exclaimed

"Sometimes they have the sensitivity of a brick. "I had to agree with her, especially the way Josh was behaving recently.

Before leaving, we exchanged phone numbers and arranged to meet on Friday to suss out local hairdressers and beauticians. We also decided to do some shopping and have lunch. To make a day of it. "At last, something to look forward to "I thought, perhaps I had just made a friend in the same boat as myself.

When I returned home it was lunch time. I discovered Josh rummaging in the kitchen cupboard looking for something to eat. I stood behind him, "There's plenty of food in the fridge and bread in the bread bin"
" Where the fucking hell have you been?" He shouted, his face distorted and his eyes blazing with anger. "To the library to check out local activities." I replied coolly "..... and shopping". I indicated the two bags of groceries I had placed on the table.
" I told you I need you here . You have to make sure the builders are doing their job properly and not taking out the wrong walls or floors. Also, I need you in the surgery later. The afternoon receptionist has a dental appointment. " " I told you yesterday" I pointed out, " I am not a builder or a practice manager. Until I get a job, I'll try and help out occasionally, but after that you will have to sort out some other arrangement"

Josh 's face was suffused with anger. He clenched his jaw and his face became bright red . I stepped back, away from him. " Fucking hell! " he burst out " I told you. You are not working, you can help me here until we have a baby...then you'll have plenty to do " " Josh " I said, still remaining calm " we have never discussed any of this. You have just decided MY future without consulting me in any way" . He still looked enraged. " I thought it was what we both wanted " he stated " It's the way things are supposed to be " " What do you mean 'supposed to be' ? According to who ? " I demanded " according to any right minded person " he replied " anyone with morals and family values ". I snorted ...then started to laugh ...he sounded like some 1980s politician .

No Refuge

" Don't you DARE laugh at me" he shouted, coming nearer until we were almost touching face to face. " Only dirty old slags do that ! I thought you were better than that " he spat , and took me by the shoulders, pushing me against the wall. I felt frightened , he had changed from the loving husband I knew into some sort of chauvinist monster. I pushed him away from me . He glared, his mouth contorting with rage, " I'll fucking show you what can happen to slags like you. You disobey me and you'll be punished .....it's the only way to control your behaviour...the only way you'll learn !"

I was sobbing by now, tears coursing down my cheeks. I felt sick, with knots in my stomach , my body trembled. " Josh, Josh ...stop it please ..stop it ....I'm sorry ". I begged, apologising for what, I did not know . " Ah sorry now are you ? Make sure it's not too late . That fucking scrubber in the skip was sorry ...but it was too bloody late for her...Ha ha " He half laughed and half sneered, drawing his lips back and baring his teeth like a rabid dog. He turned quickly on his heel and left, slamming the back door behind him. I sank into a chair in a heap, trying to make myself as small as possible. What was wrong with Josh? Was it my fault? Should I try harder to be a better wife? ....and what did he mean about the body in the skip ? .....

CHAPTER FIVE

Jodie

I knew I had to pull myself together. It was obvious Josh and I needed to talk , but sitting in this chair feeling sorry for myself wasn't going to do any good. I decided I would quickly check on the builders progress , them make myself look respectable and go over to the surgery to stand in for the missing receptionist.

The renovations were going well and the plastering in what was going to be the new kitchen, was practically completed. We spoke about the next section of work to be done, and checked out timings and cost. Everything seemed to be going to schedule and budget, which was a great relief. This was some good news that I could tell Josh, which might boost his mood. I reallyb hoped it would. Perhaps it was the stress of the job, the building work and the move that had affected him , and hopefully he would soon be back to his happy , loving self.

I felt more optimistic as I got ready to work in the surgery. I put my long dark hair up in a sleek chignon and put on a smart pair of black trousers and peach blouse . I added a black longline cardigan and applied some discreet makeup. Yes, I thought, that's the right image for a doctors wife , and chuckled inwardly to myself. Picking up my bag I went next door.

I arrived around ten minutes before the doors were due to open in the main waiting room for afternoon surgery , which was 2pm until 6pm. Josh was working alone at the moment, still trying to entice patients to his surgery.

When his father died, the two other GPs who worked with him, also left the practice. One, who was in his sixties, decided to retire, and the younger one decided to move to Nottingham to take up a clinical post as a physician in the hospital there. Josh inherited the house and surgery, but with no other doctor working, he had to complete his full G.P training before he could take over the practice.

He had completed his residency in the University Hospital in Cardiff. However, to become a GP he had to do eighteen months supervised practice in a GP s surgery. I had met him in Cardiff,(where my mother lived,)when I was there for a weeks holiday. I was working as a lecturer in Liverpool, which made it difficult for us to have a relationship. However, we started seeing each other occasionally. Josh began looking for vacancies in the North of England and managed to get a GP position in Manchester. This made It easier to meet up and soon we were spending most weekends together .

He told me how much he wanted to live back in the Welsh Valleys and take on his fathers practice . I could empathise. I felt pretty rootless myself , having moved around a lot as a child because my father was a career soldier and we all moved from posting to posting. He had died in action five years previously and my mother had settled in Cardiff, her home town and where I had actually been born (my brothers had been born in Germany and Cyprus) . I had gone to University in Warwick and then found a post in Liverpool . I didn't really feel that anywhere was home.

We soon realised that our feelings for each other were getting deeper and deeper. Josh persuaded me that we could make a happy life together and settle down in his home town. He proposed to me , and I resigned my job just before his GP training ended. We lived together in his flat in Manchester for a few weeks, prior to getting married in Cardiff, and then moving to Merthyr Tydfil.

Josh's parents were both deceased. His mother died when he was seventeen, and he was an only child. Therefore, it made sense to marry in Cardiff as my mother and most of her relatives lived there. My two brothers Eddy and Steve came to the wedding with their current girlfriends and we invited friends from all over the UK . I thought dreamily of our wedding day and the love I felt for Josh as I walked down the aisle. This had only been two months ago, surely things were not going badly already? No, I decided, it was all to do with getting used to living together combined with all the upheaval we had been through. It was all a matter of compromise and getting used to each others ways.

Once the surgery took on more patients and Josh could employ another GP or so , I was sure that he would once more be the easy going man I had dated in Liverpool.

My optimism seemed to be well founded. I was just about to call the first patient, when Josh came out of the consulting room . He sidled up to me , and, with a sexy smile, said " Sorry I was grumpy earlier on. You look gorgeous. I've booked a table at a lovely little restaurant for us after surgery ends, so we can have a romantic meal together." I positively beamed , as he picked up the patient files, he gave me a pat on the bum and returned to his room.

The evening surgery seemed to go quite quickly. There was a steady flow of patients, and most of them seemed very friendly. A couple commented on my finding Candice's body. Mrs Sinclair whispered ,"Her husband's been charged you know. He suffocated her apparently ..... Some say it was to do with a SEX. Game! " she raised her eyebrows in a shocked expression. " I wouldn't know about that " I said " I only saw her legs." This piqued their interest and Mrs Sinclair and her friends questioned me on how I knew she was dead, and what her legs looked like and how long she had been there. I answered their questions the best I could, but for some reason didn't mention that one leg appeared to be damaged . I have no idea why I didn't say anything, I just somehow thought it was information I should keep to myself.

Josh saw his last patient at 6. 15pm, an elderly man with a small stoop. He left just after 6.30pm as the cleaner was arriving, and Josh quickly followed, leaving the consulting room shortly afterwards. " Right, lets get off " he said winking at me " Put your coat on girl...you've pulled " I giggled and the cleaner stared at us both as if we had two heads.

The restaurant proved to be a small Italian Bistro, located just on the edges of the town centre called " Arriverdeci " . The waiter showed us to a small table , in a quiet corner, near the window. There was a checked table cloth and the obligatory candle in a bottle. Despite its "typical" app earance, the food was superb. We both had steak with a mix of Italian sauces , garlic bread as a side dish and Cassata for desert. It was truly the best food I had eaten in weeks. We had mostly scraped by with beans on toast or fish and chips from the local chippy. I couldn't wait to get a proper cooker and range installed.

Tonight was such a delicious surprise. I decided to sit back and enjoy it. We ordered a bottle of wine which made me feel even more relaxed and Josh suggested another. Soon, I was feeling warm and satisfied as the food and wine wove its magic.

" I'm sorry for being so moody recently " said Josh, as we sipped coffees , after the meal. He certainly looked more relaxed than he had in the last couple of days. " Thanks for the apology, but to tell you the truth I was really upset by the things you called me ". " I know , but I seem to have so much to worry about recently. " " Maybe, but you shouldn't take it out on me. I've never seen you like that before . To tell you the truth it's only been since we moved here " " What do you mean? " his voice became sharper " Well, you never seemed to mind me working , or anything when we lived in Manchester . Now, you sound like you want a fifties housewife . ". " Oh, don't be silly. It's just that we're thinking of having a baby , and I thought that it would be silly for you to start work only to get pregnant and have all the stress of working up until the birth and then organising maternity leave " " I think that's up to me , don't you? And anyway, I'm not even pregnant yet. It might take ages" " Why should it? We're both healthy aren't we? " " As far as we know. It can still take some time though " " I was just trying to be considerate" he looked down, a small pout on his face, like a naughty child. " Oh well. forget about it for now " I sighed.

No Refuge

" But what was all that about the dead woman...Candice? " I prompted breaking a period of silence, " What do you mean? " this time he sounded wary. " Well, you said she was a scrubber. You said she was dead because she didn't say sorry.... and the way you reacted when I told you about the tattoo ...well it was as if lightening had hit you . Off you went without a bye or a leave! "

" Mmmmm. Well I didn't want to say anything , patient confidentiality, and that. When you described the tattoo I knew who it was because I had seen her in the surgery ...as a patient . She had mentioned being afraid of someone, but I hadn't taken any notice ...thought she was putting it on a bit for a medical certificate. Then , when you described the tattoo.....well, I realised she might have been saying the truth. I felt guilty, and knew I had to tell the police ...so that's what I did" he tried to look shamefaced, but didn't quite pull it off. To tell you the truth I was not convinced " It doesn't explain what you SAID " I protested " " Said? What do you mean said? " he looked back and forth shiftily, as if the answer was written somewhere in the room. " that she was a scrubber and died because she didn't say sorry in time " I repeated slowly. " Ummm, Ohhh that was nonsense....I was angry . I mean, well....she was a bit loose. I knew her husband. I've known him since I was a kid, we went around in the same gang together for years. I've heard rumours since coming back that she's been cheating on him with every Tom, Dick and

Harry. This must have made him pretty mad "

" People say that she was a good wife , do anything for him.

" well umm. ...they've charged him with her murder....haven't they? So I meant she can't have said sorry soon enough to him .....because he, umm , murdered her . I know it was stupid . I was in a foul mood. Sorry . " his head was down and he looked up at me without moving, so I could see his eyes , like those of a puppy dog, peering through his eyelashes " Oh.....I ....see" I said' not believing for one moment ,a word he had said

We left the restaurant and caught a taxi home. Josh tried to hold my hand, and I allowed it to rest coolly there, without actually pulling away.

I hurried to bed when we arrived at the house, piling on my woollies against the cold. Josh soon followed . He turned towards me and began kissing my brow, and trying to fight through the layers of clothing to reach my skin. I quickly turned around, my back to him. " Not tonight Josh, I'm too tired " I murmured " goodnight " . He didn't reply, but thankfully turned over and went to sleep. I lay awake in the dark, sleep eluding me. I had a great deal to think about .....

CHAPTER SIX

"Honey"

The doctors surgery certainly looks very posh and contemporary, thought Honey as she sat on one of the curved eggshell blue chairs in the waiting room. The receptionists desk was all chrome and granite, with a shiny looking tiled black floor and mirrors and windows giving the illusion of light. She had asked to see the doctor, but had to register with the surgery first , and then be examined by the nurse who took her weight, height and blood pressure . She was now waiting patiently to see Doctor Harrison.

Her name really was Honey, Honey Sullivan to be precise. Her mother always had a fanciful side to her and imagined a petite daughter with deep blonde hair, blue eyes and a sweet disposition. In the event, Honey was large boned, mousey haired with brown eyes and a tendency to fly into a temper if anyone annoyed her. She hadn't been feeling well for ages now, but found her old doctor , in the top surgery, a bit fearsome. She knew Josh Harrison she thought, with a faint smile , which would make him much easier to talk to.

" Honey Sullivan " called the receptionist " The Consulting room , first on the right. Honey got up and made her way to the door, She gave a slight tap, and heard Josh's voice boom out " Come in " . She pushed open the door and entered the room, sitting in the chair placed at the side of the doctors desk.

Josh looked up and his eyes opened wide with surprise " Honey, " he said " What on earth are you doing here? " he didn't seem too pleased, to tell the truth. " The same as anyone else" she replied " I'm ill " " I would have thought you'd go to a different doctor " " No, I decided it would be easier to talk to you . Terrible what happened to Candice weren't it? " Josh went slightly pale " better if we don't talk about her " he said " oh, oh ..right . But is was her husband killed her...she didn't die in the club..did she? " " No, she didn't " agreed Josh. " but I'd prefer it if you didn't mention the club in connection with me , at all " " Ok, ok , keep your hair on. Little wifey won't find out ...dontcha worry bach" she pronounced the sentence with a thick Welsh accent. 'shes taking the piss now" thought Josh.

In a professional voice he asked " What seems to be the problem Mrs Sullivan? " Honey looked worried now. " I've lost weight ...without trying, about two stone in the last six months. I'm very tired, and in the night I'm having these terrible sweats ...so bad they soak the blankets. I feel like I've got the flu most of the time, and now I've developed a cough. ". " Mmmmm go behind the screen and take off all your clothes besides your bra and panties. I'll call a nurse in, so I can examine you " " never needed anyone else there before when I stripped off , Josh, cariad" she teased, Josh scowled and picked up his phone to call the nurse in.

Honey got dressed and sat back in the chair by Josh's desk. He was writing quickly on some forms. " Well " she said " What's the verdict? " "

..... Not sure yet " he replied, continuing to write. " You have to go for some blood tests and a chest X ray . When you leave my room, go to the door with Haematology written on it and give them the form with the plastic bit on the front, a nurse will then take your blood. Go up the hospital with the other form, and take it to the x ray department. I should have the results within three days, so call back then , and I should have more idea as to what is wrong with you. We'll go from there . ". " Can you give me any clue, Josh? Stop me worrying, like " " Sorry, it could be anything from anaemia to a virus , it wouldn't be fair for me to guess and then be completely wrong. " " Oh, I see. " Honey looked downcast. " I'll be off then, see you later in the week ..... and don't worry, your secret is safe with me . ". she gave him a wan smile and a little wave. Josh breathed out as she shut the door behind her.

No Refuge

He gave a deep sigh. ' as long as Jodie never finds out ' he thought.

Honey left the surgery with mixed emotions. She was glad that she had been examined so thoroughly and was having all the tests, but worried as to what could be wrong. She had the two little ones to think about . Who would look after them if she had to go to hospital or something? Glen wouldn't bother, that's for sure . He'd probably farm them out on his mother , and a miserable old cow she was an' all.

Lost in thought, Honey reached home before she realised. She could see the twins playing some game in the living room, with Glen reading the paper with his feet up. No chance of him getting tea ready then, she thought.

Honey stumbled into the house feeling very, very tired " Where you been then?" " asked Glen " I'm starving here " " I've been to the doctors. Told you I was going " " oh aye, what did he have to say then? " " That I got to rest... it's probably anaemia " the twins ran to her, their chubby little arms wrapped around her legs . She bent down and kissed them , feeling their soft, still toddler-like skin. " Anaemia " repeated Glen " me mother had that, and she was right as rain. Get some Guinness down you , that'll do the trick. "

Honey didn't reply, she just went to the sink and started peeling potatoes. Her shoulders drooped down with weariness " think I'll have a night off from the club " she said to Glen " No way Jose " his voice rose " we need the bloody money . Have a few drinks...you'll be as right as rain. Try the Guinness like I said. I don't want you talking anymore nonsense. ". he picked up his paper and continued reading . Honeys eyes filled with

CHAPTER SEVEN

Josh

"Where the hell are those papers ? " muttered Josh , partly to himself, and partly to Jodie " What papers ? ". " The ones to do with the surgery and the practice licence ". " take a look in your bureau the builders put it in the corner of the main room " Jodie sighed, he never could find anything by himself. Josh left the room to dig the papers out.

Having found them, he shouted out to Jodie " I'm off to the solicitors ...be back later! " " OK ..see you " Josh got into his car and quickly pulled away from the curb. He drove to the town centre and parked in the new car park where the cinema used to be . Nostalgically, he walked away from his car, remembering the happy times he'd enjoyed in that cinema with the old gang . His thoughts turned to Chris, Candice's husband who was now charged with her murder, and remanded in custody. I wonder what really happened ? he thought . He had heard the rumours that she had died of strangulation , some saying it was to do with a sex game. He conceded that it might have been during sex, but no one had mentioned the damage to her leg which Jodie described. It was this that puzzled Josh. It puzzled and worried him .

If her death had any connection with " The Club" , then the police might start digging, although he was pretty sure that Chris would keep his mouth shut. Perhaps he should have let Honey talk about it when she came to see him, perhaps she had more information. There again, she had seemed to think it was straightforward, hadn't she ? This worrying was no good , he had better go to the solicitors and sort out these papers, getting back in time for surgery.

Josh crossed the road in Glebeland street and walked through the alleyway to the bus station, cutting across the precinct to his solicitors at the end of St Tydfils Court. He did not notice the burly man watching his progress. His steely grey eyes followed Josh as he passed the shops in the small precinct. He wore jeans and a thick , hooded fleece. ' You are in for one big shock soon Doctor Josh' he thought to himself .' How much will you pay to stop your pretty little wife finding out about your activities... or would you prefer me to persuade her to join in? I think I'd like that ...yes, I'd like that very much '. He saw Josh enter the solicitors doorway, and turned around, walking back towards the car park. ' Time to leave a little message for the doc ' he thought.

•••

Jodie

Standing by the back door , I pulled my thick woollen jacket further around my body . I took a long, satisfying drag on my cigarette . The pleasure of smoking it had driven me to stand outside in this freezing weather.

It always amazes me how Josh's nostrils could detect even the faintest whiff of smoke in a room, or on clothes. I must be sure to spray myself with " Febreze " before I go back into the house . Ever since the night of 'the body in the skip ' as I constantly think of it , I've gone back to smoking. I have hidden my cigarettes, lighter and Febreze spray , behind a loose brick in the old outhouse which is situated a few yards from the back door.

Taking another drag, I lose myself in the pleasure of the smoke entering my lungs , soothing my anxiety. Then I blow it out into the freezing air to form abstract shapes. ' am I just imagining things '? I keep asked myself. I have never had any reason to doubt Josh before. Why would he lie about the deceased Candice ?

Perhaps he was in such a state that he said stupid things about her. He was a friend of her husbands , maybe he was so shocked when he heard she was dead that he reacted out of character ...shouting at me .... rushing off...then trying to blame her for her own death . I decided that the best thing I could do, was to put it to the back of my mind and forget all about it.

I vowed, there and then, to make sure we settled down happily in the community and that we started to enjoy life again and stop worrying about the house, and the practice. I would try and get Josh to calm down and face life with a more relaxed attitude. It was also time to inject some romance back into our relationship. Perhaps I would conceive a baby …..and that would make all the difference . Feeling more hopeful, I hid my stash behind the brick, sprayed my clothes and went back into the house.

CHAPTER EIGHT

"Honey"

Wearily Honey entered "The Club" ten minutes late. She felt as if she would like to lie down on one of those plush velvet chaises and go to sleep. Fat chance she had of that. She had five hours of dancing ahead of her.... when every bone in her body ached and her head throbbed with fatigue.

Stan, the boss, saw her entering the dressing room, or undressing room as it should be more accurately referred to . He gave her a stern look, but strangely didn't comment on her lateness. Last time he had, Honey had retaliated with a verbal lashing ....perhaps that's why he was quiet today.

She opened her locker and removed her 'costume' ...a gold sequinned bikini. She also took a bottle of body lotion to slather over her skin making it slippery and glowing. Honey stripped off her outdoor clothes, applied the lotion, put on her bikini and sat at the dressing table.

Lara was sitting on one of the other stools applying make up " How's it going , babes? " she asked in her perpetually friendly voice " Oh you know, so....so " replied Honey " " Glen boy getting you down is he? ". " You know what he's like " shrugged Honey " He'd have a heart attack if he had to pour himself a cup of tea " " All the bloody same these men. Glad I live on my own " Lara, a slim long legged blonde , got up and made her way to the door " she you laters love " she called as she left the room.

Honey could see her pale face and dark eyes in the mirror . She couldn't go on show like that. Deftly she applied some golden bronze makeup to her face, blusher and silver eyeshadow. Using a pencil she outlined her eyes and applied copious amounts of mascara. ' that's better' she thought ' I only look half dead now " Honey twisted her brown hair into a knot, clipped it up on top of her head and attached a small gold feathered head dress. This twinkled in the light, and drew attention from the lank ness of her hair, and the drawn look on her face. She stood and looked in the mirror, slipping a pair of gold stilettos on her feet. ' Good God she was getting thin, There was hardly any skin on her bones. 'She had to adjust the bra top to make it smaller and insert some ' chicken fillets' , to enhance her cleavage. 'Thank God she didn't strip, the punters would have been really disappointed with her 'fried eggs." She tightened the ties on the bikini bottoms, she didn't want any unforeseen accidents.

Honey was ready for her first pole dancing stint of the night . As long as no-one wants any 'specials' I'll just about manage it she thought. She knew the dance routines backwards; "the slide and turn" , The rock and roll". " Up and under " and "sexy snake " . She only had to hear the music and she automatically carried out the moves.

Pole dancing was at the top of the hierarchy in these type of clubs. A pole dancer did just that...danced with a pole. Wearing a skimpy outfit, she would gyrate through a series of dance moves....sexy ..yes. Pornographic ...no. The punters watched but could not touch . In fact, they could come no nearer than the barriers constructed around the area of the poles. These were the respectable girls...the elite ...and all were trained and accomplished dancers.

It hadn't been Honey 's first choice of career, but she had gone to dance lessons since she was a youngster, and had a real talent. She met Glen, and stupidly left her family to live with him. Her parents didn't approve of him. They thought he was a seedy little crook who had an aversion to real work . They proved to be right, but Honey was stubborn, and at that time , madly in love with the dark eyed , sexy charmer. She didn't even mind when he introduced her to Stan and " The Club" . At least the lap dancing gave her a chance to show off her talents. By the time she realised what a loser Glen was and how he lived off her, it was too late, she was pregnant with the twins. Honey realised she was stuck. This was her life, for the foreseeable future.

Pole dancing was not all that was available at the club. In certain rooms there were lap dancers , who danced on the table immediately in front of the punters. Again , no touching was allowed, but the dancer gyrated and thrust her tits and fanny at the blokes sitting there. Of course " extras" could be purchased...such as private lap dancing sessions and a variety of sexual liberties taken, up to and including, full sex

The piece de resistance in the club was " the Cellar" where 'specials' could be purchased. This was a set of inter-connecting rooms which catered for every possible sexual taste or deviance you could imagine,(with only one or two exceptions) . It had the full range of SMBD and was only available to platinum club members who were sworn to secrecy. However, for Stan and the consortium , it was a real money spinner.

Honey had started as a pole dancer and was still a pole dancer. When money was extremely tight a few years back, Stan...and Glen, had persuaded her to do some " specials".Reluctantly, she had agreed. The acts she agreed to, were mostly related to her taking the part of a Domatrix , and to tell the truth, she found it boring, if tiring on her arms from wielding a whip. Some of the other practices Honey thought were revolting, but she had never been involved in them . The late, lamented Candice, however, had been a large part of that scene. This bothered Honey, but she had heard that it was Chris, her husband ,who had killed her " accidentally" at home .... But she still wondered..

The music started and Honey began gyrating around her pole. Her mind blank as she carried out the moves...the twists and turns ...she couldn't tell you how many men were watching her , let alone what they looked like . She concentrated on the kids costumes she had to make for their school play, and whether or not she could get the material from the market tomorrow. The music played on ....

After 40 minutes she was allowed a break. The dancers had a 5 minute break after the first 40 minutes, then a half hour off after a hour and a half. Honey had a quick glass of coke and a visit to the toilet, then she was back on the podium. She was very tired tonight, and she had noticed some bruises on her arms and legs, which hadn't been there earlier. She wondered if she had been careless and bumped on the pole or if it was to do with her 'anaemia ". Some of the girls did double shifts of dancing...but they relied on drugs like speed or cocaine to keep going. Honey knew she could easily get some, but didn't want to go down that route. What she wanted was to get out altogether ... she sighed...she would be bloody glad when she was too old.

In her half hour break, Honey went back to the dressing room and lay back with her eyes closed, on one of the old chaise longues that had been placed there. She could sense someone looking at her, so she opened her eyes to see Stan sitting on a nearby chair. " What do you want? " she asked irritably, fed up at being disturbed " " A bloke wants you for a special " he said pressi twenties and a tenner into her hand, " No, " she replied trying to give the money back to him " aw c'mon Honey. He asked especially for you ...he's one of our most generous clients ...he might give you a big tip " " I'm tired ....I want to go straight home when I finish my shift " " Tell you what .....You can finish dancing early and see him. Then you can go home at the normal time " " Really. ? You're not having me on now are you? " this was a good deal, thought Honey ...extra fifty quid, home on time, she wouldn't have to tell Glen about the money and might even get a tip on top. " OK them I'll do it " she told Stan " Right, come down the cellar about 11pm ." " Ok, see you " Honey shut her eyes again for the last few minutes of her break, trying to reserve every ounce of energy in her body.

Just before 11pm Honey stopped dancing, to the dismay of her audience, and returned to the dressing room. Some of the men had shouted " come back" or " you're the best...simply the best " at her as she left ' I've still got it then ' she thought, even if I'm old, Ill ,and knackered. It actually gave her a bit of a boost ...well for five minutes, anyhow.

She took her dressing gown off the hook in her locker and put it on, then she tottered down to the entrance to the cellar.

No Refuge

The cellar's entrance was actually a concealed door. A corridor led off to the left from the main entrance of the club , just past the cloak room. It was papered with a dark , patterned wall paper, which in the dim lights was very difficult to see. Down the length of the corridor were several doors which lead into offices and store rooms. All were of a light wood and had name plaques on them . At the very end of the corridor , was what appeared to be a plain wall. However, if you ran your hand down the far right hand side of the wallpaper there was a switch , which was concealed in the pattern . It was virtually undetectable to the naked eye.

Honey ran her hand down the edge of the pattern and felt an indentation. She pressed it, and a door opened inwardly . Honey stepped through the entrance on to a small square landing. The door closed behind her, and a light came on. In front of her was a staircase leading downwards to a dimly lit room. Honey stepped down and arrived in the largest of the rooms , with all sorts of equipment fixed to the walls and ceiling. Large chests which contained more instruments or articles which may be required were also placed around the room.

Stan was already down there , with a man of medium height, small build and sparse hair. Honey recognised him, he had been one of her " specials " in the past . He was some sort of local dignitary , but she had to call him " Baldrick " (the same name as a character from the ' Black Adder series) . Goodness knows why , she had never asked .
Stan quickly left and Honey was alone with " Baldrick " . " Same as usual" he whispered " You're the best at this " .

Turning her back on him , Honey rolled her eyes ' now what did I use? ' , she searched her memory, then went to one of the chests and removed a few articles which she placed on a table. She turned back sharply to Baldrick, having put on a pair of leather gloves. " You weasley little lump of shit ! " she shouted in a commanding voice " You have been naughty, very, very, naughty......haven't you ? ". " Yes" he replied meekly " What happens to naughty boys ? " demanded Honey " they get punished " he whispered " Yes, they get punished, and you must be punished.....take off all your clothes. "

Baldrick complied, watching Honey, who had now picked up a whip with a fine lash, which she cracked around him as he removed his clothes.

Once naked, Baldrick stood there, looking, to Honey's eyes, totally pathetic, if not idiotic. Sometimes, she really didn't know how she stopped herself laughing. ' I must have acting ability ' she thought. Honey sat down on a solid wood chair . " Come here " she commanded, and made Baldrick lie over her knees, his scrawny little bum sticking in the air. She proceeded to smack him with as much power as she could, ensuring that the leather of the gloves marked his buttocks. She could feel his penis growing larger against her leg, he was starting to get excited. She knew from experience that he wouldn't ejaculate until she had completed the full array of " punishments " which he desired.

Honey continued punishing Baldrick for over half an hour. He ended up handcuffed to a bed, face down, by his wrists and ankles and electrodes placed on his balls. The bed was slatted and a mirror was on the floor so that they could both watch the proceedings. She applied random electric shocks until his penis become hard and totally engorged, then she started telling him how 'dirty' he was and applied carefully aimed whip lashes to his buttocks until he ejaculated all over the mirror.

Honey was sitting in the chair, waiting for him to dress, when she noticed one of the other girls, Jess, leading a punter into the small room at the far end of the cellar. He was still fully dressed and Jess had her dressing gown on. Honey did a double take...she knew that punter, even though she had just glimpsed him as they passed by. Honey stood up to get a better look, angled from one of the large mirrors placed on the ceiling and walls directly opposite the entrance to the small room . Yes, she was right, it was him ...it was Doctor Josh ...now why on earth was he back here, when he had his lovely new wife at home ? Men she thought, are never satisfied. I should know, in this bloody game.

No Refuge

Baldrick, now dressed, sidled up to Honey. " Thank you for a wonderful night , my dear " he whispered pressing another fifty quid into her hand, " my pleasure " she replied, smiling wryly.

At last Honey could dress and go home ...and sleep. Still, she definitely had enough money for the kids material now, and some to put away for herself . She also had a mystery to solve . Why was Josh Harrison back here, after all this time?

CHAPTER NINE

Jodie

"Yes, I can't wait.I'll see you in the cafe in half an hour " I said to Anita on my mobile " Don't be late " she trilled " I've got a surprise for you ...a treat for us both " She wouldn't tell me any more, insisting that it wouldn't be a surprise if she did. I could hardly wait, I hadn't had much to look forward to recently.

Josh and I had hardly spoken since the other night, although I had come to the conclusion that I was making a mountain out of a molehill and he hadn't really done anything wrong ....a few ill thought out words ..that's all, and I'd acted as if he'd told me he'd been cheating. No wonder he was pissed off with a moaning, ungrateful wife , who accused him of god knows what , when he was doing his best to build up a practice , in order for us to have the house, and life, of our dreams.

To make amends, I had purchased an electric slow cooker in the supermarket yesterday . This morning, I had prepared all the ingredients for a chicken casserole and put it in the cooker to be ready by this evening. I had also made a fresh cream trifle ...which I knew Josh loved, and I was going to try and make the Formica table and rickety chairs look romantic and inviting by using a table cloth, some candles and the crockery we'd had as a wedding present. Tonight we would have a dinner a deux , in our own home. I would also buy a couple of bottles of wine, to help set the mood . Who knows ? Perhaps tonight would be the night we'd start a baby.

When I reached the cafe, I spotted Anita straight away. She was practically bubbling over with excitement, and stood up to call to me immediately. " Jodie, Jodie ...here ....over here" she cried. I reached her table and noticed a younger woman sitting with her. Anita greeted me like a long, lost relative, which I felt was a bit over the top considering our short acquaintance... but perhaps she was always that sort of effusive person. " Jodie ! This is my daughter Caitlin, I mentioned her to you " " Oh yes, yes , hello Caitlin" I said , simultaneously sitting down, and nodding at the girl.

She was probably not far from my age, around 29 or 30, her hair was blonde and cropped short. She wore studs in her ears , and a stud in her nose. Her bright blue eyes looked moist and slightly bloodshot , as if she had recently been crying. Caitlin murmured " hello" then looked down at her lap , she seemed to shrink into herself . . " I wanted Caitlin to come with us " said Anita " But she was having none of it. She wants to go hill walking with her partner, Sally, this afternoon, and says she's not the type for a " make over "in any case "

" Makeover ? " I repeated " we're having a makeover ? " "Well yes,I thought it would do you good, do us all good in fact " said Anita , smiling. Secretly I wondered if she had bought this for her daughter, and I was a substitute. Well , never mind , even if I was , I'd still enjoy myself , I thought and it would only be a waste if it was already booked. "Well nice meeting you " mumbled Caitlin, getting up and leaving the cafe , " I don't know what's wrong with her " whispered Anita,as we watched her making her way out of the cafe, her shoulders hunched and her head down. " I couple of years ago, she'd have been well up for a bit of glam. It's nothing to do with her being a lesbian " she said to me, defensively " she's always been that way inclined. Until she met this one though, she loved looking her best..... designer dressers, shoes...the lot ...and it's not as if she appears happy. " Anita picked up her handbag, shaking her head sadly. She took out a tissue and wiped the corner of her eyes. "You think it's her partners influence do you? " I asked, tentatively " Oh , it's nothing probably. Don't mind me, I'm just being a silly old woman " she said, waving the tissue, as if to ward off any negative thoughts, and replacing it in her bag.

No Refuge

My coffee arrived just at that moment. I could see Anita didn't want to talk any more about her daughter …she had that shut off look people get, when a subject is closed. Instead, I bent towards her eagerly, and said …." well tell me about this make over we're having then".

We were in " New Waves ", a hairdressers and beauticians which had just opened at the top end of town. In order to attract new customers they had introduced a "Special Offer" of a 'New Waves Makeover' for £30. The package included hair, make up and style advice. It was a basic package, but if you wanted any additional services you could pay extra.

Myself and Anita poured over the hairstyles booklet, giggling like teenagers at some of the more extreme styles . " Oh go for it " she urged me, after hearing about mine and Josh's latest argument, and all the disagreements we'd had lately " let them make you into a sexy siren ….so you can knock his socks off" " But he always says he prefers me with the natural look " I protested. " I haven't changed my image since we met. " " tut, tut all men say that …but you should see their reaction when you become the seductive vamp …he'll be all over you! " I wasn't entirely sure. I had worn my longish, dark hair straight for years, or put up in a smooth chignon for work. The make up I wore was so discreet, people mostly thought I didn't have any on, …the only time I'd had professional make up had been for weddings (including my own) and then I'd stuck with a natural look and sheer lipstick. It was tempting though. I felt in a bit of a rut, with no job and constant stress. Perhaps a change of look would give me, and my marriage, a welcome boost.

Anita splashed the boat out. She had her shoulder length brown hair cut into a stylish bob, with a deep auburn colour wash, which brought out all the reddish glints in her hair. For make up she had the " day out " effect, with just a touch of brown and beige eyeshadow and a lipstick which was a pale rose, adding colour to her lips, but not overtly obvious. Her foundation was a match to her skin tone with the merest touch of blusher to hollow out her cheekbones. It was a youthful look and took about ten years off her age …Anita was delighted . "Just wait until Ray gets a look at me " she exclaimed " he won't be able to keep his hands off " and she giggled....a funny little trill of a sound. This set me off, although I was in the middle of my hair "do" .

The hairdresser and Anita, persuaded me to go for the 'glamour look.' Especially after I confessed that I had had the same hair style for the past 15 years - since I was about 16 or 17. My hair was dark brown, and parted in the centre. I wore it straight ,to just past my shoulders . Sometimes for work or other occasions I put it up in a chignon or French pleat. "urgh....old fashioned " commented the hair dresser, and pulled a face.

She decided to give me a side parting, and cut a half fringe. Then, she would wave my hair in a natural fall over one shoulder with a diamanté clip to hold it back on the other side. A dark colour wash would also bring out the shine and shades in my hair.

I was enjoying the experience . Sitting there, being pampered, my hair washed , styled and dried for me was so relaxing . I should do this more often I thought. The only visits I had previously had were for a dry hair trim about every two months or so. There was no comparison . How boring and dull my everyday life was at present . I began to wonder if I was slightly depressed.

My make up session was a major discussion between the beautician, Anita and myself. Anita insisted I carry the " glamour " look started by the hairstyle, through to the make up and the beautician insisted that a stronger, more defining make up would really suit me. " Your features need definition to bring out their shape and depth of colour " she insisted, starting with plucking my eyebrows into a perfect arch. I gave in and decided to go with the beauticians recommendations.

The foundation and powder was darker that I would usually use, but I must admit it brought a glow to my face . The beautician used a bronze blusher which emphasised my cheekbones, and purple eyeshadow in three shades, finished with highlighter cream on my eye lids to bring out their hazel colour, followed by deep midnight mascara. My eyes looked enormous! Especially when she also used midnight eye liner. I could hardly believe this sultry woman was me . We had a discussion about my lipstick. I wanted natural nude, whilst the others wanted me to wear a deep red. We ended up with red orchid , which was a definite red but with a lighter tinge. This outlined my mouth so that my lips looked wider , with a pout . Who was this woman? This dark haired siren? The look was so different to my usual drab appearance , that I was practically speechless. Anita looked at me in awe. " You look like that woman off the telly...you know... the one from X factor ....Nichole.....sch ..something " "Scheringer" I said. " Yes...her" " no way ...don't be daft " I laughed, though to be honest, I could see some resemblance.

We left " New Waves" arm in arm, giggling like a pair of school girls. We had given the stylists a substantial tip , and now Anita insisted we were going to look at some clothes shops. " I've got no money left " I protested , having spent a fortune on make up and hair products to replicate my look . " C'mon , you told me you haven't bought any clothes since you left Manchester . Anyhow , you need at least one sexy outfit to go with your new image . " persuaded Anita. I didn't need much cajoling.

We toured a few high street chain shops in the precinct, without luck , until I spotted a small independent retailers at the bottom end of the high street. The clothes were more expensive, but you could see that they were good quality. Anita bought herself a pair of slim line trousers with a flattering tunic top in a deep salmon colour detailed with interspersed tiny diamanté stones . I tried on several dresses , which were quite nice and flattered my figure, but didn't have that "wow "factor .

Then I saw it .... A red dress, shaped neckline, figure fitting , skirt cut on the bias, knee length . I tried it on ....and well...it fitted perfectly. The colour enhanced my dark hair, and suited my skin tone . It was a beautiful shade ...not an overly bright orange red, but a deep cherry lustre. The neckline was quite low, but fitted my bust, allowing just the right amount of creamy cleavage. The skirt was slightly flirty, and swung just above my knees in undulating folds , due to the amount and quality of the material . This length suited me as it showed off my shapely, slender legs. The sales woman asked my shoe size and brought over a pair of high heeled, strappy sandals in the exact same shade. I put them on ....the outfit was complete.

Anita actually clapped . The saleswoman said " that is THE dress for you. You would swear it was individually tailored . It looks so beautiful . Stay there, I want to take a picture. ". She scampered off to the back of the shop and returned with a camera " smile " she commanded , taking snaps from various angles. She made me twirl around and took some more photos. " I'll use these for advertising" she said " that's if you don't mind? " " not at all " I beamed , thinking 'I must look good in it then. ' " My goodness, Jodie you have to buy that dress...and those shoes " encouraged Anita.

It was only then that I looked at the price tag £ 120 ! I think I probably turned white, even if it was hidden by my make up . The shoes were £60 . " Ummm arrr ...I don't think.." I began " Now, Jodie, " burst in Anita "you haven't treated yourself to anything. You told me yourself that Josh had bought a new set of golf clubs when you arrived here , in order to play in the Morlais Golf Club . They cost a pretty penny ...more than the dress and shoes " she had guessed what I was about to say. I thought about it , and it was true that Josh had bought a set of clubs . " Yes, alright then, I'll take them " I said determinedly , before I could change my mind. The saleswoman smiled, and packaged them up before I had a chance to think. I handed over my credit card, and left the shop with my new purchases.

" The way to spend a lot of money in one day " I said to Anita as we returned to our cars " Pah" she snorted " We deserve it...as they say in the advert ' because I'm worth it ' " she made a funny pose, with one hand on her hip and the other in the air, wrist bent. " I bloody well hope Josh thinks I am " " He won't know what's hit him , when you show him your new look ...he'll think he's got a new wife " we both laughed at this. I must admit I had noticed a few admiring glances as we had walked through the town . That was something that didn't usually happen to me. " I'd best be off" I said to Anita " I want to get the place looking

No Refuge

the best I can , for tonight's seduction scene " Anita laughed " give me a ring ..and tell me all about it " she giggled " well, perhaps not ALL ". We said our goodbyes and got in our cars. I was looking forward to tonight. Lets make this a night to remember I thought.

I arrived home, luckily before Josh had finished evening surgery, although he tended to end earlier on a Friday. I unpacked all the shopping, hanging my new dress at the back of the clothes rail.

In our tiny kitchen, I checked the casserole , and cut some pieces of fresh French bread, which I put in a wicker basket. The trifle looked delicious and the crockery was piled up on the side of the table with two settings of cutlery. I moved them, and took the Formica table into our makeshift living room. We had received a set of white linen tableware for our marriage . I lay the tablecloth over the table , set two places and put the napkins out. I brought the crockery from the kitchen and set it on the table together with two candle holders and red tapering candles.

Looking at the clock , I realised that Josh should be home at any minute and made sure everything was ready. Lighting the candles, I sat down to wait . My plan was to to serve the casserole, then nip upstairs, touch up my makeup and put on my new dress and shoes. I smiled to myself.

A few minutes later, I heard Josh come in from the surgery. He dropped his bag at the side of the doorway and sighed . I hope he hasn't had another bad day , I thought. "Hi Josh" I called out " I'm in the living room " He came in and stared at the table and candles " What's this in aid of ?" He asked " I thought it would be a good idea if we had a romantic evening in together. I know we've been arguing lately, and we're both under stress . I want to make up for nagging you about that Candice...I realise I was making a mountain out of a molehill "

" Thats quite a speech.....thank you for realising how much stress I've been under. Don't know what you're moaning about though. " I tried not to react to this comment, so I ignored it " Sit down and I'll bring the dinner in . I bought a slow cooker and I've made you a chicken casserole, with fresh cream trifle for dessert " " Oh....been spending again " sneered Josh. I still kept quiet. I was determined to make this evening a success.

I went into the kitchen and returned with the basket of French bread and a plate of casserole. I placed the dinner in front of Josh " Hmmmm be a change to eat a decent meal for once " he murmured, stabbing the casserole with a fork " Hey! What have you done to your hair? " " I've had it styled ...special offer at a new hairdressers ...do you like it? " " It's ok.....I prefer it as you usually have it " I glared at him, but he didn't notice as he was tucking into the chicken " Just nipping upstairs to change " I trilled merrily " In to what?" "you'll see " .

I made my way to the bedroom and changed into my new dress. It even looked gorgeous in the old mirror we had placed in the corner of the room. The lights from the bedside lamps made it appear to shimmer. I slipped on the shoes, and renewed my makeup , making sure my lipstick was glossy enough to emphasise the pout. Finally, I just tidied up my hair , combing the half fringe so that I could peer at Josh seductively. Satisfied , I went back downstairs, via the kitchen, picked up my plate and sashayed into the living room .

I placed the plate on the table, and sat down opposite Josh . He continued eating, and I began to eat my casserole. I had placed a bottle of white wine on the table, and I noticed that Josh had already helped himself to a glass. " Will you pour me some wine please. Love? " I asked, holding out a glass . Josh picked up the bottle and started to pour into my glass, then he looked at me . He appeared somewhat taken aback. I smiled, and he just continued to stare . Looking at my red, sensuous lips, and down to the cleavage of my dress. His eyes practically devoured me and I smiled even broader .

" Stand up " ordered Josh. I stood, still smiling. I tossed my wavy hair over one shoulder and pouted at him . I stuck out one hip and placed my hand on it , in a sexy pose. I was enjoying this. I had never felt so sexy and sensuous, it was a heady feeling.

No Refuge

I placed one leg in front of the other, displaying my slender ankles and long legs, enhanced by the high heeled sandals. Josh stood up from behind the table and walked towards me, I gave him a lascivious look . He picked up his arm.......and with all his strength.....slapped me ....right across my cheek. The blow was so hard and unexpected that I fell to the ground. " You fucking whore! " he shouted " Get up ...it was just a tap. " I was bewildered..what had I done? Why was he acting like this? I tried to struggle to my feet, but kept slipping, I couldn't seem to get purchase on the floor. I slipped off my shoes and scrambled to my feet.

" What the fucking hell are you up to? " he demanded " are you thinking of becoming a call girl or something ? You look fucking disgusting ". " Josh..Josh... It's a new dress....sob...a makeover...thought you'd like it...sob " tears were running down my face, but my biggest emotion was bewilderment . I just didn't understand. Nothing made any sense. Josh came closer to me again. He reached out for me, I shrunk away.

" Don't you fucking move away from me " he whispered in a threatening way. " Come here " he put his arm around my waist and pulled me to him " I'll give you what you fucking want......cunt " . His grasp was strong and painful, he pulled me towards the stairs.

Still holding me tightly, he caught my hair, pulled it back , and moved his other arm to loop under my armpit, his hand pressing on the back of my neck " come on you fucking bitch,I'm taking you upstairs and I'm going to fuck the arse off you......just like you deserve " he pulled me into the bedroom, my legs all scratched and bleeding from the bare wooden stairs. " stop....stop.. please Josh..stop...you're hurting me " I cried and screamed. I couldn't move.. he had me in an arm lock. He threw me on the bed, face down, and I immediately tried to get up . He hit me across the back of my neck , pinned me down and held my two arms above my head . I could feel his knee between my legs as he got on top of me . His free hand ripped the material of the dress and he tore my panties off. I felt a stinging pain in my back and my thighs . I was crying , sobbing and pleading, but no longer screaming . I had no breath left to protest. I was shaking from shock as he thrust himself into me. The pain was excruciating. This man that I loved was raping me and the pain was unbearable. I was dry and resistant as his thrusting tore at the lining of my vagina. Thankfully, he came quickly . He pushed me away from him with an expression of disgust. Then he got off, ran downstairs , fumbled by the door ....and left.

I was left, lying in a crumpled heap. Stunned and shocked. I had no idea what to do. My mind seemed incapable of rational thought. Deep, deep inside me , the first flame of anger started to burn, but it was only a very tiny spark . It would take a long time to become a blaze and even longer to extinguish.

CHAPTER TEN

Josh

He pulled some of the files off his desk and moved them to the top of the filing cabinet. Wearily, Josh realised he could not face sorting them out and filing them under the correct headings. He really needed a medical secretary. There was no one to type letters, chase up appointments, do the filing or 101 other administrative tasks which were beyond his remit. The paperwork was building up.....even more so, since they had taken on a sudden influx of new patients who had moved from their previous surgery due to some sort of dispute over appointment times.

To tell the truth, Josh was getting bloody fed up with all this administrative work, and especially with Jodie's attitude. She knew how important it was to build up a thriving practice. Essential in today's economic climate and all the restrictions placed on the NHS. There was also the house and it's renovations that had to be paid for ...and the longer the builders took, the more money it was costing. Jodie did nothing to help.

Josh had managed to scrape enough from the budget to pay for two part time receptionists, but this was not nearly enough staff, they were really struggling. His ambitions of running specialised clinics was putting a great deal of pressure on the three nurses the practice was currently allocated. They had no admin support, apart from the small amount the receptionists could provide. Several important records had already been temporarily misplaced. He was extremely worried that something urgent would be lost, causing problems for the patient, the staff and himself. He drew his fingers through his hair in frustration.

The more he thought about Jodie, the angrier he got. She was fully aware of the whole picture, the pressure and the work. She should be here, supervising the builders and making sure they were working to full capacity. She should be giving a hand in the surgery with the secretarial duties. Jodie could quite easily sort out the files, chase up appointments and construct the clinic timetables . But where was she? She had swanned off to town with the new friend she had made in the library , in order to have a 'girls day out' full of pampering and shopping , whilst he was left here in the shit! Josh growled angrily under his breath , she was becoming a right selfish bitch , he thought.

There was a knock at his consulting room door. It opened to reveal Sheila, one of the receptionists . " there's two police officers to see you Doctor Harrison , shall I show them in ? " she asked . Josh was taken aback…what was this about? His mind ran through possible scenarios , including the recent death of Candice. He took a deep breath, to compose himself, and said " Please show them in Sheila, thank you "

She ushered the two officers into the room. Josh shook their hands. One was a male officer in his forties, heavy built, tall and with a strong , no nonsense handshake, the other was a woman, around her mid thirties, slim ,with a weaker, yet just as determined , handshake. The male officer introduced them; " Hello Doctor Harrison " he began " I'm Detective Inspector Ross, and this is Detective Sergeant Dawson " he indicated towards the female officer. Josh offered them both a seat and sat down behind his desk. " How do you think I can help you officers? " he asked, leaning forward, with his hands clasped .

The two police officers shifted in their chairs, trying to get as comfortable as possible. Inspector Ross wore trousers in a sage green, with a toning tweed , sports jacket . He had on a cream shirt with a small green stripe, and a dark grey tie with some sort of emblem on it. 'Very dapper' thought Josh.' He's obviously got a wife who looks after him ' . This observation was partly borne out by the presence of a thick gold band on his wedding finger.

No Refuge

Sergeant Dawson was dressed in a navy suit with a pencil skirt which stopped just below her knees. She had teamed this with a white blouse, dark tights and a pair of flat, black shoes. She crossed her legs demurely, but Josh got the impression that she was uncomfortable in this tailored outfit, and would be more at home in something more casual and less restrictive . It was something to do with the way she held her body so rigidly as if she was afraid she might move awkwardly and blow the whole ensemble to pieces.

"We'd like to talk to you in connection with the death of Candice Roberts " said Ross , his eyes
meeting Josh's , slightly narrowed with suspicion. " I believe you were acquainted with Mrs Roberts ? "
"Yes, she was a patient. " " When did you last see her?" Sergeant Dawson was writing busily in her notebook, as Ross kept up the questioning. " Let me see....mmmmm...about two or three weeks ago when she came in here with her husband Chris " " What did she come to see you about? " " Sorry,, that's confidential information, and I cannot disclose it unless you have a warrant which obliges me to release that information to you, " Josh and Inspector Ross locked eyes.The officer reached into his inside pocket and brought out a piece of paper " We are well versed in the Data Protection Act these Days, Doctor Harrison " he said , opening the paper for Josh to read. It was a police warrant to disclosure any information and any records etc pertaining to Mrs Candice Roberts . " Very well" agreed Josh. " She came to see me because she was suffering from a urinary tract infection. I examined her, took a sample of urine and prescribed some anti-biotics. She also told me that her "nerves " were bad. That she felt someone was following her and she was scared " " What did you advise her to do ? " " Well , nothing really. I thought that perhaps she was exaggerating, in order to get a medical certificate or that it was her imagination. In any case, Candice was a strong character, easily able to stand up for herself. Not someone to be scared . I told her if she was still feeling anxious in a couple of weeks, to come back and see me. She seemed happy enough with that. " " I see. What about her husband ...Chris Roberts . What was he like? " " I only exchanged greetings with him on that occasion. He remained outside when Candice came in. I know him from school though. We were in the same schools and went about together as youngsters.

He always seemed a mild mannered, quiet bloke to me, to tell you the truth. ". " Did Candice say she was afraid of her husband?" " No, on the contrary. She made some jokes in the vein of 'she'd give him what for 'if he didn't do some household repairs for her. I can't remember exactly what she said, but she certainly wasn't scared of him. " Josh smiled, and shook his head in disbelief.

The two officers appeared to relax, and Josh thought that they would probably now leave. He was aware that he had patients due to see him and they would be waiting impatiently, for their appointments. " Well, if that's all officers " Josh said, getting to his feet " I'm sorry I couldn't be of more help. If you want to see her medical records just tell my receptionist and she will photocopy them for you " He made to walk around from behind his desk, to see the officers out.

" Excuse me, Doctor Harrison " said Inspector Ross " have you heard of a place in town called " The Club?" " There's lots of clubs about " replied Josh " Do you know it's name ? " " It's official name is Club Paradis .....but it's locally known as just 'The Club, 'in fact , most people are probably unaware of its real name " " Mmmmm....yes, now you mention it, I have heard the patients and some other people talking about it ......something to do with pole dancing isn't it? " " Yes, it is officially a pole dancing club " Inspector Ross gave a cynical look together with a sarcastic tone of voice , as if he knew that it was a cover for other business.

He looked straight at Josh and continued " Have you ever been there, sir ?" " Ummm...no, not as far as I can remember". " Mmm...I see " murmured Ross, making a note in his pad. "Were you aware that Candice Roberts worked there! Sir ? " " No ....I can't remember her telling me that " Josh shock his head " Your memory seems a bit hazy, if you don't mind me saying so , sir " Josh said nothing. He was feeling uncomfortable and worried about the answers he had just given. Should he admit he'd been there? It could look suspicious now, if someone had told them they'd seen him.

" Your wife found the body , didn't she doctor? " asked Sergeant Dawson " Yes, in the skip we had hired for the building work " " Did she mention anything about the condition of the body to you , sir ? " " Yes, yes, actually she

No Refuge

did. She only saw the body's legs ....but she said that one leg looked damaged, with flesh hanging off it like pieces of meat. It really upset her, she was immediately sick, and couldn't look any more. She called you straight away. " " Yes, that's correct sir , we have Mrs Harrison's statement. " Inspector Ross butt in " Have you any idea how that injury could have been caused to Mrs Roberts' legs , sir? " he asked " No, none whatsoever. I never saw the body. If I had........ well maybe I could have guessed ...it would depend on the type of injury , the marks, damage ,or any other factors " " Would it surprise you sir to know that the foot and ankle had been hacked off by a sharp weapon? " " Is that what happened ? " asked Josh, genuinely shocked. His face paled and his eyes widened. " You seem surprised sir " stated Ross " Well I am, I would not have thought Chris would be capable of doing anything like that " Josh's voice became a squeak, and he looked away. He could feel perspiration breaking out on his forehead. " Do you know why her foot was hacked off sir? " " No " " Because she was handcuffed by her ankles to something when she died, and the perpetrator couldn't unlock the cuff to release the body " Josh said nothing . Just stood there looking at the police officers, wishing to God that they would just go away and leave him alone.

" The foot was found under more of the rubbish in your skip, sir. Were you aware of that? ". " No . My wife didn't say ...I don't think she knew " "Unfortunately, we haven't found the handcuffs . Have you any suggestions about where it may be , sir? " " No, off course not! " exclaimed Josh " Why on earth should I ? " " I was just asking sir, there's no need to get upset ". " I am NOT upset" cried Josh " Now, if you have nothing else with which to waste my time, I suggest you leave. I have patients to see." " We have nothing else at the moment sir. Thank you for giving us your time. I'm sure we will call back again in the future. If you remember anything pertinent, such as a visit to " the Club" I would appreciate it if you could give us a call . " Ross handed him a card " We'll see ourselves out ...thank you sir". The two Officers left the room , shutting the door behind them.

Josh sat down at his desk. He was surprised to notice that he was visibly shaking. He put his head in his hands and groaned . ' Oh my God, what was all that about ' he wondered . He had lied to the police, and then they gave him information which suggested that they thought he might have had something to do with the murder. He should have told them the truth. But if he did, Jodie could find out and they might arrest him for some other offence or something . He wasn't even sure if anything he had done HAD been against the law. Parts of the club may be operating illegally , but this didn't necessarily mean that the customers could be arrested .....well he hoped not, anyhow. " Oh My God...what was going to happen next ? "

Josh managed to pull himself together and continue with his surgery. His mind kept drifting away from his patients and he could feel frustration and anger building up inside his body. Why was he a victim to his needs? What had made him seek out these practices. He thought it would all go away when he met Jodie. She was such a beautiful, clever , yet fairly innocent girl. She dressed conservatively and non-provocatively. The opposite to all the girls he had used and shagged in the past. She should have been enough to satisfy him. To get rid of his deviant urges.

Perhaps that was part of the problem. She wouldn't even indulge in the mildest of S & M practices...not even silken scarves or a blindfold. He had asked her teasingly on their honeymoon and she had refused, saying that she ' found all that stuff repulsive '. The only sex she enjoyed was the 'emotional, loving welding 'of 'two bodies together '. She insisted that sexual satisfaction was all about pure loving emotions that were produced in the mind, not the body. Well it wasn't in his fucking mind . His body and mind needed cruelty and pain to find satisfaction.

Josh managed to stumble through the evening's surgery. All he wanted to do was go home, have a few drinks and go to sleep. He wanted to forget all about today . The work, the pressure, the builders and most of all the visit from the police . He wanted to put Candice and anyone associated with her, completely out of his mind . The best would be if he was left alone , and Jodie said nothing which could ignite his anger.

He left just after six o' clock , and wearily made his way home, dropping his bag at the side of the door as he entered the house, and sighed.

No Refuge

Jodie called him and he went in to the living room , where she had made an attempt at a 'romantic meal' . It turned out to be a chicken casserole which she had produced after purchasing a slow cooker. He was so fed up and tired, that he could only stab at the chicken with a fork. He would have preferred a sandwich in front of the telly tonight. Before she sat down to eat, Jodie had told him that she was going upstairs ' to change ' . He noticed that she had had something done to her hair. ' More bloody money again ' he thought ' which we can't fucking afford .' And what's this about changing? Not clothes as well? Gallivanting about whilst I've been working myself to death, unable to cope , and problems hitting me at all sides. What the hell does she think she's up to?

Jodie came back downstairs and sat opposite Josh. He noticed her hair, her make up and the cleavage revealed by the dress. He stared at her in disbelief. He couldn't believe his eyes. She looked like a fucking whore. She was dressed like those girls he had pleasured himself with in the past. She wouldn't try any of their practices....but she was bloody dressed and made up like one of them !

To Josh's total amazement, Jodie stood up and smiled at him with the knowing smile of a cheap whore She stood as if she was for sale , willing to be tied up and beaten and fucked until she couldn't move. She had been his " little miss nice girl ", in her Laura Ashley clothes , her straight dull hair and her plain, freshly washed face .....that was what had attracted him to her . Now she appeared as if by magic, to have transformed herself into human trash , a fucking little slut , whilst he had been trying his best to work, work, work for them, to keep his darker urges in check , and to try not to complain when she didn't help in the house or practice ......how did she repay him ? By becoming this fancy trollop.......and the joke was ...she didn't have a fucking clue as to what it meant, how to behave ....she probably thought the sex would be ' a meeting of emotional minds, soft and gentle and vanilla '. Well he would fucking show her.

Josh grabbed her tightly. Twisted her into an arm lock and dragged her by her fancy hair, up to bed.

He'd show her what sex was like as a fucking slag ...she'd dressed like one, now she could act like one. He needed it anyway...he needed to inflict the pain and feel the resistance. He threw her on the bed face down and pushed her into the duvet, hitting her across the back of her neck, getting aroused at the sight of the welts rising on her skin.

He ripped aside her fucking red dress, pulled the material and scratched her thighs, deeply with his nails, relishing the blood he drew and the shape of the stinging wounds. He ripped off her panties, making sure he stung her with the elastic and she cried with the pain, causing his cock to become harder and harder. His penis was fully engorged with a lust he'd never felt with her before in their previous sanitised love making .

Scratching and gorging with his fingers, he pressed and pushed them inside, until he could open her fanny wider and thrust himself into her, slapping her arse and causing her to buck with pain...oh how he relished the pain. He could feel his cock cutting in her dry and tight vagina....he hoped he made the cunt bleed. He'd show her what sex was like for a thankless whore , who did fuck all but spend money on herself to make her look like a parody of the real thing . She had to be punished...and he made sure he punished her.

Josh ejaculated. He looked at the welts and scratches on her body, the blood on the duvet cover , and threw her to one side with a snort of disgust. He left her there , to her own devices and stormed out of the house. He needed more , he needed pain, he needed to be totally satisfied.

Reaching "The Club" , Josh showed his card and entered the vestibule. He looked around wildly " Where's Stan? " he asked the cloakroom girl " I'll get him now sir " she replied , used to clients in all sorts of moods . She picked up the internal telephone and pressed the number for Stan's office " A platinum client is here, Wants to see you " she said into the mouthpiece.

Placing it back on the receiver she smiled at Josh and said " He'll be here in a few ticks sir, " Josh waited, tapping his foot impatiently , until Stan rounded the corner. " Ah Sir," he said, smiling at Josh " How can I be

No Refuge

of help to you this evening ? ". " I want a girl . A very 'special 'girl......if you know what I mean " he whispered gruffly to Stan " Yes certainly sir. " Stan took out a small book from his inside pocket . " Jess is available...just the job. Caters for all your tastes, sir. However, she IS very expensive" " I don't mind the cost ....get her for me " Josh's eyes were blazing , there was a glint of madness in them.

Stan made his way to the dressing room. Jess was sitting there, filing her nails. " Got just the job for you darlin' " he said " A customer who hasn't been in for a while ...but has perverse tastes .... J.H....been with him before? " " Oh aye . I know the one ....Big bloke? " " Yes that's him ...but he seems a bit wild, shall me say , tonight " " Don't worry " reassured Jess " I can handle him . The whips first and he' ll soon settle down " Jess gave a wicked smile, and narrowed her eyes. " Fine....follow me ." declared Stan as he held his arm out with a flourish for Jess , and she followed him out to work on calming down her 'wild' punter.

CHAPTER ELEVEN

Jodie

I woke up and realised that my limbs were all aching, and I felt sore and bruised. For a moment, I wondered if I had been in some sort of accident. My head throbbed as I tried to move. Gingerly I uncoiled my body and looked around . ....then the memories came flooding back. Josh, my husband, had raped me .....abused me ...hurt me . My face felt wet, I didn't realise that I was crying.

Looking out of the window, I could see streaks of light just starting to appear across the horizon . It was morning I realised, so I had been lying there a long time in my tattered finery. The dress I had been so pleased with was now torn and stained, not even good enough for floor cloths . My hair was like a crows nest ....sticking out around my face. Where had Josh gone? He had run out of the house but that was around eight last night , where had he stayed ? ....why did I bloody care ?

I made my way downstairs, boiled the kettle and had a hot cup of tea with plenty of sugar. .....for shock, I rationalised. How I would love to have a hot bath, bathe my wounds and injuries, allow the water to soothe the physical pain and hopefully make me feel less dirty......I felt soiled, degraded and used. It was a horrible feeling. I just wanted it to go away. What shall I do?

I returned to the bedroom and took off the torn garments and thrust them in to a black bin bag. I washed tentatively with cold water, and put on clean underwear, a pair of loose jeans and a baggy top. I brushed my hair thoroughly, although the waves remained . This made me feel marginally better. I stripped the bed, and put the duvet cover and sheets in a large laundry bag , ready for collection. I still felt dazed. Unable to fully believe what had happened and no idea why. What had made my previously loving husband do this? There had been no signs before . Not in Manchester or Cardiff.....not for the first few months of our marriage......had he suffered some sort of breakdown? I was totally bewildered. All I knew at the moment was that I didn't want to be here any more. I didn't want to see him . I needed time to think. I shoved some toiletries and a few clothes into a bag, locked up the house, got in the car and drove to Cardiff. I decided to go and stay with my mother. I didn't give a shit about the surgery or the bloody house...let Josh sort it out. The embers of anger were starting to glow.

During the drive, I had to plan what to tell my mother. I wasn't going to go into the gory details . I thought perhaps the best line to take was that we had argued due to all the stress of the house and the practice . I would tell her that we both needed some time apart for us to take a break from each other and get our thoughts into perspective.

I arrived at the front door of my mothers three bedroom semi. She had lived there for the past five years, since my dad had died, and she still missed him terribly. He had not been a 'new man' by any means . He was strict but fair, which worked well with my brothers, but not so effectively with me...but then, I could twist him around my little finger. I also missed him...I really wished he was here now, I was sure he could sort out all my problems. Tears welled in my eyes again.

My mother was shocked to see me standing there when she opened the door. "what's the matter love? I didn't know you were coming. " " I've had a row with Josh....oh mam...." I started sobbing, so much so, I couldn't speak. "There, there love...come in and tell me all about it". She put an arm around me and led me into the living room, sitting me down on the sofa.

My mothers living room was a cosy, welcoming place. She had the walls painted in a plain cream, and the carpet was beige. She had taken this decor as a

No Refuge

blank palette and she had injected her favourite colours. There were two sofas - one red and one black, covered in soft, cuddly cushions, in gold, crimson and silver. on the floor she had placed a multicoloured mat in front of a modern fireplace, with abstract ornaments placed on top .Dotted around the room were small lamp tables with varying lamps, of all shapes and sizes The walls were decorated with brightly coloured paintings which were my mothers own work. She favoured abstract whirls and curves or gigantic bold flowers Above the fireplace was a large screen TV. The overall effect was of a warm, embracing place; optimistic, safe and secure ...just what I needed .

My mother brought me a cup of tea, the panacea of all ills. She placed a small table in front of us, sat down with her own cuppa and asked me what was wrong. I had just about managed to stop crying , I was dabbing my eyes with a tissue , realising what a mess I must look. " We've been arguing about the house and the surgery mam . We've both been very stressed and it's really getting me down. " The words tumbled out. My mother looked at me with questions in her eyes. She looked a bit sceptical about what I had just said. " You seem very upset, too upset, for just being stressed about the building work and Josh's practice " she implied, looking straight into my eyes, as if for clues. " Well, I did find that body I told you about mam , and that freaked me out ....I think that's what started it . I was like a scalded cat in the house ....very jumpy ....and Josh wanted me to supervise the builders and help with the admin in the practice. " " Yes, it must have been awful to have found that body in your skip, the thought of it gives me the shivers ....but as for helping with the admin and seeing to the builders ....well, that doesn't seem too unreasonable " " But mam, I was all nervy and scared. I applied for jobs and wanted to do my own work, not just be a helper for Josh " " Well love, sometimes that's what marriage is about. Making compromises, giving up what you want to do for a while, helping your partner.

You haven't got a job yet have you? ". " No, not yet ...but I've applied ". " I see....but if you haven't actually GOT a job.....then why not help out? " I started to feel annoyed. Here was my mother sticking up for Josh . Admittedly, she didn't know the full, horrendous story, but I wanted my mam to be on MY side ...about everything. I started to pout. She put her arms around me " Now,

don't pout, my lovely ....you've always been a pouter "she gave a little chuckle " I can tell you're very upset...I was just trying to sort of balance out what you told me. Perhaps it's a combination of the stress of finding the body and living in what is virtually a building site with no proper facilities. Difficult for both of you when there's so much to do and that's probably causing friction. "
"Mmm maybe " I muttered, leaning against my mother and enjoying her cwtch. We just sat there quietly, for some minutes. It was lovely to feel protected and secure ...I thought Josh would make me feel like that, but I felt quite the opposite about him at the moment ....he felt like the enemy.

I was now ensconced in my old bedroom which my mother had always kept for me. Feeling so rootless during our childhood, mam had decided when she bought this house that one room would be allocated for me and one (bigger room) for my brothers, so we always had somewhere to stay, if we needed to. My youngest brother Eddie still lived at home when she moved in so he had actually occupied the " boys room" for a couple of years until he moved away with his job.

I hung my meagre number of clothes in the wardrobe and put my underwear in a drawer. It was furnished with a white bedroom suite, including a large triple mirror on the dressing table. The walls were painted in white with a tinge of apple green. An oatmeal carpet covered the floor. More of my mothers art hung on the walls. The duvet was white with sprigged green and yellow flowers, and matched the curtains. A fluffy white rug was by the side of the bed. It was a light, pleasant room. I had to say this about my mother ...she had good taste.

She had got me wondering about how much of our problems had been my fault. Had I been very selfish not helping Josh out and not supervising the renovations? Did this send him over the edge.... Together with my transformation .? He had often expressed his dislike of " tarty " women, with revealing clothes and heavy makeup. When he had seen " Kat Slater " on Eastenders, he had actually become quite angry, saying it was disgusting the image of women they put on television, degrading the whole gender. He'd often said how lovely he thought my fresh face, plain, neat clothes, and natural hairstyle were. We'd had a gentle, caring style of lovemaking. In fact, he hadn't

No Refuge

touched me for months after we started seeing each other. Not until we were engaged and living in Manchester , to be exact. Josh always sad that I was a goddess, far too good for him, and he didn't want to sully me.

Was this all my fault?

Previous boyfriends had accused me of being cold, and unresponsive. I had only had two other 'lovers ' . The first was a boy the same age as me in college. I had drunk quite a bit , and he tried it on. I was fed up of being teased about my virginal status so I went for it. It was a big disappointment. He was drunk as well and neither of us remembered much about it. I only saw him a couple of times after that, and we never had sex again . The second one was a fellow lecturer in Liverpool,who I dated before I knew Josh . We went out for a few meals together, about three or four dates, when he became very passionate one night after I had invited him in for coffee. I tried to enjoy it, but found I felt nothing much. He just got on with it, never tried to please me or use foreplay and soon ejaculated. This put me right off and I thought I would be alone forever .....until I met Josh . He was so considerate, that I could relax and not worry about sex . When we finally did sleep together, he was very gentle and brought me to orgasm by using foreplay. I thought I had found the ideal man.

The more I thought about it, the more I could see how much I was to blame. I had put all the pressure on him. I had left him to do all the work whilst I went out and had a makeover and did shopping . I had then dressed up like the type of woman he loathed, when he was probably feeling fed up and needed some homely comforts. I hated myself. I was obviously no good as a wife or lover . Instead of pulling together, I had nagged about getting a job of my own, and doing nothing in the meantime . I had even dismissed the importance of having a baby and looking after myself . What a right cow I had been .

I took off all my clothes and went into the bath room. I filled the tub with hot soapy water and bathed my body. It was lovely to have a hot bath again, how I had missed it. I gently swabbed the sore parts of my body -inside and out. Soon I felt much better, shampooing my hair and rinsing it off with the shower attachment. It felt squeaky clean. I felt cleansed and fresh again. I got out of the bath, and wrapped myself in a soft, warm fluffy towel. I applied some antiseptic cream to my wounds and inside my vagina....it was smooth and cooling. Then I sat by the dressing table and brushed my long dark hair, ' this was the cause of a lot of trouble ' I thought angrily , remembering how Josh had pulled it back , and dragged me by it saying I looked like a slut with that hairstyle. I could see the remnants of the waves in the wet tresses.

I took a scissors from the drawer and started cutting my hair. I cut away at the dark lustrous locks which could look so tarty . I cut it all around the back and sides until it came to just below my ears. ' there ' I thought ' one less thing to worry about...one less feature that can make me look a slut . ' I felt better. Cutting my hair off had felt liberating . I was less anxious . I knew things would work out . I lay on the bed and fell asleep.

CHAPTER TWELVE

"Betty". (Jodie's mother)

Betty had taken out some ingredients from the fridge and was making Jodie one of her favourite meals; Gammon, potatoes, kidney beans and parsley sauce . ' She can't be eating properly with no proper cooker in that house ' she thought ' I bet everything is either takeaways or fish and chips ' . She worked away merrily, humming a little tune, it was nice to have someone else in the house with her, someone to look after. Although to be honest ,she was happy enough with her sister Joyce living nearby, and the friends , old and new , she had in Cardiff .

Betty thought that Jodie probably needed a short break after her row with Josh. They had both been living under quite a bit of pressure since moving to Merthyr. Josh had inherited his fathers house and practice, but it needed a lot of expensive renovations, and, because the surgery had been closed for the past 18 months, he also had to entice new people to come there. . There was no existing list of patients already in the practice.

In Betty's opinion, Jodie was in the wrong not helping Josh as much as she could with the house and surgery . Instead, she had been looking for a new job, and leaving him to it. Their plans for a baby hadn't even been taken into account. For goodness sake, when you got married and started a family you had to make compromises, and sometimes sacrifices. Look at Betty, herself. She had travelled about from place to place for over 25 years, following Ken's postings. In some places she had felt very lonely indeed, and it was always difficult making new friends . But that's what you did, if you wanted a successful marriage. She'd had Ken - a strong, reliable husband......and three beautiful children . That was her life and her family. You hadn't seen her nagging him to leave the army and settle in one place...she knew how much it meant to him...it was his life . The problem was....it had also been his death.....a tear sprang to her eyes which she quickly brushed away.

Betty checked the pans boiling on the hob, and speared the vegetables with a fork. They were nearly ready . She would sit down with Jodie and have a nice chat. Betty would make her see the error of her ways , and maybe Josh could come down for the day . They could go out ..make a treat of it, and settle their differences. She smiled to herself , all would turn out ok...just wait and see.

The problem with Jodie was that she was spoiled. Ken had worshiped her ' his precious girl' , and she could twist him around her little finger. The boys were the same. They protected their sister , and she always charmed them into fighting her battles for her. Any trouble , and Jodie never got the blame ...one or other of her brothers would take the punishment for her, and she would get away scot free. Because she always got her own way with her father and siblings, she thought she could do the same with Josh .....no wonder they had argued.

Josh had actually rung about half an hour ago to see if Jodie was there. Betty had told him she was , but that she was having a lie down and it would be better if he rang back later. He told her that they had had a big argument and to tell Jodie he was sorry. What more could he do? Betty thought that Josh was a good son in law. He had bought her an extra Mother's Day present because she was ' the mother he no longer had '. When they stayed in Cardiff, Josh had been really helpful with little jobs around the house . He also treated Betty and Jodie to theatre tickets and trips to the cinema as special " mother and daughter " day outs AND he had such nice manners ......everyone said so . Even Joyce said that he had a ' lovely bedside manner ' ..and Joyce had something negative to say about everyone !

No Refuge

The kitchen table was set with the 'Poppy' crockery that Betty was collecting from Dunhelm Mill . She almost had a full dining service , and was hoping for the breakfast bowls for Christmas or her birthday. Carefully she took down a ' Poppy ' mug and made Jodie a cup of tea, Dinner was almost ready , and Jodie had slept for several hours. She decided to take up the tea and wake her , then come back down and dish up.

Betty entered the bedroom and immediately noticed what looked like a hairpiece on the floor. She placed the cup of tea on a bedside table and bent down to pick the 'hairpiece' up . To her amazement , she saw that all the carpet around the stool and the dressing table was covered in mounds of hair ......Jodie's long dark hair . What on earth.......? She turned to look at Jodie sleeping in the bed. Her hair was sticking up in clumps ...what had possessed her to cut her lovely hair off . This was a total mystery to Betty .

She gently shook Jodie , " wake up love, wake up....here's a cup of tea for you " Jodie moved her head back and forth slowly. Then, she opened her eyes and looked around as if disorientated. " Where ...what? " she began " You're in your bedroom in my house" said Betty " You had a row with Josh..remember? " Betty was concerned that Jodie had suffered some sort of breakdown and it had affected her memory . " Oh, oh, yes " smiled Jodie " thanks for the tea mam " she picked up the cup and took a sip . "umm Jodie, don't mind me asking......but what have you done to your hair?" " Hair? Oh yes, decided I wanted a change ...fed up of it being long . " " OK dear, ...well, dinners ready, I'm going to start to dish up ...are you coming down , now? " "Yes, mam. I'll be down in a few minutes " Betty left the room and went back downstairs to sort out the meal.

Betty set out the plates and dishes . She got two wine glasses out of her glass cabinet and opened a bottle of white wine she had chilling. ' Hopefully this will make Jodie relax and she'll talk to me. Perhaps she's more upset than I realised , may be she's suffering some sort of depression , like Martha Lewis' girl...she shaved her hair off ' thought Betty, biting her lip , anxiously . She'd do her best to help Jodie , if she confided in her. Perhaps she ought to phone

Josh and ask him to come down ? Betty flapped about, not knowing what to do for the best.

A few minutes later, Jodie entered the kitchen. She had dressed in a clean pair of jeans and long blue jumper. It was obvious that she had tried to do something to her hair by brushing it and using some sort of gel or spray. However, Jodie had originally fallen asleep on it when it was wet , and her hair still looked like a half plucked chicken. Betty tried not to stare .

They sat down for their meal, and Jodie seemed quite chatty and normal, although Betty was still a bit wary. " Josh phoned" said Betty " Oh yes, what did he say? " Jodie smiled " He said to tell you that he was sorry ". " oh that's good. I'll give him a ring later." " He said he'd phone you this evening " . Jodie smiled again and continued eating her dinner " This is lovely , mam, I really miss your cooking " " Thanks love, you and Josh can always come down and have a meal - especially as you haven't got a proper kitchen. You could come for Sunday dinner. I think Eddie'll be here with his girlfriend " " That would be great mam. Thanks " They both ate in silence for a while. Neither of them knew what to say ....there was an elephant , (or a shorn sheep), in the room .

Finally, Betty could keep quiet no longer " Why did you chop off your hair ,Jodie love ? " she asked . Jodie looked her in the eyes " I felt as if my old hairstyle was holding me back. Stopping me being properly grown up, being a proper wife to Josh. I didn't want to be that person anymore. ". " Why didn't you go to the hairdressers and have it cut properly? " " I don't really know, I just wanted it done then, immediately .....I suppose I was still upset " " So you think you will be going back to Josh? " Betty voiced this question tentatively . " Oh yes, of course mam " she cried, with a big smile " It was just an argument. I'll go home tomorrow, and ......I think you're right .....I need to do more to help Josh....stop being selfish " " Oh I'm so glad " cried Betty beaming " I hated the thought of you two breaking up . " " Don't worry mam, I just think things had been getting on top of me. " " Now, don't let that happen again. phone me , or come down and visit, before things go too far . " " I will, I promise, mam " " I think though, before you go home , you should go and see my hairdresser " Betty smiled , Jodie nodded her agreement.

That evening, Jodie had a phone call from Josh and they spoke for about an hour. He said he was sorry and begged her forgiveness for his behaviour.

To his surprise, Jodie readily forgave him. She even said that she would help him more with supervising the builders and sorting out the admin relating to the practice. He mentioned them having a baby, and she giggled like a young girl, saying she couldn't wait and would enjoy " practicing " .

Josh wondered if he was having hallucinations. He had never imagined she would forgive him so easily , and be laughing and joking with him . Perhaps she had secretly enjoyed the rough sex? They say all these prim girls are whores underneath. Well, whatever the reason, he certainly wasn't going to look a gift horse in the mouth. She promised she would come home the next day , which suited him down to the ground , he could have another night with Jessie first. That ought to keep him happy for a while and he'd be able to keep his darker urges in check. Josh said goodnight and went to " The Club" with a smile and a spring in his step.

The following morning , Jodie and Betty visited the hairdresser. Marlene, Betty's regular girl looked appalled at first " What were you doing? No one cuts their own hair these days .....you need training. what sort of look were you aiming for ? " Jodie explained that she hadn't thought about a " look " , she just wanted shorter hair, she was fed up with it long " you can do what you like with it " she told Marlene .

Jodie wanted to look plain. She didn't want Josh thinking she looked like a whore . She didn't want men to lust after her . Marlene cut and shaped, brushed her hair this way and that, tried different partings and used straighteners and tongs .....finally she had finished.

Jodie now had a short, sleek, bob. Layer cut at the back , and slightly longer on to her face, in the front . Her parting was at the side , with a soft feathered fringe. Jodie was glad to have short hair ....what she failed to realise was that she looked amazing. The cut emphasised her dark eyes, making them look larger , her mouth seemed wider and her graceful, creamy neck was now in view. Betty gasped....but wisely , said nothing.

CHAPTER THIRTEEN

"Honey"

The ring of the alarm bell was sounding in the distance. Honey heard it vaguely, but tried in vain to open her eyes. She was so tired. Suddenly, she felt a large bump, as the twins landed on her body, shaking her and shouting " Mammy ". " Mammy " " Get up " . The combined weight of the two five year olds - Sam and Sally, plus their prodding and attempts to wake her, made her force her eyelids apart. She looked into their smiling, delicious faces, and felt a pang of anxiety. What if she was too ill to look after them ? She had her results today from Doctor Harrison .

Honey dragged herself out of bed and quickly washed and dressed the twins, then herself. Glen, as usual, was blissfully sleeping. He was putting a few hours in at " The Club" later on, manning the small, daytime bar, putting out leaflets and checking the premises. He didn't start until 12 noon, and finished at 5pm ....lucky bugger. She was supposed to work 7 pm till midnight, tonight, dancing and gyrating, using what little energy she still had.

" Mammy have you done our costumes? " asked Sally, her innocent little face covered in jam, from her breakfast toast. "Yes, indeed I have " replied Honey proudly. She had used some of the tip from her " special " and purchased the material from the market. Sally now had a full skirted Edwardian dress and Sam's knickerbockers, shirt and waistcoat were hanging up in his bedroom. The dress rehearsal was tomorrow, with the full production on Wednesday.

Bustling about, Honey gathered their bags , gym kit and other paraphernalia together. The twins struggled with their coats as she was pushing them towards the kerb outside the house, and into the car. Quickly she drove off, managing to arrive at their school just in time to avoid a late mark. Honey gave them both a quick kiss and a hug, and waved them in through the school door.

' Now, to face the doctors ' she thought nervously, as she drove towards the surgery.

Entering Josh's waiting room, Honey could see that it was busier than the last time she was there.

'People must be moving to his practice, 'she thought. This increased her trust in him, and she hoped he had a diagnosis which could be quickly, and easily treated. " Mrs Sullivan " came her name over the tannoy system . " Consulting room one , please. " Honey got up, her palms sweating , she rubbed her hands together .

" Hello Honey" said Josh, with a look of concern on his face . " How are you feeling today? ". " Still very tired " Honey replied. " Yes, I'm not surprised " Josh consulted his notes " Your results are back, and I'm afraid they give us a reason for concern "

Honey could feel her stomach turn over with anxiety " What do you mean ? " " Well, your blood test shows that your blood cells have some abnormalities. You most definitely have anaemia , but it could be a little more serious. I'm afraid you will have to attend the hospital for more tests " " What do you mean? what could it be? ". " We can't be sure at the moment. You could have pernicious anaemia or some other type. Worse scene scenario is the possibility of Leukaemia. ". Honey put her hand to her mouth, startled " Oh, I see ...... what do you think? "

" There is genuinely no way I can tell. Your x ray showed a chest infection, which I can give you antibiotics for , and of course that is making you feel worse. I have a note here for you to take to the hospital for further blood tests and a bone marrow biopsy. We will know more after these . "

No Refuge

" What treatment will I have? " " Wait for the diagnosis, before discussing treatment ". Josh cautioned. " Here's a prescription for the tablets to cure your infection, and according to the test results , you will start appropriate treatment. Try not to worry, you are young and usually healthy. This means that whatever we find, you can be successfully treated " Honey tried to smile, but tears started to fall down her face. She took a tissue out of her bag and dabbed her eyes. " I'm worried about my children " she sobbed " Your children can't catch your illness -Don't worry " " It's not that. I've no -one to look after them if I go into hospital, or I'm too Ill to do so . "

" Haven't you any family? " " No..." Honey thought about her parents who had banned her from their house, and her siblings who she hadn't seen for years, and her sobs got louder. " Oh , I'm so sorry " Josh tried to comfort her, his face full of concern

" You are married though. What about your husband......surely he can help out ? " "Glen? ...... He's about as useful as a chocolate radiator . He'll farm them out somewhere , saying he can't cope " Josh pulled a face indicating disgust with this man who wouldn't help his wife and children , in a time of need.

" What about friends ? " he asked hopefully " None I could leave the kids with " " If you like, I could put Social Services in touch with you " " No way, Glen would have a f...., awful fit if a social worker came to the door " she stumbled over her words, trying to prevent swearing. Josh smiled wryly. " Lets cross that bridge when and if we come to it . "

"You will have to stop working, anyway " stated Josh "What do you mean ? " Honey was appalled . " I can't ....Glen would....well ...he would be upset " she put her head down trying not to give too much away. " You have an infection for starters.....you could collapse, your heart could be affected ...anything " Josh couldn't believe his ears. " If you have to have treatment for ....a...um... blood disorder , then you would have a compromised immune system ...and you would be obliged to rest . Otherwise you would not recover ". " Ohhh ". Honey looked even more unhappy.

"I'm sorry to have to have given you all this seemingly bad news. I think you should talk to your husband and try and sort things out with him " ' oh aye' she thought , ' like you've sorted things out with your wife ?' Aloud she said " Well goodbye, Doctor Harrison , thanks. I'll go to the hospital for these tests and what then, do you want me to come back? ".

"Make an appointment for a week today, we'll have more of an idea with the results, and can talk over options . Goodbye, take care. ". Honey left the consulting room, worried not only about her health but about the children, work, money and of course, Glen.

Honey was too upset to really notice anything that was going on around her. The news was awful . More terrible than she had imagined . The illness yes, but the children and not being able to work - well that was far worse. Glen would go ballistic! Her life wouldn't be worth living, even if she recovered.

Last week she had barely been able to dance anyhow. ' I suppose when I get really ill, I won't be in any shape to work ' she thought glumly. She remembered that last night and the night before Stan had sent her home an hour early . The club had been quiet , and Stan had said " Get off home with you, you look knackered " she was so relieved and Glen had been out, the kids were with Doris May from next door , so he didn't even know. If he queried her pay she'd say the tax had gone up …he'd never realise.

Honey stumbled out of the surgery, her eyes blinded by tears . She couldn't see where she was going and bumped straight into Jodie " Ooof!" she exclaimed . Jodie held her up straight , balancing her carefully. " My goodness , what's the matter? Why are you crying ? ". " I'm Ill and I don't know what to do..." Stammered Honey. " Oh ....look here...come and sit down inside the house for a bit...get yourself sorted out, a bit calmer....I'll make you a cuppa ". Jodie put her arm around Honey's shoulder , and led the weeping woman inside to the kitchen.

No Refuge

They sat on the old kitchen chairs, either side of the wobbly Formica table. For a while, they just sipped the tea in silence, then Honey spoke :" thank you so much for this " she practically whispered. " Oh, it's nothing. You said you're ill, is there anything I can help you with? " " Not really. I have to have some more tests and medication. Then probably some treatment. It's the kids and work I'm worried about. No-one to look after the kids , see....and no work means no money "

Jodie was at a loss as to what to say. " Oh , what have you done to your hair? " Honey suddenly burst out . Jodie was taken aback , she could feel her colour rising " I had it cut.....I was fed up with it long .....I know it's not very flattering..... ". " No, I didn't mean that . I think it's lovely...it really suits you . You look , well , amazing " " Thanks " said Jodie, knowing that Honey was just being kind. " I mean it...it was just such a shock...like I didn't realise who you were ...Josh..Doctor Harrison's wife.... I've seen you about before, but with long hair ! " Jodie just smiled.

" Tell me about your children " said Jodie. Honeys face lit up " They're twins - a boy and girl- Sam and Sally . They were five in November...little tinkers they are " she laughed " always up to some mischief or another...nothing nasty mind. They're in their school play tomorrow ....something to do with history...they've got to dress up in 'period costume '-that's like, olden days. I made the outfits myself " she beamed with pride .

"You must be talented. I'm hopeless at sewing " confided Jodie " Yes, but I heard you're some sort of top notch Lecturer - I couldn't do that " " it's no big deal -I just studied hard and learned lots and lots about English Literature , now I teach other people all the stuff I learned . Bet you could lecture on your job. ". " My job? I don't think there's any jobs for lecturers in "Lap Dancing " " You're a lap dancer? " Jodie was surprised and fascinated " I bet you can move bits , I've never tried moving " she laughed " I don't know about that... but you've got to be very flexible " chuckled Honey . " Oh I'd love to have a go ". " When I'm better, I'll show you some moves if you like ". " Brilliant ! "

exclaimed Jodie excitedly . She could do a " performance " for Josh, she thought.

"Where do you work? " Jodie asked " It's a place called " The Club Paradis " but most people know it mostly just as " The Club " it's in Bethesda street . " " Oh I know...I've past it in the car. I'll call in one night when you're dancing " Honey became a little worried. She didn't want Jodie to find out about Josh ....it would hurt her too much, and Honey had decided she liked this woman . She could become a good friend ." I probably won't be working there anymore. I have to rest ...Doctor Harrison's orders . Come when I'm better - well arrange it, and you can have a go on a pole ". " Great, I'll look forward to that. "

They continued chatting for a few more minutes , then Honey had to go. She said her goodbye to Jodie and returned to her car. 'That's a good friend to have ,' she thought. 'She was interested in my pole dancing and didn't act as if I was a prostitute. There's not many ' respectable ' women act like that. Her husbands a good doctor, but I wish he wasn't such a Dick-head when it comes to what he gets up to in the club. '

However, Honey had more pressing things on her mind than Josh and Jodie's marriage . Honey was terrified of telling Glen she had to stop work . As well as being worried about the illness, the treatment , and what would happen to the children. Her stomach was turning over, and Honey looked down at her hands to see that they were shaking.

CHAPTER FOURTEEN

"Josh "

He was at home waiting when Jodie returned. He had cleaned up the living room as much as was possible and bought Jodie a large bunch of roses and a vase to put them in. He had arranged them with gypsophila , and placed them on a small side table .

Josh heard Jodie's car pull up, and her steps tap tapping as she walked around the outside of the house, so that she entered through the back door.

He stood there with anticipation.He was going to apologise once more and give her a hug. In truth, he couldn't believe his luck that she had come home and actually forgiven him ! He had never been so harsh and cruel to any other "normal" girl in his life, let alone his wife . He never thought he would have attacked Jodie like that, but there again, he never thought she would dress like a whore. The image of her like that started his headache again and he clenched his teeth. Josh pushed the image from his mind.

Jodie entered the room. The first thing he noticed was her hair ' what the fuck.....' He thought ' was she deliberately winding him up .....looking so bloody beautiful? ' " Jodie" he said, holding himself in check, " what have you done with your hair? " he was trying to control his breathing, he was starting to feel anger building up in him " Oh, sorry its so ugly....I wanted to look plain ...but maybe this is a bit much " she dropped her head in embarrassment . Josh gave a deep breath of relief , she had no idea how good she looked. She had done it to look plain!

He rushed over to her and gave her a hug. She winced involuntarily, but then tried to relax. " Please forgive me Jodie, I'm so sorry " Josh pleaded " I told you , I forgive you. I realise how much pressure you were under, and how I failed to help you. I didn't think of your feelings, or when I dressed up like the sort of woman you loathe " . Josh kept holding her and kissed her gently , " You are wonderful " he said " I should never have reacted the way I did . " He stepped aside for her to see the flowers . She smiled and looked t him with love in hr eyes " Oh thank you Josh, they're beautiful " she whispered.

They ate a takeaway that evening and watched some drama on the television, trying to get everything back to normal . Josh asked Jodie " What plans have you got for tomorrow? " " Nothing really -except watching and negotiating with the builders of course" she smiled " Do you want me to help at the surgery at all ? " " I wouldn't mind if you could try and sort out some of the correspondence for me ...that would be a great help". " Ok I 'll do a couple of hours on it ". " Thanks so much Jodie ...I do love you, you know ". " I love you too Josh "

The rest of the evening passed companionably. They were both very tired and went to bed quite early, dressed up in all their pyjamas and woollies. Josh fell asleep almost immediately, whilst Jodie read a novel for a while. There was only a good night kiss....no attempt at anything more. Josh was determined to take it slowly and gently.

●●●

The following morning was cold and chilly. Still wrapped up in piles of clothing Josh ran around the small living space turning on the electric fire and blow heater, hoping foe at least a little warmth before work. Josie did the same. She made tea and toast on their basic equipment, ensuring that the large hot mugs of tea warmed their hands as well as insides. Unbelievably, there was frost on the inside of the windows ...Jodie broke some off in the "kitchen " . . "I'll be bloody glad when all this work is finished and we've got a proper home " said Josh " Me too.....I don't fancy getting pregnant and having a baby whilst its in this state ". " I hope it's only going to take another 5 or 6 months to complete ! ".

No Refuge

" Yes, well you never know. I'm always afraid they are going to find something else they are going to have to do ...like they did with the electrics ".

" Oh yeah " Josh's face dropped and he looked morosely into his cup. " Oh well " Josie smiled " No good sitting around here miserable . You get over to the surgery, I'll greet the builders with all my requests, then ill come over to look at the paperwork in your place...OK? ". " Yes, OK. " Josh gave her a peck on the cheek and left to go next door.

It was good for things to be back to ' normal' thought Josh, but he was still scared that he might ' blow up ' again. It had been easier when they hadn't been living together. It had also been easier when he was away from Merthyr to tell the truth.

Perhaps he should never have come back? When he'd lived in Cardiff, he used to come to " The Club" a few times a week, but when he moved to Manchester he was too far away. He had found a similar bondage and S&M club there, but at weekends he was with Jodie , so he would keep away. Although he'd still visit it about once a week, it was less frequent than in Merthyr.

Josh had vowed to himself when they moved back that he wouldn't return to his old ways ....but the urge was too strong. How he longed to "punish those slutty girls " it made him feel omnipotent and in total control, as well as relieving his sexual tension. He had tried....but got too irritable and angry. After a session at " The Club" he felt calmer and more contented ....it was like a drug. A drug he was addicted to. He hadn't decided what he was going to do yet,not in the long term, he had no strategies.

Josh also had another niggling worry. About a week ago he had returned to his car, which had been parked in the Castle Car Park in town , to find a note stuck between a windscreen wiper and the glass. It had read " Telephone 01685 712830 as soon as possible . This is in your best
Interests. " He hadn't known what to make of it, but then decided , it must be some new type of advertising ploy, and if he phoned , he would find someone trying to sell him double glazing or life insurance.

The problem was however, that he had received several phone messages since then, which had the same number, telling him to phone or he would find things would start happening that would be to his DISadvantage . The tone of these were starting to get more and more threatening. He had to do something. Josh decided that he would telephone the number and get it over with.

Arriving in the surgery, Josh picked up a pile of letters from the doormat , just as Sheila arrived. She was on the morning shift this week, taking it in turns with Moira the other receptionist. " Good morning Doctor Harrison " she said cheerily , " I'll just put the kettle on, shall I ? " Josh smiled at her, nodding agreement. He walked into his consulting room and sat at the desk. There were four voice messages for him . Three were simple requests or questions, whilst the fourth was another of those threatening entreaties to telephone that number. Josh decided to do it straight away.
number. Josh decided to do it straight away.

Nervously, Josh pressed the buttons and heard the ringing tone at the other end , it was soon answered, " Hello, who's calling? " came a deep, male voice . "Umm...arrr, doctor Josh Harrison. You left a message for me to call you " " About time Doctor Harrison. I believe I have left you several umessages. " the voice had a menacing under tone. " So sorry " Josh mumbled " I've been very busy ". " Anyway , now I've finally got you to ring ....I want you to come and see myself and my colleagues. We have a proposition for you ..one you can't refuse "

" What proposition? What colleagues?" " Calm down Doctor Harrison .... We want to meet with you in " The Club " and discuss the matter ". " "The Club, why the club?" " It's connected " the man said mysteriously. " When are you available ? Doctor Harrison " . "I suppose I could meet you this afternoon. I have no patient appointments at the surgery. We run the baby and toddler clinic with the nurses, also the family planning........They could ring me if some issue cropped up that I am required to deal with" " Very glad to hear it Doctor ...... we will see you at 2pm .

Use the side entrance , wouldn't like to have you seen by all and sundry, now, would we ?" " OK, I'll be there " " My name is Vincent by the way......

just ask for me. " "alright. Vincent Goodbye " "Goodbye" they both put down their telephones.

Josh put his head in his hands ' What on earth do they want off me? . ' he wondered ' knowing my luck, it's bound to be something bad '.

He continued the rest of the morning surgery. Josh saw a steady stream of patients, including Honey and made several referrals and appointments with specialists . Jodie came in and dealt with some letters and filing. They had a coffee break together and he told her he would not be in the surgery that afternoon as he had a meeting with the Local Health Board. Jodie said she would do a bit more admin and then see how things were getting on in the house and rustle something up for their evening meal. Everything seemed to be going smoothly, for which he breathed a sigh of relief.

Josh turned up at " The Club" shortly before 2pm. He went to the side entrance as requested and knocked. The door was opened by a large bulky man, with a shaved head and a gold earring in his left ear. He was dressed in a smart dark suit
which had obviously been tailored individually for him as it fitted his frame perfectly. Josh frowned, he thought the man looked slightly familiar. " I am here to see Vincent " said Josh The man extended his hand " Pleased to meet you Doctor Harrison. I am he " he shook hands vigorously. " I am glad that you are so prompt, everyone else is already here .....follow me "

Josh had never been admitted through the side door before. It led into a dark passageway which appeared to be panelled in wood. Occasionally there was a portrait painting of someone or another on the wall. There was carpet on the floor, which was patterned , and at one end a very old looking sideboard with books and a lamp on it.

They continued down the passage, turning left at the far end . There was more light now, as windows were fitted on this part of the corridor. They were the old fashioned high sash type ...in need of modernisation. Finally they reached a door which Vincent opened . Inside, were four men, sitting at an oval table.

The first one Josh recognised as Stan, next to him was a man sitting up as if in charge and Josh recognised him as Gwilym (Wil) Griffiths, who was a local Councillor, the head of planning and sewerage. The other two men were strangers. The first was young, in his twenties, athletic build, wearing a shirt and loosened tie. Blonde with a shaved head, he appeared as if he wanted to be somewhere else. He was all fidgety with suppressed energy. The final man looked the epitome of a successful business man. Dressed in a suit, shirt and tie ...all expensive, all immaculate. He had short, well groomed, dark hair and piercing blue eyes. No - one did any introductions. Stan offered Josh a chair.

"Hello Doctor Harrison " said Stan " glad you could come to our meeting". " I didn't really have much choice " answered Josh with a wry expression. " No, I suppose not " Stan agreed. " We'll I'm going to leave the talking to the chairman of our consortium... I think you may already know him ....Wil Griffiths " he indicated the Councillor.

" Yes, Hello Councillor Griffiths " said Josh, emphasising his status " Hello Josh, call me Wil. This is Vlad " he nodded towards the fair haired, young man, who smiled at Josh " and "Henry " indicating the "businessman" who gave a tight half smile. " We do not need surnames when in this company. We represent the consortium who own "Club Paradis" and a number of other establishments around the country. There are far more members than this tiny group, but we have been given the authority to make executive decisions when necessary. " he smiled. Josh returned the smile and nodded his head " OK, but where do I come in ? " asked Josh.

" Well, Josh. You are a platinum member of this club and you are a doctor. This is where you come in. ". " I don't understand " Josh looked puzzled " We have decided that we need a doctor, especially in the case of some of the dangerous sexual practices we offer our clients. We also need someone who will be totally confidential ......you are the ideal candidate. " Josh shifted slightly in his seat, he was a little uncomfortable with the way the conversation was going.

No Refuge

Wil continued " Recently, as you know , a woman,Candice Roberts died . In fact her body was found by your wife, I believe ? " Josh nodded " She had a missing ankle and foot, which was found with her in the skip. The story being put about is that she died as a result of sexual bondage and asphyxiation play with her husband , and when he couldn't get her out of the manacles he cut her foot off to release the body . He can't remember where he subsequently got rid of the manacles, but thinks he threw them in the sea. ". " Yes, the police told me that...they came to interview me " " That story is a complete fabrication " said Wil.

" Candice worked here, and a very wealthy and famous client took a fancy to her. He paid thousands for her to be his sex partner, the Sub to his Dom. Her husband Chris, had full knowledge , he did some work here as well. Anyway, this man had a sexual fetish or paraphillia which he could never get satisfied . He wanted to cut off a woman's limb. He had an obsession with amputees, He had sex with amputees, but that didn't satisfy him enough . "

" I know about this" said Josh " I studied the paraphilias." He explained ;

" Acrotomophilia refers to a paraphilia in which an individual expresses strong sexual interest in amputees. It is a counterpart to apotemnophilia, the sexual interest in being an amputee.

Some people question whether amputating one's own body parts or operating on a partner for the sake of sexual pleasure is ethical. "

" There you are " exclaimed Wil " You've been a help already.We understand the ethics, but if both parties have consented then its fine with us. In the event, Candice agreed , for a very substantial sum of money, to let him cut off her ankle and foot. He gave her a lot of painkillers, and then aroused himself and tranquillised her by using erotic asphyxiation .

He had brought her to breathlessness several times in the past ....it was something she was used to . She was partially suffocated when he carried out the amputation. . However, after he did it and took his extreme pleasure, he realised she had become unconscious. He called Stan for help , but unfortunately his attempts at resuscitation failed ...she was dead.

Her husband Chris is taking the rap, saying it was 'a sexual game of erotic-asphyxia gone wrong and that she had been manacled to the bed...you know the rest. There is no manacle to find ...one was never used. We have hired him the top barrister ,and if the jury accepts his story he is likely to get a short sentence, in fact it may be suspended and he won't even go to jail. "

" I still don't see where I fit in " said Josh " The way we see it is, if you had been here , or we could have contacted you quickly, you may have saved her life. There may be other such incidents in the future " Henry butted in " you can check the girls sexual health at regular intervals ...that would be a relief for them and clients would pay more. Injuries from activities...even from the pole dancers could be treated without making up excuses at A and E. "

" Thank you all for your confidence in my skills " said Josh " But , to be honest I'm working flat out now in my practice . I'm the only Doctor" Henry smiled " We will pay you to hire a locum to cover for you ". " What if I don't want to do it? ". " I am sorry, but then we will have to persuade you . We have a record of all your activities in the club. We are aware of all your sexual proclivities. There's even some video footage you wanted filmed yourself . We would have to give this information to your wife if you won't co-operate, and even worse, to the GMC. who do not approve of these activities as they bring disrepute to the profession and you will most likely be struck off " he shrugged his ". shoulders. " I hope it won't come to that. "

Josh frowned " I have to agree then, don't I ? " 'fraid you do. But you will be well paid, and we'll throw in free membership. Think of the duty you'll be doing to the community ……..and we know you'll keep confidentiality. ". " Just one more question said Josh " Why did Candice tell me she was afraid some man was after her? ". " I don't know, unless she was getting fed up of her "masters " attention . Anyhow, it's all academic now". " Yes, I suppose so " agreed Josh.

The four men stood up, Josh followed them. They shook hands on their future "partnership" and bid him goodbye. Vlad handed him a wallet with

No Refuge

phone numbers and other information relating to "The Club" . " I zink zis vil be a great benefit to uz all " he said, smiling . Josh nodded.

Stan showed Josh the way back out via the side door. Walking back to the car, he could see some benefits to this job . He would have total access to all facilities, at all times. He would be monitoring the girls health and sorting out any medical problems immediately . He only had to think of a way to tell Jodie about it all , in a totally sanitised version, of course, and everything would turn out fine .....he would even have a legitimate reason for being there.

What Josh did not realise was that he was getting more and more sucked into a dark psychological web from which he would never return.

CHAPTER FIFTEEN

"I'm sorry you were so worried about me. Yes, I had to go to my mothers for a couple of days...a bit of an emergency ....yes , ok , ...meet you in the cafe at 1 o'clock............byeeeee " I put the phone down on Anita . I was feeling a little guilty to be honest, because I had practically ignored her since the row with Josh. I had been back from my mothers for several days now, and hadn't even bothered to get in touch with Anita.

I know it's illogical, but a little bit of me blames her for what happened between me and Josh that night. I mean she arranged the makeover and she persuaded me into that dress and shoes....if she hadn't interfered, then Josh and I wouldn't have argued. I'll have to make sure that she has nothing to do with my looks and wardrobe again. I will meet her today , I think she's a lovely woman , and we get on well. I just have to be careful, that's all.

I've seen Honey once or twice up the local shops. I feel so sorry for her having to work, when she feels so ill. She's having a bone marrow biopsy tomorrow. I said I'll go with her . Strangely, I haven't told Josh about our friendship. I think he might not approve, considering her occupation ......he would hit the roof if he knew I was bothering with a pole dancer. I suppose Honey is one of those girls he doesn't approve of.

I also have another concern, I've been short listed for a job in the University of Glamorgan ....I would absolutely LOVE to do it . Senior Lecturer and Researcher in modern Literature.........but how do I tell Josh? He wants me to help him here , and get pregnant , not bother with work . My bloody heads spinning, I don't know if I'm on my feet or my head half the time. Could I take a job? Is it feasible?

" Goodbye! " I cried merrily to Josh as I left the surgery around 12.30pm to pop down to town and meet Anita in the cafe. I had been sorting out the referrals, X ray requests and Consultants letters since 10am, showing my willingness to aid Josh in the admin side of the practice.

" Where are you going? " he responded
" Thought I'd pop down town for an hour or two " " Why? "
" Well...there's one or two things I need to get, and I thought it would be a change....I've been in the house or surgery all week "
" What about me? ....where do I go then? "
" You've been out with your friends a few times this week. remember? ".
" That was connected with work....that extra job I told you about ".
I said nothing. I didn't believe he'd spent every one of the nights he'd gone out negotiating a "doctor on call " job in a club. That could have been sorted out in half an hour or so, did he think I was stupid?

However, I said nothing. It would be pointless and he'd only have some snide remark to come back at me with.
" Josh, I need to buy some feminine things...personal...you know ".
" Oh...ah ...alright then..but don't be long ... I'll be expecting you back by three ".
I gave a loud, audible sigh. . What's all this control about? I wondered, was he always like this and I didn't realise?
Could be. I mistook his control for concern when we only met at weekends. We were always together then.....walking, eating or love making. There was no need for him to ask where I was going because I was a stranger in Manchester and never went anywhere without him. We were stuck together like glue. Now the glue had gone, Josh wanted to get another tube but I was firmly anti-adhesive....I started to laugh, this proved I was cracking up! .
Chuckling I made my way to the car and drove off.

No Refuge

Anita was already in the cafe, and again greeted me like a long lost relative. She got up and gave me a great big hug

" I've really missed you " she extolled, " I was worried when I didn't hear from you "

"Sorry, I had to go to my mothers unexpectedly...family stuff ...you know. It was so busy I had no time to even ring "

" never mind, you're here now ....My God .....you've cut your hair ".

I was getting a bit cheesed off over comments about my hair by now, to tell the truth ...but I suppose it was my own fault

" Yes, felt like a change "

" But you'd just had a change ...the waves and curls " " I know, but that made me realise how long and heavy it was so I c...I had it cut off "

" Wow, well normally I'd think how terrible to get rid of such lovely long hair....but to be honest with you ...you look fantastic ...all eyes and mouth and cheekbones ".

" Thanks, but you don't have to pretend . I know it's made me a real plain Jane ..but I don't mind. " Anita gave me an odd look, but said no more.

We finished our coffees and I told her I wanted to go to the library to get some more books. I wanted some relating to the area as I had heard that Merthyr had an interesting past.

" Oh Yes " said Anita

" It was the capital of Wales once, larger than Cardiff. The iron masters ruled the town and were cruel and promiscuous...there's loads of stories about them . "

" I love reading things like that ....Literatures my subject, so I will read anything of course, but history is so fascinating......Talking about Literature I've been short listed for a Senior Lecturers post in the University of Glamorgan ". " Oh well done! When's the interview? ".

" Next Thursday ...but I don't think I'm going ".

" Why ever not? ".

" Josh wants me to stay home, help with the builders and the practice ...and have a baby "

" Is that what you want to do? "
" Yes...no...oh I don't know ....I really don't know " .

We walked around the library , picking books. Anita recommended some about Merthyr, but apart from that, she was unusually quiet.
" I know you must keep your voice low in he library " I whispered " but you've stopped talking altogether . What's the matter? ".
" It's not me it's you "
" What do you mean? ".
" Remember what I said about my daughter and her partner ? How she'd changed and was doing as her partner said, and wasn't happy ? ".
" Yes "
" Well you seem to be the same . Caitlin has ended it with her. She said it was suffocating. Jill didn't want her to meet her friends or do anything she wanted. Jill was controlling her, and Caitlin was depressed....so she finished it . She feels much better already. back to her own self, dressing up and going out . I'm so glad " Anita smiled , lighting up her whole face, then she continued " I don't like to say it...but you seem like she was . Josh controlling you. Not doing what you want to do ".

At one level, I could recognise some truth in this, and I could feel myself blushing
" No, it's not like that at all " I said out loud " what Josh wants makes a lot of sense . He can't afford a secretary at the moment, so if I do that , it's a financial help. The builders do need supervising, you know how they can easily do things wrong or laze about ....they need someone urging them on. We both want a family ....a baby. It makes sense for me to not get embroiled in a job and them get pregnant "
" Why did you look so happy when you mentioned the Job and so sad when you said you probably won't take it' then? "
" Just ...in an ideal world ..I could have the job as well "
" You CAN have the job. It would more than pay for a secretary, even for someone to 'whip the builders into shape ' if that's what you want "

No Refuge

Anita snorted " A baby will come when it's the right time....and you can go on maternity leave these days...there was none of that about when I had my children "

I looked at Anita, and thought deeply, them I took a deep breath.

" No I can't " I said " I can't have it all. "

By some sort of telepathic agreement, we both said no more on the subject. I refused to go to any clothes shops, but we went to the chemist and I bought what I needed.

" I'm awful sorry, but I've got to get off now " I said to Anita , watching the time.

" Aww so soon. I was hoping we'd have another coffee "

" Sorry ..perhaps next week. I have to see if the tiles have arrived and that they're the right size and colour"

" Oh yes, I see. Phone me and we'll meet up next week "

We gave each other a hug, and I walked swiftly to my car, parked in its usual spot. I placed my parcels in the boot , and got into the drivers seat.

Turning my key in the ignition it failed o make a sound . I tried again and again...nothing

' Oh no ' I thought ' what's the matter with the bloody car ? ' I just sat there for a few moments . I was feeling so low that tears came to my eyes. I told myself to stop being so stupid. I could phone the RAC and they'd sort it out. I could even phone Josh and he'd come and get me.

I rubbed my eyes and started rummaging in my handbag for my mobile phone . I couldn't find it. I started to panic. Where did I have it last? Recounting my steps I thought and thought. I had used it in the cafe because I wanted to check a number with Anita, but I hadn't seen it since. Did I leave it there? Usually, I just place it back in my bag automatically. I tipped the contents of my handbag on to the passenger seat. Brush, compact, purse, tissues, loose coins, lipstick, two pens, even a small notebook and some old sweets ...but no phone. I looked on the floor, under the sets , in the glove compartment (how could it get in there?) , it was no where to be seen. I got out of the car and retraced my steps to the cafe.

" Excise me . I seem to have lost my mobile phone, has anyone handed one in ? " I asked the woman behind the counter in the cafe " not as far as I know love. Hang on a minute ...." " Doris...Doris ...anyone handed in a mobile ? " she shouted down the room . After a few minutes Doris came back " No, love . Sorry no phone , and no one else's seen one either " " Oh thanks " I replied despondently and left the cafe.

I decided to ask in the library, and crossed the road. I was getting very tense and jittery by now, and felt as if someone was watching me. I looked around and thought I caught a glimpse of a tall man in a dark suit who passed by and disappeared around the following corner.

" Excuse me, I was in here earlier. I wonder if anyone has handed in a mobile phone ? " I asked the young , female librarian. " Mmmm I don't know of any . I'll look in the lost property book . When did you lose it?" " around lunch time 1. 30 pm or so" the librarian looked in a box under the counter and also the "Lost Property " book. " nothing, sorry " she finally declared. I left the library and decided to go back to my car, get the details for the RAC and find a pay phone.

Walking back to the car, I was convinced I could hear someone behind me. I'd stop, the steps would stop, I'd start ...and so did they . I could feel eyes boring into the back of my head. I hurried with quicker steps, turned the corner, faster and faster towards the car ...I reached the door . A large hand covered mine as I placed it on the door handle.

" Hello, Mrs Harrison " said a deep voice. I turned slightly and looked up. A tall , broad man, dressed in a dark expensive suit stood by my side with his hand over mind . He smiled . He was good looking in a dark, slightly foreign way " who are you? How do you know me? " I asked. " Allow me to introduce myself ...I am Vincent, a friend of your husband Doctor Josh Harrison. He may have mentioned me ? " " No..o he's never mention you ".

No Refuge

" We'll, I am quite hurt about that. I thought we had become great friends recently " he turned his mouth down, in a mock sorrowful look.

" Ha ha ...how do you know Josh ? "

"I'm one of the men in the club we've been keen to recruit him to "

" Oh, you're one of the " boys" keeping him out so often "

"Guilty as charged ". He held his hands up in mock surrender "what's up? You seem pretty wound up over something "

"My cars broken down, and I've lost my mobile phone "

"Il soon sort that out . Here's my phone ...call the recovery service , and I'll give you a lift home " he handed me his mobile.

" Do you know the number of the RAC? "

" it's in my contacts ...I'll call it. " he took the phone back off me, and pressed a few buttons, then handed it back. " talk to them "

I explained the situation, gave all relevant details and was told they would be at least an hour. Vincent took the phone off me"we will leave the car keys under the driver seat and the car unlocked.

You can repair and deliver to the ladies house. There is no way she can remain here. Alone, for an hour or more, I will take her home " he told them decisively. His voice was such, that no one would argue.

" Come on, pretty lady, take my arm " Vincent offered me his arm , and I linked mine through it. We walked a few rows down the car pack until we reached a silver Mercedes. It gleamed in the sunlight. This was one of my favourite cars, and I knew this was top of the range. Vincent opened the passenger door and helped me in. He walked around to the drivers side and opened the door, grinning at me as he slid into the drivers seat, on to the soft black leather interior. I noticed he had a Saint Christopher hanging from the mirror, it glinted in the light sending off rays of rainbow colours which played on his cheek. I was fascinated by the dappled effect on his skin.

" We pulled out of the car park onto the main road. Vincent was a good driver and the Merc was so smooth, it was like moving on a cloud of air. I noticed that we were travelling in the wrong direction. " Vincent, I live in North Street " I protested " I know, I just thought it would be pleasant for us to go for a meal and a drink ....and get to know each other".

" No,no, no, I 've got to get home. Josh is expecting me " I was starting to panic

" Calm down pretty lady, we can have a delicious meal, a few drinks........ start to relax . Some scintillating conversation .....what more could you ask for? "

"I have to get home ...don't you see, he'll go mad "

"I don't think he'll argue with me....now ..do you?"

" I don't know..but he'll sure as hell have a go at me. Stop...please stop.. let me out. I have to go. . " . " .I don't know who you are more frightened of ...me or Josh...your loving husband " He sneered

" Please, please Vincent ...take me home ....just let me out!."

" Sorry..pretty lady ...but the answer is NO. I am anxious to spend some time in your company . "

I began to cry, tears running down my cheeks. My breath became faster and my heart beat was too fast to count. I could feel my head spinning as if I had been on one of those anti -gravity rides .....becoming more and more dizzier by the moment . I felt I was going to die.....my heart was going to break out of my chest cavity ......I was spinning down...and down ....and down..... then everything went black.......

CHAPTER SIXTEEN

"Josh"

Josh looked impatiently at his watch. It was 5 o' clock 'Where the bloody hell is she?'I told her to be home by 3pm . Why does she taunt me like this?How can I be expected to keep my temper and not react? ' He got up and stomped into the reception area " Anymore patients ? He asked Sheila .
" No, that's all for today" she replied

" Any messages from my wife?"

" No, sorry doctor,nothing's come in. "

Josh looked even more annoyed. He had rung her mobile several times ... only to get voice mail . There was nothing so frustrating as bloody voice mail, he thought.

Josh and Sheila tidied up the premises, locked all doors and windows and left. Josh returned to his house next door. It was obviously uninhabited. Nothing had moved, not even the two breakfast dishes had been washed up. They sat by the bosh, pieces of toast and smudges of butter still sticking to their surfaces. ' She hasn't been back here then " Josh thought . He picked up a bottle of whiskey , which was lying on the floor in the living room , and finding a glass, poured himself a very large measure. ' if she returns looking like a slut this time....I'll fucking kill her ' he promised himself.

Josh sank into the chair ....and downed the drink in one gulp.

It was past 8 o 'clock . Josh had fallen asleep. He had spent around an hour getting himself into such a state that he thought she had been murdered, but was too afraid to contact the police. Instead, he drank some more....until the bottle was empty and he fell into a stupor. Now, he could hear bells ringing. Are they in my head? He wondered, before identifying that it was the phone. He picked up the receiver. A deep voice was on the other end " Hello Josh, it's your good friend here, Vincent "

" Vincent ...what do you want? "

" Anything missing .....Josh? Have you misplaced anything ? " he chuckled

" What? ....what? .....have you got her ? Have you got my wife? "

" We've had a lovely meal together...Josh ..steaks and salad ....some wine.. great ambience....romantic music ...mmmm. Pretty lady "

" You bastard . where is she? Have you hurt her ?"

" I'm not the one who hurts her Josh ....now ..am I?"

" Fuck you . Bring her back ! "

" I will, I will, all in good time. " .

" Now, I want her back here NOW ! "

" Patience, Josh...patience ...man. We just wanted you to realise that we can do anything we like . You will always be in our employ..........or anything could happen. Comprenez? "

" Yes, yes, ...just get Jodie home .....I understand, you bastard . You've made your point. "

" Glad to hear it ....bye ...see you soon ". Vincent rang off.

Josh quickly sobered up . He walked around the room, running his fingers through his hair, in that habit he had when tense or worried. He now knew she was with Vincent ...but what the fuck did that really mean ? Was she tied up .... a prisoner ......or treated as a welcome visitor ? Even worse, could Vincent and/ or someone else have had sex with her ? This thought made his eyes blaze with anger and jealousy. Especially knowing he was trapped ..that he could do nothing about it. He was held tightly in their grip.

The doorbell rang. Josh, who had slumped in a chair, jumped up as if scalded. He ran to the door.

"Hello, who's there? " he called out .

" Me, Vincent ....I have a delivery for you ". The unmistakable voice came from outside the door. Josh opened it. There stood Vincent with his arm around Jodie's shoulders. He was holding her tightly to him. Jodie's head was bent, she did not meet Josh's eyes .

" Thank God ....thank God " cried Josh as he reached out for his wife. Jodie came towards him , and he hugged her to him , so tightly that she could barely breathe. He loosened his grip and guided her into the living room. Vincent followed.

Josh helped Jodie into a chair ....she still hadn't uttered a word. He looked darkly at Vincent " You'd better not have done her any harm " he snarled " Harm? Me do her harm ?" Vincent chuckled " She was probably safer with me than with you "

" What's that supposed to mean? "

" Way I see it she's scared shitless of you ...what d'ya do to her ? Whip her ?"

" I haven't done anything to her "

Vincent shrugged " It's no skin off my nose what you do to your missus . All I care about is you play our game by our rules "

" I do....I have .....what was all this for ? I haven't stepped out of line "

" Just a little reminder of what we could do if necessary . To make sure you understand the contract ......terrible things contracts ...all that small print ..." Vincent chuckled again.

During this conversation, Jodie had remained silent . She sat in the chair, her hands loosely intertwined , her eyes bent, looking down at them.

" I've delivered the goods...so now I'll be on my way " said Vincent , with a salute.

" Goodnight. I hope you will leave me and my wife alone in future " Josh glared at him .

" Goodbye, thanks for a wonderful evening, pretty lady " said Vincent, looking at Jodie with an unfathomable expression on his face.

He walked with an arrogant swagger to the front door , followed by Josh , with a hurried step. Vincent opened the door and stepped out, into the cold , sharp air. Josh quickly shut and bolted the door behind him. He turned around, and went back into the living room to confront Jodie, his wife......

CHAPTER SEVENTEEN

"Jodie"

The next thing I was aware of was a splitting headache. The pain was excruciating, and I could tell light was shining into my eyes. Very slowly I prised the lids open , realising that the light was from the beam of a torch. I was lying on something which stuck to my skin, my arms and legs had obviously been perspiring and as I tried to move, the material moved with me.

I was on the back seat of the Mercedes and the leather seat was sticking itself to me. Vincent was leaning over from the front, with the torch in his hand.

."Ah......so you are back with us " he said

"Take that light out of my eyes " I moved my head to the side, closing my eyes again .

"Ok pretty lady... No problem ". He turned off the torch . I realised that it was sunset... darker than I had thought.

" Where are we ? "

"In a lay by on the road towards the Brecon Beacons "

"What are we doing here ? "

"Oh I thought we'd have a picnic . It's usually nice around here on a freezing February night " he said sarcastically .

" You know what I mean. You told me you were taking me home ...and then you kidnapped me. Now, I end up here on the mountains "

" You are not on a mountain, and I haven't kidnapped you. I just wanted us to have a meal and a drink together. Get to know each other ...then I'll take you home "

" I want to go home now"

" Sorry, no can do pretty lady. Don't you want to get to know your husband's friends? You'd think a wife would be interested in her husband's work. "

I was starting to feel panicky again. My heart was beating too fast and my mouth was dry. What if all he said was just a pack of lies and he was going to rape me ...or worse . I started gasping for breath.

" Huh ..huh...huh .. Hurr ..." I forced out of my lungs. Vincent held a flask to my mouth, I gulped, ...it was whiskey . It burned my throat, then I felt the warmth of it travel down to my stomach, I took another gulp and it felt easier to breathe.

Vincent opened the back door of the car .He half supported and half pulled me out of the back seat and into the front passenger seat. He fastened the seat belt , then crossed the front of the car and got in behind the steering wheel, He started the car, pulling out onto the country road.

The headlights of the car caught a stray rabbit, running to its burrow. The animal was petrified, it's eyes shone in the beam of light . I could sense it's fear, my nerves jangling in empathy. The rabbit ran off.

" You must be hungry. I'm taking you for a meal" Vincent's tone brooked no argument .

We drove probably a mile or two, then turned into an old large building through a wide gateway and on to a curving drive. There was a sign at the side of the gate which was illuminated with spotlights: " Nant Ddu Lodge " .

" Good food here " muttered Vincent

Vincent escorted me out of the car , and in through an old wooden door with large brass hinges . We found ourselves in a tiled passageway and he ushered me into a room on the right hand side, which had a rustic appearance. It consisted of a large old bar, with brass fittings, wooden tables and chairs, set out with cutlery ready for customers. Behind the bar was a large blackboard , which listed the " chefs recommendations " .

No Refuge

There was an appetising smell ....a mixture of curries , spices and other mouth watering dishes. Vincent sat us down at a corner table, with me on the inside and him opposite .... His large frame filling the chair plus blocking the space between us.

He ordered a bottle of white wine, after I had meekly nodded my agreement. The waiter gave us both a menu and read out the recommendations on the board. Vincent ordered a sirloin steak , French fries, onion rings and tomatoes. I managed to persuade him that a salmon salad was fine for me , after he tried to entice me to eat something more substantial. I knew I wouldn't be able to eat at all. Did he think we were on a bloody date?

"How did you and Doctor Josh meet ? " Vincent made an attempt at conversation .
"I met him first in Cardiff , in a pub with friends "
"How long ago?"
"About two and a half years or so "
"When did you get married then ? "
"Four months ago....Why are you so bloody interested in Josh and me ? "
"Just chatting, wondered how much you knew about him ..that's all . "
"What's that suppose to mean ? "
"Nothing...just inquisitive ....I've known him for years ....since he lived here as a boy "
I found that very difficult to believe . I could never imagine Josh being a friend of someone like Vincent . It seemed so.....incongruous.

I took a large swallow of wine .
"What was he like as a boy? " I asked, couldn't help myself. I was very curious. Especially if he really did know him.
" Much the same as he is now I suppose. "

Vincent moved to the left as the waiter arrived with our meals, and placed them in front of us.

We started to eat. Vincent got stuck in, eating as if he was ravenous . I nibbled at the salmon, taking small portions on to my fork , I felt nauseous.

"I want to go to the ladies room " I said
"Now!? ... Have you got to go now? "
" Yes, I'm afraid I do. ". I tried to get up, out of my seat, but I found there was not enough room.
" Hold on...hold on..." Vincent stood up and moved his chair back. He then pulled out the table and took hold of my arm. " There you are...come on... " he held me tightly by my biceps. I tried to shake him off... " Let go. I'm perfectly capable of going to the toilet by myself " I protested
" You've been Ill you fainted earlier. I'd feel better if I escorted you . "He looked directly into my eyes making sure I got his message.. His eyes were deep, dark blue. An unusual colour like a bottomless pool, I felt as if he was drawing me in. I averted his gaze.

We walked together to the Ladies room, with his arm tightly around me. He ushered me in through the door, and took up sentry duty outside.

Once in the room , I used one of the cubicles, then searched around for an escape route. The only door was the one I had entered by, so my only option was a window. The end cubicle had a high window which could, however , be reached if you stood on the toilet seat. Unfortunately, it was too small for me to ever struggle through. .

There was no other way out, so I washed my hands and splashed my face hoping to stop the nausea. Looking in the mirror , I could see that I looked awful . All white face and dark panda eyes. My hair looked windswept and I had no handbag or comb.I tried to tidy it a little with my fingers. Vincent had kept my belongings in the car.

There was nothing for it but return to the restaurant with my captor.

No Refuge

I opened the door, and there he stood. Greeting me with a "friendly " embrace around my shoulders. We walked back in unison to our table, and continued to eat the meal. It looked delicious, but to me it tasted of cardboard and gravel. I drank some more wine, however, trying to blot out my emotions.

In an attempt to restart the conversation, Vincent asked :
" Did you know about your husbands involvement with the club? "
"Yes, he said you want him to be a sort of doctor on call "
" That's all he told you, is it? "
" Yes, what else is there to know? "
" Oh well, he's your husband. You'd better ask him. "
" What are you trying to say? "
" Let's just say, Josh developed certain 'tastes' when he was younger ....and he likes to indulge them at times ."
"What tastes ? what are you talking about? "
"Haven't you noticed ? ....he sometimes likes to be a bit ...umm..ahh... different? "
"No! No, not at all. "
" You do surprise me .....his nickname was 'Josh the Impaler "
" You're talking in riddles now. ". I didn't like the direction of the conversation, I wanted to get away from it. I could feel fear building up in me .... there were things I didn't want to think about right now
" I can tell you....... "
" Never mind that.... ," I broke in " Why have you brought me here and when am I going home? " Vincent looked taken aback. However, I could see his expression soften after a moment or two. I believe that he realised the pain it would cause me, and he understood.

Looking at his watch he said " Actually, I think I can take you home soon . I just wanted to get to know you, pretty lady, as I said . My bosses, however, wanted to make sure your husband understood exactly what he had taken on, and what could happen if he refused to play ball. "

I said nothing to this, realising that Josh had got himself into something right over his head, that he couldn't possibly handle.

Vincent ordered two brandies "A nightcap for us both, pretty lady.....cheers". He held up his glass and we clinked glasses. I drank it down, thankfully.

"You're too good for him you know" he said, staring into my eyes again, those dark pools mesmerising.

I stared back, trying not to be drawn in., "Who am I good for then?" I asked, regretting the words the moment they left my mouth.

"Me" he replied. I looked away.

We returned to the car. I got into the passenger seat without any protest. He drove in silence as we negotiated dark, weaving roads, where the moon peered spookily through the tree branches and owls could be heard tooting to each other.

Finally we reached a main road, the orange sodium vapour lamps giving a clarity to the highway and the buildings. We still maintained a silence. Vincent had phoned Josh to tell him we were on our way....home.

We arrived at the house.

Josh opened the door, he pulled me in to the passage, and held me close to him, so I could scarcely breathe. He led me into the living room and sat me gently on a chair. I started playing with my hands, becoming hypnotised by the intricate patterns I could weave with my fingers. Trying not to think of anything.

Josh and Vincent were talking. I was unaware of the words in their conversation. The front door shut. He returned to the living room .....he came towards me, ready to confront me, Josh .....my husband.

CHAPTER EIGHTEEN

"Jodie "

Josh sat down in the chair next to me. He turned to face me, his eyes bright and the lamp casting a glow over his features.

" What happened? " he asked. Not in the sympathetic tone I needed so much to hear , but in a harsh, demanding voice.

I cringed slightly, pushing my body back into the chair. " What on earth do you mean? " I replied.

"What EXACTLY happened?" He demanded again.

" I was coming home and went back to the car, which was parked in the Castle car park " I answered, as steadily as possible " The car wouldn't start. The ignition didn't turn . I tried several times. I decided to phone the RAC. Unfortunately, I couldn't find my mobile, I searched my bag.....everywhere.

I returned to the cafe and library but no one had handed it in. I decided to go back to the car, get the RACs number and find a pay phone.

When I returned, Vincent was there . He told me he was a friend of yours and phoned the RAC and offered me a lift home. "

"Why didn't you wait for the breakdown man to arrive? " Josh butted in .

" Because they said it would be an hour, and I didn't want to sit there on my own, "

" For your information. The RAC brought the car home at 3.15pm. And your mobile was on the front passenger seat "

" I didn't know that. I didn't want to hang about , alone for ages in a car park ....I couldn't find my phone ...I don't know how it could have got there. "

" Why didn't you borrow Vincent's phone to call me ?"
" He offered me a lift ...a lift home "

" So you didn't think twice about going in a car with a strange man ?"

" He said he was your friend, He knew your name, where we lived. He told me he knew you from school "

" So ...you just believed him? "

"Well ....yes "

" What happened then ? " his tone was still harsh , I could feel myself curling up inside.
" We drove off in the car, then I realised he was going the wrong way "
" Did you say anything? "

" Of course I did! I told him to take me home. I said I had to be home, that you were expecting me, I cried, I panicked ....I got in such a state that I fainted "

" You fainted? "

" Yes, I was terrified "

" I've never known you faint "

" Well I can assure you I did "

No Refuge

" What then? "

" I woke up . It was nearly dark and we were parked in a lay by at the side of a lane. I was still scared, I begged him to take me home. He refused. Said it was too early ..... Instead , he took me to a place to eat. The " Nant Ddu Lodge " it was called "

" Ohh...very posh....nice date was it? "

" I was petrified . I didn't know what he might be capable of. He ushered me inside and ordered food and wine. "

" Why didn't you just walk, or run out of the restaurant ? "

" I couldn't get out. He sat so I was hemmed in, I was scared he'd chase me, hurt me. I went to the toilet, but he came to the door with me and waited outside. I looked for a way out...but there was none. The toilet window was tiny, I couldn't possibly twist through it. We returned to the food "

" Why didn't you alert the barman? A waitress ? Pass them a note? Anything ?"

" I was too scared. he could have dragged me outside and killed me before they could do anything! "

" When you left, why didn't you run back in , tell the manager and hide ? "

" I'd heard him telephone you . I knew he was taking me home , so I just sat in the car, not saying a word, waiting to get back "

" And here you are ! " he declared. " My faithful wife " his voice was mocking . He stood up, opening his arms wide as he spoke . Pretending he was introducing me to an audience.

He brought his face up close to mine " Did he fuck you ? " he spat out.

I nearly toppled the chair over as I tried to move away from him.

" How could you even think such a thing? "

" Because I know what you are like ...I know what women are like ....sluts ... the lot of them! "

" I've never cheated on you, or given you any reason to suspect me "

" That just means you've been clever. What about those blokes you went about with in Liverpool? "

" They were friends ...just friends " I slumped, defeated, back into the chair.

" Was he good? Did Vincent make you come ? Did he want to do 'perverted ' things with you?"

He sneered, standing over me. He put his hand on the back of the chair and the other on my leg, moving it up to my panties.

I felt disgusted. I turned my head away from him . I didn't answer his questions, just tried to ignore him.
In an even voice , I said " Josh, I'm very tired. I just want to go to bed "

" Bed, bed .....yes you can go to bed. But I'm coming with you. Don't you dare undress and wash unless I'm there . "

Now , I was puzzled . What tangent had his brain taken ? Why did he have to accompany me to bed ? I had no strength to argue so I just agreed .

We picked up the bottles and glasses from the floor, a pizza box, which contained the remnants from a meal Josh had ordered. I tidied the couple of

No Refuge

cushions and throws we had . When finally, the house was as neat as possible , I climbed the stairs, Josh was directly behind me .

We reached the bedroom.....freezing as usual . I began undressing. I took off my jeans and top and carefully folded them and hung them on the clothes rail, reaching for my soft flannel pyjama bottoms .

Just as I slipped off my panties, Josh lunged for them . Shocked, I just moved away. To my amazement he took them to the old, large, standard lamp we were using in the bedroom, and began examining them under the light. He looked this way and that, and even took some scrapings with a small sodden spatula and placed them in a specimen bottle !

" What on earth are you doing? " I exclaimed

" Looking for evidence ."

" Evidence? "

" Yes, of someone else screwing you. "

" Josh, you are going mad " I felt hurt and angry.

" There's some blood here "

" It's my period . I told you...this morning "

" Oh yes ! That makes it even worse. " he snarled

Josh put the panties to one side and began to undress himself . He put on a track suit bottom and tee shirt. I , by now ,had also undressed and been to the bathroom to wash, and change from tampons into a sanitary pad.

I was longing to lie down and just sleep this whole bloody nightmare away ...how ironic , I thought. I hoped and prayed that Josh would stay strictly to his side of the bed . I needed peace..... physical and mental peace.

I had just curled on my right side, my back to Josh, when I felt his arm snake around me. ' That's OK ' I thought " I can put up with that ' . Then.... he put his left hand inside the waistband of my pyjama bottoms . He started to pull them down, and initially I began to resist. " Oh , you can fuck him, but you can't fuck your loving husband " He whispered menacingly. I froze, actually became immobile.

Josh continued his journey , pulling at my waistband, until it became loose and slipped off easily. Then , he removed my panties. The sanitary towel was stuck to them, so it came off in one pull. He threw my garments to the floor and flipped me over on to my back.

I did not resist , I lay supine, my mind blanking off every bad thought which threatened to enter it. What was the point of resisting? I'd only get hurt. Let him do as he pleased, he couldn't touch the real me.

He mounted me, pulling my legs open, he thrust his hard penis into me. I continued to lie there, like some broken doll. Not moving, not speaking , just limp limbed. I knew this was just as much rape as that night, a few weeks ago. Only this time, I would suffer no pain.

I did not feel aroused, or lubricated....but it did not matter....my flowing blood was wetness enough. Josh humped away...... Thrusting and grunting... with one final shove, his body shuddered , and he fell on top of me. " Now you've been fucked by a proper man " he said.

I lay there until his breathing became even, then I pushed his body off me and wriggled away from him. I got out of bed and pulled at the soiled sheet until I could remove it. Josh grunted as I manoeuvred it from under him.

I took the sheet , my panties and pyjamas and put them all in a large bowl to soak with stain remover , and left them in the bathroom. I washed and put

No Refuge

on clean clothes and a sanitary towel, and opened the bottom drawer of an old chest and removed one of the sleeping bags we had used when camping.

Back in the bedroom, I turned the quilt up on my side of the bed. After opening the sleeping bag and laying it down on the mattress, I zipped myself up in it. I pulled the duvet over me , turning away from Josh. I finally felt warm and comfortable

I didn't want to think. I didn't want to face up to the hell my life had become. I just craved sleep. My mobile phone was now on the bedside table... it bleeped a message .....

"sweet dreams pretty lady "

CHAPTER NINETEEN

"Honey"

Honey was leaning against the wall at the end of her street, smoking a cigarette. Her nerves were jangling throughout her body at the thought of today's tests at the hospital . She needed someone to take her and then return for her a few hours later, because she might be groggy after the anaesthetic. Then she needed to rest for the rest of the day .

'Fat chance I have of that' ,she thought, as the warm smoke hit her lungs. Glenn would expect his tea on the table , the kids seen to , and fresh clothes ready for his boys night out. She also had a shift at 7.30pm , which she had managed to persuade Stan to make a three hour one, as it was Tuesday, usually a quiet night.

She was waiting for Jodie who was picking her up. There was no way she wanted her, a doctors wife, to come to their house this morning and take in the sight of Glenn, snoozing on the sofa in his boxers, scratching his balls , slurping the odd drop of tea and making crude comments.

They had arranged to meet on this corner after Honey had taken the twins to school. She hadn't even asked Glen to take her. What was the point? He thought she had ' women's anaemia ' and wondered why she couldn't just drink a few glasses of Guinness to cure it.

"All this 'doctoring' is a fucking waste of time in my opinion, making mamby pambys of people." He told her. "I haven't been ill in my life...and I never get all tired and exhausted like you moan about....."he had boasted.

No, that's because he never did fuck all, she thought bitterly. Why was she tied to such a no-good , lazy , waste of space, she wondered for the umpteenth time. Not because she loved him, that had gone long ago.

Honey spotted Jodie's car turn the corner and pull up beside her. She prepared to get in, when, to her suprize, Jodie got out. " did I see you smoking a fag? " asked Jodie
" Yes, just put it out "
" Can I have one ? " she asked beseechingly.

Honey took two fags from her packet and they had one each. Jodie lit Honey's first, then her own." Whew...that's better" exclaimed Jodie, taking a deep drag .
" Didn't know you smoked" commented Honey
" Josh disapproves of it, but at the moment I don't give a flying fuck. "
Honey looked at her in amazement..... Then looked at her properly.
" You look bloody awful....worse than me ....you should be having these sodding tests "
" Do I ? Look awful , I mean "
" Yeah, like death warmed up...only someone forgot to warm you "
" Cough...splutter..ha...ha " ..I nearly chocked then ! You're a right laugh Honey "
" But you do...you're all pale and waxy looking "
" Let's just say I didn't have a good day yesterday. " Wanna talk about it? "
"Maybe later. We'd better be getting you to this hospital first " Jodie insisted.

They arrived at the hospital within fifteen minutes. Jodie found it very difficult to park ..especially anywhere near the front entrance. They ended up on a piece of ground towards the side of the hospital which was merely mud and gravel . It was nearer the doors than the top of the large car park, even though it appeared to be a part of the waste ground.

They reached the large automatic glass doors , which opened to allow them to enter a tiled foyer. Another set of doors then gave them entrance to the reception and waiting room area.

The receptionists were all enclosed by a horseshoe shaped wooden desk, marked out in sections for different clinics and departments. Honey handed in her letter and was returned it with instructions for the location of the day surgery unit . This was outside of the main area, towards the in patient wards. It was located down a corridor towards the left of the lifts on the ground floor. They carefully followed the yellow signs and line on the floor, which was also painted yellow.

As they were walking towards day surgery, Honey noticed on the walls, some beautiful artwork which had been donated to the hospital. Honey was particularly impressed by an oil painting of the Castle which stood at the edge of the town. It's grey walls and towers looked so strong and impenetrable .

Other pictures were landscapes of scenic places around the borough , which made you want to visit them, and just laze there in bright sunshine .... tranquility and calm.......This was certainly needed to recover from illness, but it was the strength of the Castle Walls which impressed Honey the most. She sensed that she would need this quality more than any other if she was to recover and be there for her children ....this Castle would be her inspiration.

They reached the day surgery unit, and Honey gave her letter to a nurse in a dark blue uniform. " Ah Mrs Sullivan " she said " Follow me "

They both followed her to a bed in a small ward of about eight cubicles. " I'm sister Laine" the nurse introduced herself " Any questions, just ask me. I will be around later to check your details and explain the procedure. If you could just undress and put on the hospital gown and paper panties that are laid on the bed , I shall come and see you afterwards. Your friend can stay with you until you are about to go in for the procedure."

She turned to Jodie " you can come back to collect Mrs Sullivan two hours later. If no one comes to collect her she cannot be discharged, due to the anaesthetic. ". Jodi and Honey nodded. the sister walked off.

Honey quickly undressed and donned the gown and panties . " plenty of practice " she tried to joke, but her voice broke into a sob.

" Now you are going to be fine. They will discover what is wrong, you will be given treatment, and then you will be cured. Believe me, I'm a doctors wife " joked Jodie

" OK " Honey laughed.

" If there's anything you want to say, or talk about ....go on. I'm here "

" Not really a lot . But coming in here, seeing the hospital in all it's starkness, noticing so many fellow patients in different stages of health ,I was pleased to see those oil paintings on the corridor walls "

" Yes, I feel it adds some humanity to the place , and also reminds you of the beautiful places just on our door step "

" I agree. But I found the painting of the Castle especially emotional. That's the one that inspires me ...it's strength , it's durability in some ways, it's determination. When I'm on the road to recovery , I want to visit Cyfartfa Castle and learn even more about it. "

" I'll come with you ....and we'll take your twins...they'll love it . You can soak up the atmosphere and see where your inspiration comes from "

" That's a date " Honey gave a beaming smile and Jodie smiled back.

No Refuge

When Jodie had left, Honey was wheeled into the operating theatre and given some sedatives and a local anaesthetic . The biopsy was taken . After it was completed , Honey fell asleep glad for a chance to rest.

At 3pm Jodie returned and collected Honey. They drove to her house, where Teresa, one of the mothers from the school had picked the twins up as arranged, and was waiting for them. Glen, was out , probably at the club. Honey knew he would be out and to tell the truth was glad of it , the last thing she needed was his demands and stupid opinions.

Jodie helped Honey into the house, as the twins ran ahead.

She felt really tired and slumped onto the sofa. Jodie sorted the two children out with some toys and they played happily in the living room. Jodie made tea for them both , and they sat drinking it. " Thank you so much for today, I would never have managed without you. I have to phone the doctor on Thursday to find out what's happening and get my results .....I'm scared to be honest "

" It was no trouble , that's what friends do. I know it's scary, but I'll be with you when you get your results. Then, we can work out a plan for your treatment and recovery. We can have days out with the kids...all sorts. For now, take one day at a time. Don't forget you have to rest for the rest of today and tonight. That's enough to think about for now.

" Pigs will fly before I have that! Glen will be in around 6 pm and want his tea, his clothes ready for tonight , and I'm working at 7 .30pm. "

Jodie was appalled. " You can't ...he'll have to do it himself, and you must ring work and tell them you're not coming in. .... You e got to! "

" I can't ! " Honey was starting to cry " " He'll play hell.... make life miserable for me and the kids . Shout and perform......he won't give me any money . " she was breathing quickly now, getting herself into an anxiety state .

" Calm down love, calm down, " said Jodie , thinking how in some ways their lives resembled one another. Was this what they had recognised, and sparked their friendship? Both with abuse husbands?

Jodie decided that the state Honey was in, it would be better to give her some practical help. Sometimes that is worth more than all the sympathy in the world. " Ok then " said Jodie " Just lie there and I'll sort out as much as I can "

Honey was lying on the sofa, pale and wan. Tears ran down her cheeks , she looked like someone who had reached rock bottom , and she had no energy to pull herself up. She was worried about her health and the fate of the twins . All fight was seeping out of her.' Thank God Jodie's my friend 'she thought , as her eyes slowly closed and she fell asleep.

By the time Honey awoke , Jodie had cooked a chicken casserole for the family's tea, and finished a basket full of ironing, including Glenn's clothes.

As soon as she heard Honey stirring ,she made her a cup of tea, brought it in to the room , and sat down. " Everything's done...so you don't have to worry . The only thing I haven't managed was to phone your work, but I don't know where it is "

" Oh don't worry, I'll sort that out " Honey quickly reassured her. "Look, I will ring you tomorrow, and if I feel better we'll go out to the shops or something ...do. something nice ...it will be a thank you for today. "

" I won't be here tomorrow , Honey. I'm sorry, but I will see you in a few days when you get your results" . "

" What do you mean....you won't be here ? "

" I'm going to my mothers in Cardiff .....I'm leaving Josh "

" That's why you looked so ill this morning is it? "

No Refuge

" Yes, I expect so...I didn't want to tell you until you'd had your biopsy "

" Why? Why are you leaving him ? "

" Because he's abused me, raped me , hit me ...that's why . Also he's involved in something at " The Club" , to do with treating their girls , I think. That, I wouldn't mind, but some thug called Vincent kidnapped me for a few hours yesterday and scared the living daylights out of me ....all to show Josh who was boss. When he did take me home ....you'll never believe this ...Josh blamed ME ! ...then he abused me ".

Now it was Honey's turn to be appalled. She knew about Josh's activities in the club, but didn't think he would treat Jodie like that. She also knew Vincent and how scary he could be. She had to think carefully about how much to tell Jodie . She didn't want to cause her any more pain, so decided not to tell her about Josh and his activities with girls in the club.....yet. She would do so if needed for divorce proceedings. However, there were some things she could tell her.

" I am shocked " said Honey " That you should have to have gone through such pain. " The Club " is where I work. I know Vincent, he's one of the consortium of owners , and yes, he can be scary ...particularly with his size. I must admit I've never heard of him harming a woman , although he has sorted out some men, who have been troublemakers.

I didn't know that Josh had an arrangement with the club, but it makes sense that they get a doctor involved. There are often injuries that they would rather keep quiet , especially when it involves some 'unusual activities ' . You though, should never have been involved in it .....by Josh, Vincent or anyone else. "

" What do you mean by unusual activities ?"

" Well, I do pole dancing, which it's licensed for and inspected. So are the lap dancers . But some girls do other things .....sexual activities , you know "

" You mean prostitution "

" Yes, but not just straight forward prostitution. They use bondage, S&M , all sorts of sexual perversions are catered for.....and some can be quite dangerous. "

" Oh, I see. So a doctor might be needed for those injuries or to resuscitate someone "

" Yes, exactly "

" Why did they choose Josh? "

" Mmmm I don't know ....perhaps because he hasn't started his practice here long , and he needs the money. Perhaps they were too wary of the older doctors . Maybe someone knew him from school or something "

" Vincent said he had known Josh since they were children together. "

" There you are then! ....that could explain it . "

" Vincent didn't hurt me you know .....he actually took me for a meal . "

" Oh well " chuckled Honey " that's not a bad kidnapping "

" No, it was the return that was terrible . How do you find working in the club?"

" Alright ...I don't have anything to do with it except for the pole dancing. My boss Stan is OK really. He's been letting me go home early recently since I've been Ill "

" So I find a kidnapper and you find your Club boss treat us better that our own bloody husbands "

No Refuge

" Yes, now you mention it , I suppose you're right. "

" At least I can go to my mothers. Isn't there anywhere you can go? "

" No. Mt family disapproved of Glen, so I ran away from home...and they disowned me "

" Have you tried to contact them since? "

" I sent a letter when the twins were born, but I never got a reply "

" Perhaps you should try again, they may have changed by now. Want to see you...and the children"

" I don't expect so, they're a stubborn lot perhaps it's best to let sleeping dogs lie"

" Just think about it ……. I'm sorry I will have to go I'll telephone you later, "

" I understand " Honey stood up and hugged Jodie

"Take care, " she said " You to "

Jodie left Honey sitting on the sofa as she made her way to her car and her drive to Cardiff.

•••

As predicted, Glen arrived home, ate his tea, changed and left. He scarcely spoke to Honey, and didn't mention the hospital or asked her how she felt.

She felt like he invisible woman to be honest, but was glad that Glen didn't physically attack her, as Josh had done to Honey……that would have been intolerable !

Honey went to work . Pale, fatigued and Ill . Stan to his credit , looked worried when he saw her, and thought ' why the hell did she come in for Christ's Sake …….. Bet it was to do with that arsehole of a husband she's got '

He kept an eye on her, and watched when she appeared for her first dance. It was obvious she couldn't do it. He caught hold of her arm as she walked towards the side of the stage. Honey turned sharply towards him….. and passed out cold.

He caught her in his arms , and couldn't let go. There was no way this poor woman was cavorting about tonight . He carried her to the dressing room and arranged a taxi home for her. When she came round, Stan was sitting there with a look of concern on his face. He handed her her clothes and told her to get dressed " Don't come back until you are better……don't worry about that husband of yours ..I 'll put him in the picture " Stan's tone was grim.

Gratefully, Honey accepted Stan's advice and took the taxi home. She let herself into the house and sent the babysitter off. The twins were fast asleep , and that's how she wanted to be…in bed.

She was thankful to Stan and thought " looks like I've got a protector after all…what a surprise" Honey smiled at this thought. Sometimes when you needed help, people did turn up in the unlikeliest of places.

The only worry now was the test results ……

CHAPTER TWENTY

"Jodie"

I arrived at my mothers around 7 o'clock . I saw her car parked in the drive, but there was also a red sporty type Citroen, parked behind hers . I recognised this as my Aunty Joyce's car. My heart sank.

All the way down , as I was driving to Cardiff, I thought about what to tell my mother. She's going to think me mad leaving Josh again after a few weeks, without some feasible explanation.

I was scared, and embarrassed to tell her the truth, but didn't know what else to do . I had just about decided to tell her all ...except for some of the more gory details, when I saw Aunty Joyce's car ! There was no way I was telling her. I might as well broadcast it on the Welsh news ...with extras . Because that's what Joyce would do ..she loved scandal, the worse the better , and the more popular she would be with her cronies especially as she added on her own inventions.

I left my case in the car, and knocked at the door. My mother opened it . A shocked expression came to her face, with not more than a little suspicion.
" Jodie..why are you here, I wasn't expecting you " she cried " let me in mam , and I'll tell you " I pushed past her on the doorstep and made my way to the living room , where Aunty Joyce was sitting .

Her eyes lit up. I had no illusions , it wasn't because I was her favourite niece or that she enjoyed my company...no, it was the fact that I might be the harbinger of juicy gossip or some bad news . I know I might sound rather unkind about my aunt, but that's just the way she is, always has been.

" Well, hello Jodie ...what are you doing here? " Aunt Joyce sat forward, full of interest. My mother followed into the room, bringing me a cup of tea " Drink this love " she said, as she handed me the pink mug.

I took a deep breath, there was no way I was revealing the truth with my dear Aunty sitting there
" You remember I said I was looking around for some work ? " I said looking at my mother, who nodded slowly " I had a telephone call from Cardiff University this morning , asking if I would be interested in a temporary lecturing post whilst the English lecturer was off having an operation.

The problem is, they want to see me before classes at 8.30am in the morning. You know what the traffic is like on the A470 at that time . So I decided it would be an opportunity to see you, have a catch up, stay the night , then I will be bright and refreshed to go there first thing "

" Oh that's great Jodie, just what you wanted " exclaimed my mother, still giving me a suspicious look that Joyce couldn't see. My Aunty looked rather disappointed

" How's that lovely husband of yours then Jodie? " asked Joyce
" Fine, as fit as a fiddle and working hard " I plastered a cheery smile on my face . (Dramatics Society for me next, I thought).
" Oh I'm so glad " Joyce nodded " For a moment there , I thought you'd left him " she gave a chuckle, I joined in.
" How could you ever think anything like that ..he..he" I smiled even harder at her.

My mother raised her eyebrows and said nothing.

We talked for a few minutes about Joyce's " brilliant " son, Daryl and her " Beautiful " daughter Lorraine , and their recent achievements.

No Refuge

Daryl was a trainee finance officer for the council, and apparently had been chosen as "employee of the week " ..."a great honour" declared Joyce " all those hundreds of people working there and he was noticed " you could practically see her preening.

We all knew that the council took turns per week in the 'environment of equality " to choose everyone at least once a year or so. However my mother and I congratulated her and agreed that Daryl was indeed, really ' talented '.

Lorraine had been approached by a model agency who had spotted her " exceptional good looks " Joyce boasted

" Oh where was that? " asked my mother

" In the city centre, near John Lewis "

" Just came up to her? "

" Yes,,a man with a camera around his neck . Said he represented a top modelling agency " said Joyce

" What's the agency called ? " I enquired

" Oh can't remember " Joyce brushed it off

" But she's going to his studio in Lisvane to have shots taken ...he says she has the potential to be as famous as Kate Moss "

My mother and I had to fight to keep a straight face. If you knew my cousin Lorraine you would understand.

Not to be unkind, you would describe her looks as ' pleasant " and her figure as " slightly chubby " . She was about 5 foot 4 inches tall, with short, spiky red hair, and wore skirts which showed her panties.

Lorraine also had a liking for low cut vest tops and had a snake tattoo which slithered its way from her neck down her right shoulder and around her arm .

She was 18 and had left school with a BTEC Certificate in child care... and she hated children ....not really the profile of a supermodel , I thought.

" Hope it works out for her " my mother managed to splutter out without laughing.

" I think this time she has found her niche, I can see a modelling career working out " said Joyce, referring to the fact that Lorraine had tried several jobs..(.paid and voluntary), and none had suited her.

After another cup of tea and slice of my mothers fruit cake Aunty Joyce decided it was time to leave.

" Bye now, Jodie . Hope the job works out. A shame you can only get something temporary " she said, as she gave me a kiss on the cheek and a swift hug

" Bye, Betty. See you Thursday in the coffee morning in Rhiwbina . Don't forget to make some Welsh Cakes ".

" Yes, yes I'll. bring them Joyce...never fear " replied my mother .

We both waved her off from the doorstep, with me hoping she wouldn't scratch my car with her badly driven Citroen.

We watched her trundle off down the street, seemingly avoiding obstacles that only she could see. My mother practically dragged me back inside.

" What's the REAL reason you've decided to visit me? " asked mam. always straight to the point.

No Refuge

" As I said " I mumbled looking down at the floor " I've got a job interview "

"Yeah, and I've been asked to take over from the Pope "

" Josh and I have separated. It's not working out "

" I thought all had been settled after your last little tiff ? "

" That was no tiff Mam . would a little tiff have led to me cutting my hair off? "

My mother started to look doubtful.

" But ...you went home to him . Said you were helping more in the Practice, sorting out the builders, even that you were trying for a baby ...what happened ? "

" Before I came down here last time, he had started being nasty to me ...I told you that. It was a bit more than just nasty words. He had started getting violent . He shook me, slapped me across the face...stuff like that "
My mother looked shocked.

" Why didn't you tell me this before ? ....what's happened now? "

" I didn't want you worrying, I thought that I could handle it. This time I was kidnapped "

My mother put her hand to her mouth. She was really dumbstruck , her eyes wide and moist .

" Kid napped ? Why? ...what..when ? "

" That's probably a bit dramatic , I suppose. But a club in Merthyr decided they needed a doctor on call to treat their customers and girls working there . A sort of pole dancing club with some other activities going on. Josh didn't tell me about this . My car broke down and I lost my phone. A man came along who said he was Josh's friend and offered to take me home. He called the RAC , and I agreed to a lift, but instead of taking me home, he took me to a restaurant for a meal. He and the other club owners wanted to make sure that Josh realised how important it was that he took the job, and kept it all confidential. Prove how powerful they are . "

" Sounds very seedy to me ...and to take you off like that! "

" It is seedy mam, and I was frightened. However, the man took me home after the meal....and, get this, Josh blamed me !
Said I shouldn't have let him give me a lift....but the circumstances, and he knew so much about Josh , said he was a friend. I might be naive , but that's all.
Josh was horrible, called me terrible names , accused me of all sorts . It was so devastating hearing my husband talk to me like that. ". I could feel my eyes filling with tears , I wiped them with a tissue .

" What did he accuse you of? "

" Sleeping with that man, leading him on , stuff like that "

" Did you?Did he touch you ? The man "

" No. No way. He treated me ok actually. just bought me a meal, that's all "

" Did Josh hit you this time? "

" No, but only because I avoided it . I could read his mood ....the terrible things he said. I knew if I protested or said anything back he would hit me.... so I kept quiet "

" Oh you poor , poor girl " my mother drew me to her in a big hug. " Don't worry, you can stay here as long as you like . Have a good sleep

No Refuge

tonight and we'll work out anything we need to do in the morning , you're safe now "

I stayed wrapped in her arms for ages, as if I was a child again, and my mother was protecting me from the " Bogeyman " . In truth, I think she was.

Later on. , I had a hot chocolate and biscuits ....provided by my mother , who obviously thought that it was a good idea to revert to childhood routines.

My cases had been brought in from the car and I had sorted out " my" bedroom again. I instructed my mother to tell Josh that I didn't want to talk to him if he phoned. I would ignore him if he called my mobile as I had his phone number on caller ID.
Mam promised she wouldn't listen to him , and would just tell him I didn't want to speak about anything at the moment.
When I finally went to bed, I was absolutely exhausted. I thought earlier that I would never be able to get to sleep as I was so anxious.

However, after talking to my mother, I felt as if I could just sleep my worries away...there was no need to think about anything or anyone .

Thankfully I undressed, put on a pair of comfy pyjamas and slipped beneath the seats.

I was awakened about an hour later by the ring of my mobile.

' I thought I'd turned it off' I sighed to myself, as I reached out and picked it up. I noticed the light which illuminated the number and realised it wasn't Josh's I D. ' Oh damn, ' I thought " it must be Honey. I promised her I'd ring this evening to check how she was and tell her what had happened to me . I pressed the ' answer ' button

" Hello pretty lady " came Vincent's unmistakable voice out of the speakers " Glad you've left that arsehole and are safe in your mothers house "

" Vincent! " I cried " how do you know where I am? "

" You would be surprised at all I know " he replied enigmatically

" Why have you phoned me? "

" To let you know how glad I am that you are safe. To also tell you to watch out for future developments ...... And to reassure you that I am always around. "

I didn't know what to think. I had no idea what he was on about ....developments? ......always around? To be truthful I didn't like the sound of that.

" Vincent , what do you mean about always being around and there being developments? "

" Just that even if you can't see me , I'm there . I will always look after you . The developments relate to Josh and the Club .....and your future "

I shivered involuntarily. Couldn't I get away from all this....from Josh, Vincent, the club? I decided for the moment to say nothing .

" O K Vincent thanks "

" No problem.......see you soon, very soon.
Sweet dreams pretty lady " .

He cut off the phone. I was more puzzled than ever.

What on earth was going to happen next?

CHAPTER TWENTY ONE

"Josh"

"Plop" the last blob of butter fell to the floor, leaving Josh with a piece of dried toast in his hand. He had the scrapings of the marmalade jar that he could spread on it ...or he could ....throw it across the room and shout " Fuck it !", which was exactly what he decided to do.

The anger inside Josh seemed to grow by the minute since Jody had ran off to her mothers like a silly little school girl .

'Be honest , 'he thought,' what on earth have I really done to lead her to do this? OK , perhaps I could have been a bit kinder to her when that Neanderthal Vincent brought her back. But I was worried out of my mind , and therefore in a tense state of anxiety.

In truth, she should not have gone off with a strange man in his car , whatever he had said to persuade her. I know I asked her if he'd touched her or anything...well you would, wouldn't you? .....Be worried that the thug might have ' tried it on ' or something. Yes, I agree I was in a bit of a temper at that point.

I calmed down though. We went to bed and everything was alright... wasn't it ? We even made love..and she didn't protest.....even to the point of tidying up and changing the sheets afterwards. I just can't understand her behaviour. " He was genuinely puzzled .

Josh finished his semi- cold cup of tea, wiped his hands and left the kitchen for the surgery, leaving behind him a mess of dirty dishes and empty bottles.

Jodie had only been gone a day and the plac was falling apart already. Josh vowed to go down to her mothers house tonight and drag her back if necessary.

Josh could feel the sexual tension building up in him. The more aggressive he felt, the more his libido grew.

It was something he'd had since adolescence where he used to masturbate after the other boys had bullied him, and he had been too small and weak to hit them back.

Josh had discovered over time that if pain or cruelty was also involved he felt even greater satisfaction and release. He would hurt himself ....but that was never gratifying enough, so he would hurt his sexual partners. However, usually the women he dated objected to this ...this was when he first discover the cellar in " The Club ", which appeared to be the answer to all his dreams.

The practice that day was fairly busy, and Josh noticed, with satisfaction, that the patient list was increasing and that the nurses various clinics were filling up. This would soon help to ease some of his financial worries . Things were looking good ......once that stupid cow of a wife of his stopped her silly tantrums and returned home.

Just after morning surgery ended Josh received a phone call " Hello Doctor Harrison " came a male voice , on the phone " Hello " said Josh " What can I do for you? ". " This is Stan, from the club. We would be most grateful if you could attend one of our girls as soon as possible. She became Ill about an hour ago and is not recovering. It's her breathing. ... The side door will be open. ".

No Refuge

" Oh, what..? " began Josh, but Stan broke in " No questions Doc. just get here "

" Be right there "

Josh took his coat from the stand and left the building, jumping into his car and roaring off down the high street.

Josh arrived at the club, and quickly made his way to the side door which was open as promised. He went in and walked through the dark corridor, to be met by Vincent , dressed in his usual immaculately tailored suit, blue shirt and silver tie,

" Good day Doctor Harrison " he said " and how is your lovely lady wife today? ".

Josh scowled at him , wondering if he somehow knew what had happened " Fine. thanh you " he replied , with a curt nod. Vincent gave a barely discernible smirk.

Josh was escorted to the girls dressing room where Lara was gasping for breath.

" What happened ? " he asked Stan , who was standing nearby as if on guard

" Don't really know. The client took her to one of the " torture rooms". He's not known for erotic asphyxiation, by the way. Then he shouts to me ' help" help' she's breathing funny' . So I ran in and her neck and wrists were handcuffed to her ankles and she was gasping for breath. I've been trying to help her breathe ever since, by taking her out the back ....but no improvement . "

Lara was still sitting up and Josh pushed her forward so that he could listen to her chest, how her lungs were.

Immediately Josh said to Lara " are you asthmatic ? " she nodded ," yes."

He got out a ventolin inhaler and gave it to her. She took two puffs, and Josh brought out a small nebuliser , in which he inserted three different ampoules. He then attached a mask to it, and plugged it in to the nearest electric point . Gently , Josh placed the mask over Lara's head and fixed it on to her mouth. After a few moments she was breathing easily.

" Do you take any medication for your asthma ? " asked Josh after a while.
" I've got some ventolin inhalers somewhere ....?.but I haven't really had much problems with it for a good while "
"It was the position you were in.....bent over backwards.....that slightly crushed the lungs and you didn't have enough capacity to breathe properly. This triggered your asthma. In your job, you really need to take a preventative inhaler twice a day. "

" Oh, oh thanks . Where will I get one of them ? "

" I'll prescribe Salbutamol for you now and also give you a new ventolin inhaler "

Josh got out his prescription pad, wrote on it, and handed it to Lara.

" Thanks a lot " she said

Stan and Vincent were standing there. They had watched all the proceedings.
Vincent was giving Josh a very strange look, it was one that Josh could not decipher.

After Lara had dressed and left to go home, Josh took Stan aside and asked him if there was a girl available for him, for this afternoon. He had no patients, as it was a clinic day, and so far no house calls to make.

Stan discovered that Jessie was still on shift, so he asked her to take Josh for a "special" . Jess didn't mind, she had serviced Josh before and there were many customers who were much crueler than him. Also, he always gave a very

No Refuge

substantial tip, and she was saving for a conservatory ...she would probably have enough by the Summer.

Josh and Jess made their way to one of the private rooms in the cellar. This was equipped like a mini dudgeon, with manacles affixed to the wall, a chest of sex toys , some whips in various sizes and a low bed.

Josh looked around as if deciding on his role play " You are my slave ...and I can do with you as I wish" he said to Jessie.

Jessie couldn't remember if he wanted her to be a passive submissive or a reluctant one. She searched her memory, but there had been so many customers recently that she just couldn't remember. She decided to try passive:
" Yes sir, I will obey your every whim" she muttered.

Luckily, Josh seemed pleased with that, and took off her bikini top and panties. He led her to the low manacles which made the wearer squat in a half sitting position. He then placed a dog collar around her neck with a chain leash attached , so that he could control her head movements.

Josh stripped off all his clothes and was surprised to find that his erection was only semi-hard. He touched himself and even started to masturbate, but nothing happened.
He approached Jessie and thrust his crotch into her face and demanded " suck it! " Jessie obligingly took him in her mouth , but despite all her licking and sucking. Biting and touching ..nothing happened. In fact, his cock became flaccid and just hung there, looking ashamed of itself.

Josh was furious! His aggression levels were high, and this usually turned him on so that he had a hard throbbing erection. But today, he couldn't even get it up.

He took the manacles off Jessie and pushed her onto the bed. She lay there, not sure what he wanted her to do...so she tried a seductive pose.

Josh just thrust her body back down and tried to mount her. Unfortunately, this had no effect. He thrust his genitals against hers, bashing his balls onto the edge of her bottom , but his penis refused to perform.

Jess tried to reassure him " Don't worry... perhaps you are tired . Lets just lie here a while and it may start to work " but Josh was in no mood for platitudes.

Despite Jessie's reassurances he was convinced that he would probably never have sex again. The thought entered his mind that Jodie had in some way cursed him by her strange behaviour and robbed him of his masculinity ...." That's it, it's all her bloody fault" he cried to a bemused Jessie who didn't have a clue of what he was talking about.

Josh got up and quickly dressed. He gave Jessie an extra large tip " Make sure you don't tell anyone " he beseeched her " I won't.....don't worry " she promised .

With that, Josh rushed out of the club and into his car. 'I'll sort that fucking bitch out ' he thought, as he headed towards Cardiff.

•••

Josh arrived at Betty's house in less than forty minutes .He had roared down the A470 and probably got caught on at least one speeding camera.

He slammed the car door , causing Betty and Jodie to leap up out of their chairs and look out of the window .

Jodie spotted the expression on Josh's face and her stomach began to knot with fear. What on earth was he going to do?

" I don't want to see him! " she cried to her mother and ran upstairs to shut herself in the bedroom.

No Refuge

Josh banged on the door . To such an extent that the panel of glass shook with the vibration.

" Open up! Let me in " he shouted

" No " replied Betty " Not when you're in that mood "

" I want to see Jodie "

" We'll, you can't . Go home Josh "

" No , I want to talk to my wife "

" She doesn't want to talk to you "

" Will you talk to me then? "

" Not unless you calm down "

Josh took a few deep breaths. He tried to control himself and rein in his emotions . For a couple of minutes he keep quiet.
Once he felt calmer he knocked on the door again, only this time he was much softer.

" Please let me in Betty, please . I've got to talk to someone "

" Promise you won't get angry or try to see Jodie? "
" But I want to see Jodie ......please "

" Well I won't let you in then "

A few more minutes passed. Betty looked outside the window and saw Josh leaning against the wall, his hands in his pocket.

He looked so sad and dejected. Betty could feel a faint pull on her heart strings ......a slight pity. She was a soft hearted woman at the best of times.

Josh tried knocking again .

" Please let me in Betty. I won't try to see Jodie....honest "

" OK ...but I'm holding you to that promise mind. "

Betty opened the door and allowed him in. She ushered him into the kitchen, at the back of the house , where she could best keep her eye on him.

" OK then Josh " said Betty sternly " What do you want to say? "

" Betty, I can't do anything without her " aid Josh, holding his head in his hands . " I mean it ...ANYTHING "

He looked at Betty appealingly, his eyes wet, tears filling them . One small tear ran down his cheek.

" Why have you treated her so badly then? "

" I'm sorry. I didn't realise I had . I mean , I know I can lose my temper sometimes . "

"Jodie said it was more than sometimes ...and that you hurt her physically, and accused her of all sorts. "

" I pushed her once , I know..... and I was so, so, sorry about that . I was just so frustrated at the time having to do everything by myself "

" When did you hit her ? "

No Refuge

" You know, when she came down here the first time. You know how sorry I was, I haven't touched her since ...honest ! "

" What happened this time then ? She says you called her terrible names, accused her of things "

" I was just so WORRIED..........Jodie had disappeared , then she turns up with ...this, this...man. I admit I had been drinking . She tells me he kidnapped her ....but they went for a bloody meal. Kidnappers don't take you for meals in posh restaurants....do they? "

Betty started to look thoughtful. she began to worry that Jodie may have exaggerated things. Betty remembered that even she had asked her if this man had ' done anything'

" I asked her if the man had ....you know, " Josh looked away embarrassed " You know....touched her ...or anything..." His voice slipped.

" Anyway. Whatever the rights and wrongs . She definitely won't see you "

" Betty ....please we can't give up on our marriage . I don't want to, and I don't believe Jodie does really ....can't you help ....in some way? ". He looked at her pleadingly, his cheeks still wet with the tears .

" I will try and talk to her. Not tonight though. You go home ...have a rest . Think things over. I'll get Jodie to do the same and try to persuade her to talk to you .....that's all I can promise "

Josh could see that Betty was determined. This was more than he had dared hope for, so he decided to take the path of least resistance and go back home.

" Thanks Betty. I'll ring tomorrow and you can tell me what's happening. "

Josh stood up and pulled Betty to him in a hug
" Thank you s much " he said.......and was gone.

Betty watched him get in the car and pull away. As she kept looking out at the car disappearing behind a corner, she was sure she saw a man walk out of the shadows to be seen under the street lamp.

A tall muscular man, in beautifully cut clothes. He stood there watching Josh go, then looked up at the windows of her house and gave a mock salute.

CHAPTER TWENTY TWO

"Honey"

Honey woke up with a start , she had been having a Nightmare....where her children were disappearing from her grasp. She looked at the clock ....it was 7 am time to get up and do the school run.

She put out breakfast and called the twins, her heart beating faster by the minute ....today she would have the results. She would know what was wrong and what would happen afterwards...Honey was terrified !

The twins ate their breakfast without too much fuss, and she washed and dressed them ready for school. They all piled into Honeys small car and arrived just before the gates closed. She gave them a big hug and kiss each after some protestations and wriggling.

Honey arrived back at home to await Jodie who was coming with her for support. They hadn't worked out quite what to do at the moment. It would be really awkward for Jodie if she had to face Josh with Honey ,in order to get her results . They had decided to ring first , then see what happened from there.

Presently , there was a knock on the door. Honey opened it to see , thankfully , that Jodie had arrived

" I'm so scared Jodie ...what if it's terrible news? "

" Don't worry. Whatever the results I'll be here, w e can fight it together. Most blood diseases can be cured these days...it's not like years ago. Lets find out what's what first , hey? "

" I know you are right., but I'm so worried about my kids. You wouldn't want them left with Glen would you? I wish I had my family to help. "

" I've asked you before to contact them. I don't know what I'd have done without my mother this past week. ...look times gone by now, and you need help. Surely they're not as hard feeling as you say? "

" I don't know do I ? I've never tried to contact them, but there again, they've never tried to contact me. " Honey said huffily.

Jodie decided to keep quiet. Honey was worried, it was best to go along with her for now , until they knew the full story .

Jodie had just made them both a cup of tea when Glen came lumbering down the stairs .

He was half dressed , with his trousers on, but no shirt .He was scratching himself as he looked around the room, trying to spot a clean, ironed top.

" Here's one " said Honey , handing him a blue and white striped tee shirt from the top of the ironed pile. He pulled it on over his head, trying to make it longer as his beer belly pushed out revealing a small patch of flesh.
" This bloody shirt has shrunk" muttered Glen.

" No it hasn't " replied Honey " it's your belly that's grown "

" I have a fine figure for my age "

No Refuge

" Oh aye, who's been telling you that? "

" That's for me to know and you to find out ....I've got my admirers , I'll have you know "

" Ha , I couldn't care less "

" You 'd be laughing out of the other side of your mouth if I ran off with one of them. Where would you be then? "

" Happy "

"You cheeky cow ...now get me something to eat , then I'm off out...... What's she doing here ?". He indicated Jodie.

" She's getting my results with me ...today ..remember? "

" Lot of bloody fuss about a bit of anaemia ......my mother just got on with it . "

" We'll your mother didn't have what I've got ...there's different types "

" Oh...moan..moan....moan that's all you fucking do ! Forget the food I'm off out ...to somewhere where I'll get a better welcome "

"Best of bloody luck to her!!"

Glen grabbed his fleece from the back of a chair and went out, banging the door behind him.

" Do you really think he's got someone else? " asked Jodie

" Don't know , and I don't bloody care ! ". Honey shrugged her shoulders. However tears started trickling down her face .

Jodie put her arms around Honeys shoulders . " Don't cry love , don't let him upset you "

" It's not him.....well not entirely ....I'm fed up of him being a lazy good for nothing, not caring about me and stomping off when he feels like. But I'm also so afraid for the future ....I just don't know what to do ."

" I suggest the first thing you do is phone the doctor...pity it's Josh...but that's MY problem not yours "

Honey wiped her face , pushed back her hair and got out her mobile. She looked at her contacts and telephoned the surgery.

" Can I speak to Doctor Harrison please ? It's Mrs Sullivan, I'm expecting some results "

" Hold on a moment please " said the receptionist.

A few seconds went by, when Josh's voice came on the phone :

" Good morning Mrs Sullivan " he said
" I've received some of your results ....however, there are some more which need to be analysed . I am not an expert in Haematology, so I have taken the liberty of contacting Dr Carstairs , the Consultant at PCH and he has agreed to see you.

In order to spare you unnecessary waiting and worrying , you could go to his clinic this afternoon at 2pm if you would be willing to do so? "
" Yes, yes, I would be willing " said Honey
" but is there anything you could tell me "

" As I said, I'm not an expert in blood disorders. The only thing I can tell is that it's a bit more serious than iron deficiency anaemia, which is most common in women of your age.

No Refuge

Mr Carstairs is the expert in the UK in this field, and I am sure that he will be able to explain to you what's wrong and the treatment you need to get better.

Honestly, these things are curable.....just takes treatment, time and rest. Shall I tell the hospital you'll be there at 2 pm? "

" Yes, please. Thank you doctor "

" That's fine...take care now. " with that, he put down the phone.

Honey turned to Jodie ." I'm to go to the specialist in the hospital at 2pm . Josh said he's the best consultant in the country and he'll explain everything to me "

" Good - for two reasons. Firstly, you get your results and an expert to explain to you and start your treatment. Secondly, on a selfish level , I don't have to see Josh . "

" Yes, I suppose so " Honey looked very dubious .

•••

A few hours later Honey and Jodie were sitting together in the consulting room of Dr Carstair.

The room was similar to any other consulting room. It had a desk, computer and files. The doctors swivel chair and two chairs for patients. This room had been newly decorated in cream and pale grey with grey blinds.

Attached to the main room was am examination suite with the usual couch and three tier silver trolley containing instruments and medical items.

Honey had taken in every aspect of the room, including the disinfectant smell with overtones of orange.

Dr. Carstairs himself was in his early 50s . A well dressed man, with dark grey trousers immaculately pressed and a pristine white shirt and navy tie , under his doctors white coat.

He had brown hair with a hint of ginger in it and a small trim beard . He also wore spectacles . Honey though it amusing as usually she would say ' glasses' but on Dr Carstairs, these reading implements had the gravitas of spectacles -it gave him more of a status, she decided .

" Hello Mrs Sullivan " he said , with a faint Scottish accent " I am so glad you could make this clinic today. " He held out a hand.

Honey gave him a smile " Hello " she said briefly. Her hands , she noticed were shaking with nervousness. However she took his habd and managed a trembling handshake.

He didn't comment on this, but merely turned to Jodie with his hand held out " Hello....? " he queried " Mrs Harrison " she said , and they too, shook hands.

" I expect you are waiting to hear the results of all these horrible tests we've been putting you through ? " he said to Honey . She nodded. her agreement, her mouth too dry to speak.

" You have a condition known as 'Aplastic Anaemia ' Dr Carstairs stated ' it's a fairly rare condition, and is serious. Not too many years ago, there was nothing could be done , but the good news now is that there is a 71% remission rate , and those patients consider themselves to be cured "

Honey sighed, trying to take in exactly what he had told her .

" What is it exactly ? And what treatment will I have ? " she asked, anxiously

" It's what we call an ' auto-immune disease' where the body attacks itself. In this case the bone marrow stops producing enough red cells, and the red

No Refuge

cells it does produce , the white cells kill off. This is what causes the anaemia, tiredness, pallor etc.

The first thing we do is treat you with drugs which suppress your immune system, to stop your body fighting itself. These are not without their problems.

Because they stop your immune system, you become very susceptible to any infection. You must avoid places where there's lots of people, and where you could catch something.

If you do catch a cold , measles , anything like that you will have to come straight into hospital .

Some people go into remission totally on the drugs we give them . Especially older people . However, with someone as young as yourself, the best treatment by far, which usually results in a cure, is a bone marrow transplant . This works best if the donor is a sibling with matching characteristics. "

" What if you don't have a matching sibling? " asked Honey

" Then you can go on the donor transplant list , and see if anyone on there matches you. Also , other family members can be tested and there might be a good match amongst them.

However, a matching sibling is the ideal because their genes are the same as yours ...you get half your genes from each parent ....only a sibling can have that. "

" Oh. I see " Honey was looking down at her lap, her hands clenched together making the knuckles go white .

" Do you have any siblings, Mrs Sullivan? "

"Yes , I have a brother and a sister. My brother lives in New Zealand, and my sister and I haven't spoken for years "

" Perhaps this would be a good time for a reconciliation " recommended the doctor.

" Mmmm I don't know. All this is a lot to take in. "
Honey looked despondent . Her face had formed in to a frown as if she couldn't quite understand all that had been said to her.

Jodie knew there must be more things she needed to know , so gently , she probed Honey .

" is there anything you want to ask Doctor Carstairs ? " asked Jodie

" I honestly can't think "

" " Can I ask some questions? "

" Yes, go ahead "

Addressing Dr Carstairs Jodie asked " When will you start treatment ? "

" Now, today , by prescribing immunosuppressant drugs "

" What happens then? "

" I will give Mrs Sullivan a list of possible contraindications ..um..side effects . If she has any, she must come into the hospital immediately.

I will see her a week today for blood test, and continue weekly for a while. It can take some time to get the right balance of drugs and dosages "

" OK. will Honey - Mrs Sullivan, be able to return to work? "

" No, not immediately , and not whilst on the drugs ....it's too risky unless she works in isolation. Also, these drugs tend to make you fatigued and you

No Refuge

need to rest to prevent damage to the heart. She could go back to work after recovering from a transplant. "

" So I've got to stop working ! " cried Honey

" What is your profession? " asked Dr Carstairs

" Ummm, I work with people, a sort of customer relations job . "

" I see. Yes you will have to give that up "

" What if I don't have any treatment , and carry on as normal? " Honey sounded suddenly desperate. She was afraid of what Glen would say if she gave up work.

" Then, I'm afraid you will die, Mrs Sullivan , within about six months "

Honeys already looked pale, now she turned a deathly white .

" You didn't say anything about dying ! " she cried

" I told you it was a very serious disease, and I gave you the remission rates. "

" Yes, but I thought the rest of the people, those not in remission, would just remain ill - not die! "

" Oh . I thought you understood the implications. "

" So I've got cancer have I ? "

" It's similar to the blood cancers, but there's an entirely different mechanism at work. In for example, leukaemia, the bad cells go out of control and keep growing, so we have to try and stop them In Aplastic

Anaemia your bone marrow has started fighting with itself and destroying red blood cells , so we have to stop it doing that. It's your immune system going into overdrive "

" What causes it? "

" Mostly it's idiopathic, which means it just happens and we haven't any idea why. Research has shown that in some cases there appears to be a link with certain viruses , which seem to trigger it off, but this is not yet definite. "

" Ok then, " said Honey, pulling herself together, sitting straighter and shrugging her shoulders " What's first ? "

" Here's your leaflet on side effects..... phone immediately if you have any of them . Here's one weeks supply of your first drug. This schedule shows you how you increase the dose every other day. This card is your appointment for next week - give it to the receptionist on the way out. Even if you manage to find a bone marrow donor, we need to build you up first before we can operate. "

Dr Carstairs stood up. " Have you anymore questions Mrs Sullivan? " he asked kindly

" No, no thank you, for now " Honey replied , shaking his hand.

She and Jodie left the consulting room and made their way to the front entrance.

"Do you want a cuppa in the cafe ?" Asked Jodie

" No, I just want to go home , I just want to see my kids. "
Her stomach was turning and she felt as if all the blood in her veins had turned to ice. Fear clenched at her heart.

OK love , whatever you say. "

No Refuge

They walked to the car and got in. Honey sat in the passenger seat and put on her seat belt, then she burst into tears.

Jodie put her arms around her.

" There, there , cry it out " she said.

" I want to be around for my babies . What am I going to do Jodie …I'm not strong enough to go through all this "

" I'll help all I can. Your treatment will work . You must think about contacting your sister …not just for her bone marrow ….she could also be a help and support for you . "

" I haven't spoken to her since I left with Glen…..that was 6 years ago. She hates me . She'll think I'm only contacting her now because I'm Ill and want her help. "

" In a way , you are….but that's what families are for "

Honey continued crying , as Jodie soothed her .

" What about Glen? He's going to go mad! I can't work anymore and I'll have to go into hospital and leave the kids with him …he'll go ape shit …I'm telling you "

" Look Jodie. You have to tell Glen straight. You've got a very serious , potentially terminal illness and he has to pull his finger out and look after you and the kids . If not, you'd be better off if he pissed off altogether "

Honey could hear the sense in these words…but, oh. It was so much easier said than done.

Jodie could see the consternation on Honey's face

" Honey you have to put it to him straight...for your sake...for the kids sake. "

" I know...but ...how about I leave it a couple of days.? Do my shifts for the rest of the week? "

" NO, I'll go and tell your boss, he's been understanding, he seems ok....I'll tell him all. That you mustn't work "

Honey started sobbing again. Jodie started the car and drove her home. All the time thinking " What can I do ? "

By the time they had reached Honey's house, Jodie had come to a decision.

She took Honey inside and sat her down.
She was looking terrible. Jodie made her a cup of tea, and popped next door to pick up the twins, who had been collected by Natalie.

Th twins could see that their mother was upset. They ran up to her , flinging their chubby little arms around her neck. She held them tightly, as if she was never going to let them go. Honey cried on their little shoulders , aching with love for them .

" What's your sisters phone number? " demanded Jodie

" What? Why? ....ummm not sure ...might not be her number now ". Stammered Honey.

" You know it . Give it to me . If its wrong, I'll try and trace her ! " Jodie held out her hand for the number.

Honey went to a drawer in the sideboard and took out a small blue book . She turned its pages, then she handed Jodie the book, with it open on a page which said " Valerie " .

No Refuge

" That's my sister " Honey stammered. " Oh. your mother didn't have a fairy tale name for her then? "

" No " replied Jodie , with half a smile appearing on her lips " She was very practical and down to earth with my sister's name "

Jodie, took out her phone and started to enter the numbers ...." her surnames Davies " said Honey .

She appeared to be resigned to Jodie contacting her.

The Phone rang. Then a strong, female voice answered " Hello , Val here "

" Hello, is that Valerie Davies ? " said Jodie

" Yes, Val. I just said so " Jodie was taken aback .

" Are you the sister of Honey.... Honey Sullivan? " asked Jodie

" Honey ? yes. Sullivan....she married that waste of space did she ? "

Jodie wasn't sure how to answer ; yes, meant she had married Glen, but also that he was ' a waste of space'"

" Umm yes, I suppose " said Jodie
" Who are you? " said Val

" Jodie. I'm a friend of Honeys. she's very ill "

" What do you mean? " Val asked sounding very concerned .

" She's here, at home, but she's just been diagnosed with ' Aplastic Anaemia. it's not great. "

" I know what it is " said Val " I'm a nurse".

Jodie was once more taken aback

" Let me talk to her " said Val.

"Thanks ...here she is " said Jodie , giving the phone to Honey.

" So you're not too well then , Honey bun. " asked Val

" No o "

" That Glen not treating you very well either, is he ?

" No, not really "

" Lazy good for nothing "

Honey stayed silent .

" You need some proper help girl with that illness and the kids to care for ....where'd you live? "

Honey gave her address.

" I'll be there in an hour. No arguments . You've got your big sister on your side now Honey bunny "

With that she put down the phone

Jodie Looked at Honey. Honey seemed to relax more, She lay back on the sofa, the tension leaving her body.

"' It's going to be alright she thought . Her big sister Val was coming to save her .....just as she did when they were little. "

CHAPTER TWENTY THREE

"Jodie"

I stayed with Honey, made the kids and her their tea, and we sat down to watch the news on TV. It was the usual bad news ...war, famine, murder. It always made me think that the whole world was going to hell in a handcart.

We had our own small problems here. Although Honey's wasn't quite that small....to her and the children, it was the whole world. The Welsh news came on and there was a report relating to the body I found in the skip;

" Chris Roberts 45, has been charged with the manslaughter of his wife, Marion aka Candice Roberts 39 at their house in Glaisier Road, Merthyr Tydfil. He has been remanded in custody until February 24th"

" Oh, he's been charged with manslaughter, not murder " said Honey " he'll get a lesser sentence for that, won't he ? "

" Yes, " I said, usually about 5 to 10 years, maybe less.

" He didn't really kill her you know "

" What do you mean?" I was shocked

" Candice and her husband were going to be evicted, they didn't have a penny. They've got four little ones you know. Poor little things.....all under ten "

" That's sad...but I still don't understand? "

" Well this VERY rich client ...a Russian , friend of Vlad's , offered her enough money to buy a nice house about £ 150 grand, if she would let him undertake erotic asphyxiation on her and cut off her leg ! There's a name for it ac...acrotomophilia ...that's it , when you sexually desire to cut off someone's limb.."

" Oh my God! That's gruesome " I literally felt sick.

" It is , isn't it ? I could never do that. Anyway , she was absolutely desperate, and there was no other way out. She had council house arrears , so there was no where they could go. The social services were trying to put her and the kids in a hostel and Chris to fend for himself. But she adored him you know?

You might think in her line of work , you don't get attached to men. It's not like that ...it's just a job. She loved the bones of him , and to be fair, he loved her. He worked at anything to bring money in. The problem was, there was nothing about, and one of the little ones has a chronic illness and needs constant looking after ...in a good environment......There was no other option "

" What about family? Friends? Surely there was something else? "

" No,most of the family was either dead or way out of touch. Her mother actually lived with them...so she was in the same boat...she's got the kids now . Even best friends can't take in three adults and four kids , not into the small accommodation they all live in. This was definitely the only way . She said she'd manage without a leg. The NHS would give her a false one. Since the Paralympics it was quite trendy !

She had made a bit off that client already, with the asphyxiation in the past..and always came around fine. It was just the amputation that was tricky. He got some local anaesthetic and pain killers for her.... and then he was all

No Refuge

set. She didn't seem to feel the pain. He'd asphyxiated her first, then when unconscious cut off the leg. Afterwards he realised she wasn't breathing and Vincent tried CPR but it was too late. They had to get rid of the body then... so dumped her in your skip. "

" Yeah, thanks for that...lovely that was " I said sarcastically.

" Anyhow . They reckon if they could've got a doctor she could have been saved. That's why there was so much pressure put on Josh . Chris wants his kids to have the money , so he said he did it, as a sex game and also used cuffs on her, and that he panicked when he couldn't wake her or get the manacles off , so he cut off her leg to detach the manacles. Said he thinks he threw them in the river - they'll never be found because there wasn't any! They must believe him though, to put him on a man slaughter not murder charge ."

" Yes, must do. If the jury believes him, he might get off or the judge might be lenient "

" Hope so ...but it's one hell of a price to pay for a house! "

" Oh My God...Yes " .

We both sat looking at the fireplace, lost in thoughts of what things you can be driven to through poverty and desperation. I wondered how many people would do the same thing? I bet there's more than we think.

The twins played happily with a farmyard behind us . We could hear the " moo moo"s and " baa baa"s

Just then came a knock on the door .

" Will you open it Jodie please ? " begged Honey.
I nodded and opened the door.

There stood a taller version of Honey, with dark curly hair, intelligent green eyes and medium build. She looked a competent, take no nonsense, sort of person, ideal to help Honey .

She looked at me quizzically . " Umm who are you? I'm Val " she said " Yes, yes I know , I'm Jodie Harrison, a friend of Honeys " I pushed the door open, and Honey and Vals eyes met .

" Val" cried Honey " Honey Bunny " cried Val ....and the two sisters fell into each others arms , crying.

I stayed only to gather my stuff together and tell Honey I would phone her tomorrow. I wanted the two sisters to get to know each other again.

•••

I decided that the sooner Honey's boss at "The Club " was told , the better. Just in case Val failed to be the support Honey needed or through fear of Glen's reaction and worry about money for the kids, Honey would force herself to return to work despite all the risks.

I also harboured a desire to take a look at this " Club " which mesmerised my husband and was a den of sexual predators. I had never been inside a traditional pole dancing club, let alone one which carried out other " special " activities. As for BDSM I wasn't really certain what it really entailed. I might observe nothing untoward when I was there, but I just wanted to get a " feel" for the place.

I reached Bethesda street, where " The Club Paradis " was located, around 7 pm. It was early evening, so I didn't expect the club to be in full swing.

The building was of grey stone with windows on both floors. These however, were all shut, with closed blinds . Across the front facade of the club was its name in pink neon lights which mimicked handwriting. There were steps leading up to the main entrance. A man in a black suit, presumably the

No Refuge

doorkeeper, was positioned at the top of these steps , ready to allow people in, or turn them away.

I walked up the few steps, and prepared to enter. The man in the suit approached me
" Can I help you madam? "

" Yes please, I'd like to see Stan . I'm sorry I don't know his surname . "

" I expect you mean Stan Grainger " he shuffled his feet a little " come with me ..I'll direct you to his office "

This doorman was particularly well spoken, which surprised me a little. I suppose I had made lots of unfounded judgements about this place, expecting it to be a seedy little dive full of rough talking characters.

The man in the suit showed me to a door with a plaque which read " Mr S Grainger. He knocked the door, looked inside and said " There's a lady to see you Mr Grainger, may I show her in? " a deep baritone voice answered " Yes, fine. " The doorman turned to me, and opening the door wider ushered me in.

Seated at a desk, was a good looking man in his late forties. His skin shone like ebony, and his hair was close cut to his head. He wore, as expected, a black suit, I was sure by now that this was some type of uniform. His smile appeared genuine and his deep brown eyes looked interested as to why I had called to see him.

" Hello , you wanted to see me. Are you looking for a job? " he asked

" Me? No, I can't dance ! "

" We have vacancies for other positions which don't require dancing " his smile became wider.

" N..n..no thanks " I stammered

" What can I do for you, then ?"

" I've come to see you about Honey Sullivan. My names Jodie, I'm a friend of hers "

" Honey? Is anything the matter ? " he seemed genuinely concerned. I didn't expect this from a man in his job of placing and managing sex workers.

" We'll, yes. There is actually ....she's Ill."

" She hasn't been very well for weeks - I've sent her home a few times, but that arsehole of a husband of hers forces her back in " .

I started to laugh.

" Why are you laughing. " asked Stan

" That's what everyone seems to call Glen. I'm beginning to think its his proper name "

Stan laughed with me .

" Anyway, I came to tell you that, regardless of Glen, Honey will not be back in work for the foreseeable future . "

Stan looked really worried at this information .
" Why? What's wrong ? Is it serious ? " he demanded

" I'm afraid so. She has " Aplastic Anaemia " which is a serious blood disease. She has to undergo months of intensive therapy, including a bone marrow transplant . "

" Oh No, Poor Honey . She's had enough worries in her life..and now this! "

No Refuge

I was very surprised by the strength of his emotions. I had never expected Stan to be so concerned about one of his ' girls '.

He got up and went over to a cupboard near the window. He opened a door,and bent down to what was obviously a safe. He opened it and tok something out and counted some money ...I couldn't quite see . Then he locked it all up and returned to his desk.

He handed me a pay packet with Honeys name on it, and then took a brown envelope from his desk drawer, wrote a few words on a piece of paper , and put this, together with a thick wad of money, into the envelope. he handed the packet and the envelope to me

" Here's Honey's pay up to date, and some extra money to help tide her over. Tell her I hope she recovers quickly and that her job is here for her whenever she's able to return.

Reassure her though, that she's not to worry about it. If its possible I'd like to come and see her, but I don't want to ruffle any feathers, so could you just tell her and ask her to ring me? "

He looked so sincere , I agreed to give his message to Honey. I still hadn't got over the shock of how different he was from my preconceived ideas.

" Thank you so much Stan. I'm sure Honey will be very pleased. "

" No problem Jodie, just tell her to take care, I am concerned about her you know. "

" Yes San, I know . " I said sincerely. ' You find kindness in the strangest places ' I thought.

" Goodbye Jodie "

" Goodbye Stan "

I left his office and returned to the corridor. I realised I hadn't seen much of the club, but it no longer seemed to matter.

I turned left and made my way back to the entrance , when I literally bumped into someone. I didn't need to look up to see who it was. I was aware of a tall, muscular body , a person who seemed to take away all the space. It had to be Vincent.

" What are you doing here, pretty lady? " he asked

" I've been to see Stan "

" Looking for a job are you ? " he chuckled

" No, I had to see him about someone "

" Who ? "

" It's none of your business really, but one of my friends, Honey, who worked here , is very ill and has to leave "

" Sorry to hear that , but how come you are friendly with Honey? "

" We met some months ago and just became friends -as straight forward as that "

" Oh.....it's just I would never have put you two together....you seem so different "

" Shows how little you know about us ...both of us "

He shrugged. " Yeah, you're probably right " I turned to go.

No Refuge

" Where you off to ? " he asked

" Back to Cardiff after I take Honeys wages to her "

" You're living in Cardiff? " he queried in apparent astonishment.

" As if you didn't know "

" What do you mean by that? "

" You know exactly what I mean. "

I pushed past him and out of the club into the cold night air. I practically ran down the steps anxious to get to the relative warmth of my car.
Vincent came after me, he caught my arm as I turned down the street.

" Woah…you're not trying that again " I exclaimed pulling away from him.

" I'm not going to kidnap you again….don't worry "

" I'm glad you said 'again' . That means you admit you did do it last time. "

" Well, only sort of……..I took you for a meal "

" Oh come off it Vincent. I was just a pawn to frighten Josh . All it bloody did was make him jealous "

" Jealous ? What do you mean ? "

" Oh, nothing . I've got to go now, my mothers doing a meal for tonight "

" Come and have a drink with me " he suddenly declared, catching hold of my hand.

" I told you...I've got to get back. "

"Just one ...please ...I want to apologise for making you a pawn "

The way he said it made me laugh. Against my better judgement I agreed to have one drink with him in a nearby pub . Vincent was an enigma, he was like a puzzle I wanted to solve.

We walked down the street in the direction of the town centre and turned into a pub called " The Lantern" . The building was obviously very old, with low ceilings and beams. The bar was straight in front of you as you entered , with seating either side . We took a seat towards the left, just beneath an old mullion window.

Vincent ordered the drinks. I only had an orange juice as I was driving to Cardiff.

" Right. First things first , I apologise for using you as a prawn....sorry pawn, and will you call me Vince? Vincent reminds me too much of my mother and work "

He was laughing at me , chuckling and his eyes dancing . It was the first time I had seen him relax.

" OK ..apology accepted. I'll call you Vince if you like , because its not as if I'm going to bump into you often is it? Not with me living in Cardiff . "

His face dropped a little, taking on a slight hurt look.

" I thought may be we could become friends "

" Why would we? You work for a sex club , here in Merthyr, which my husband is involved in ; and I've left here to live in Cardiff and hopefully to lecture in the University . There's nothing we have in common "

No Refuge

" You don't know that until you get to know me properly . "

I didn't reply. Just took a sip of my orange juice and looked around the pub. There was only a smattering of people in there. A couple of groups of men , in what looked like work clothes, all drinking pints. There was also four women sitting at a table waiting for their bar meals, laughing and giggling at some office gossip , no doubt. I turned back to look at Vince .

" I really must go". I insisted. My mother will be getting anxious ...she's worrying about me at the moment"

" OK . But before you go, can you tell me what you meant , when you said that ' it only made Josh jealous'?"

" When you left that night , he started calling me names, became abusive again. He said that you hadn't kidnapped me, that we had been having sex . He kept saying that , and that we were making a fool of him. It didn't matter how much I protested, he took no notice and ...... Well, never mind that...... just say he wasn't nice tome ' "

I'm sorry, really sorry " said Vince. He sounded upset.

" Why? It's not your fault how his twisted mind works "

" No, but I was the person who took you "

" Oh well it's water under the bridge now ....I've really got to go ! "

I got up and put my coat on preparing to leave,

Vince also stood and said " I'll walk you to your car."

We walked around to the small car park where I had left my car.

" Bye, Vince" I said ." oh by the way, next time you're spying on my mothers house...just knock the door and we'll give you a cup of tea "

His mouth opened in surprise, but he quickly shut it and broke into a big smile.

I bent to get in to the driving seat , when suddenly, he pulled me to him, looked me in the eyes and kissed me ...hard. I was totally taken by surprise. This was the last thing I imagined would happen. His lips were softer than I expected....I pushed him away. " No, Vince sorry. I'm not interested.......thanks for the drink though. "

Quickly I got in , shut the door , and drove off, leaving him standing there looking bemused and disappointed.

I drove to Honey's , dropped the envelopes into her hand and gave her Stan's messages.
She looked pleased ,obviously. When she counted the money, she was totally gob smacked . " I can't believe this " she muttered " It will help no end . I wont have to worry about working for a while. Thank God, or thanks Stan "

I was glad to notice that Honey seemed to be getting on well with Val and there was no sign of Glen.

I didn't have time to sit down and chat but promised Honey I would telephone her the next day .

Tired, and not to say a little shaken, I drove quickly back to my mother's. The events of the day had affected me more than I thought. Not only Honey's diagnosis, but the meetings with Stan and Vince and my re-evaluations . I wondered what would happen next to shake me ....

CHAPTER TWENTY FOUR

"Jodie"

I had been living with my mother for two weeks now. In some ways it was like being a little girl again . Having meals made for me, my washing done.... but also wanting to know where I was going and what I was doing all the time. I will have to get somewhere of my own to live, otherwise I might end up killing my loving, caring mother.

Anita was coming to Cardiff shopping today. I had arranged to meet her in the cafe at John Lewises . I was feeling really guilty about practically blaming her for Josh's behaviour that night I dressed up, after the make over.

How could I be so short sighted? I was so ashamed of myself , blaming a woman who was trying to cheer me up and make me feel better . ' I owe her ' I thought...I'll help her have a good day in Cardiff ' .

Reaching the cafe , I could see Anita already ensconced at a table. She stood up, waved and called to me in the effusive way she has . I hurriedly reached her and allowed her to fling her arms around my neck.

" Wow, you look great with your hair cut " she cried. I'd quite forgotten she hadn't seen me since I'd cut it .....we'd only spoken on the phone .

" Yes, it's different isn't it ?"

" See I told you. Once you start dolling yourself up , it gets to you , and you try different styles and fashions and experiment with colour. "

Inwardly, I groaned ' if she only knew" I thought.

"What do you want to do today? " I asked Anita
I

" I'm going to my niece's wedding in a couple of months, so I'd like to look for an outfit for that . Perhaps look at one or two tops...just browse really."

"We're in the best place to start . John Lewis has a great selection of wedding outfits .....all prices and designs . Oh listen to me, I sound like an advert for the place " We both chuckled .
" I've got a few things I need to buy as well ....so we'd better get started."

Taking Anita's arm, we began our shopping spree.

" How's your daughter Caitlin these days? " I asked.
Anita's face dropped
" She's had that Jill back . The girl pestered her after they broke up. Wherever Caitlin was , Jill would appear.

In the end they 'had a talk'and Jill persuaded her that all that " control" - although she didn't call it that....was because she wanted to care and protect her . Caitlin fell for it like a sack of coals ! They're living together, all loved up. I hardly see my daughter again.

They're even talking about getting married. I just hope she' ll come to her senses."

" Control is a terrible thing ...Josh was like that. I suppose you could say it was one of the things behind all our problems "

" Don't ever forget to be your self Jodie. Let no one else own you or frighten you. Relationships built on fear are not love...they are just those of a guard and a prisoner "

" Pretty profound "

" Been there, seen the video , got the tee shirt "

No Refuge

" You're right ...I know that. c'mon lets go shopping"

We looked around the clothes department and Anita found a hippyish outfit for her niece's wedding. It was a bodice dress and had a long, handkerchief cut skirt with panels of different designs , with one co ordinating colour of green. She also bought a matching green wrap . It looked wonderful on her. If ever an outfit said " Here I am ...it's me ". This one did . although Anita said it would cause quite a stir amongst the relatives when she appeared in it.

After that , we just browsed. I bought a long, loose knit jumper in salmon pink, which suited my colouring and Anita bought a similar one in blue for Caitlin, hoping this ' peace offering ' would make relations between them improve.

We browsed around Debenhams, and Boots the chemist, where I made some purchases I wanted. Then looked around part of St David's Centre at the stalls of small little Thai women offering "threading" for eyebrows. Their small hands worked in and out of the woman's eyebrow as if doing some very fast, intricate sewing ...it was mesmerising to watch.

Exhausted, we stopped for coffee in a cafe in the Dominion Arcade , which sold beautiful cupcakes.
Settling down with our lattes and cakes , Anita asked :
" How are you getting on without Josh? "

"Oh 50/50 " I Said, indicating with my hand "so, so. "

" Yes? "

" Well , living here, with my mother, I feel like a little girl again, who has to report everything I do . It's so confining. She even wants to know what time I'll get home from work. I like the job in the University though, even if its temporary ...it's great being back , teaching English.

The other thing is, in some ways I miss Josh. I mean we'd been together about three years and married only five months ago …I just can't stop having feelings for him , even though he's been a bastard to me.

Sometimes I think maybe I've got it wrong . Especially with my mother trying to persuade me to see him, all the time.

He's persuaded her that the last " tiff" , as he calls it, was all due to him worrying about me and then over-reacting. He's told her that he was out of his mind with worry over me when I didn't come home .

Then this man brings me back, who I say kidnapped me, but he finds out we went to a restaurant for a meal. He keeps saying to her : 'Betty, what kidnapper takes his victim for a posh meal …..what was I suppose to think? ' and my mother keeps repeating this to me! "

" That must be really annoying "

" It is . Then I think, to tell the truth, I'm not afraid of Vince, not in the least . When he kissed me last week , I pushed him away, but can't say I was worried about it. Was it really a kidnap? Was Josh right in some sort of way? I didn't have sex or anything with Vince, but perhaps I wasn't frightened enough of him…maybe I even liked him a bit ?"

" Stop thinking like that. You told me you were terrified when he took you…that you had a panic attack …Josh and your mother are manipulating you. Well Josh is. Your mother is being manipulated by him "

I looked at Anita, my eyes wide open.
" Do you really think so?,"

" Yes I do. Josh is an ace manipulator. He must have been doing it for years. The problem is, we don't know when we are being manipulated 99% of the time . "

" Mmmmm. I suppose you are right. But what about these feelings I still have for him? I also miss Merthyr and the house and surgery. I was

No Refuge

so looking forward to getting the house done as I wanted ....my first real home.

I'd started to know some of the patients, made a few friends ....especially you and Honey . It all seems more attractive than staying with my mother. "

" I can understand all that. What you've got to concentrate on now,though, is getting your own place here. You've got that temporary job in the University....you'll make friends there. You already know some people from living here in the past .....Merthyr's not that far away if you want to pop up to see friends "

" Yes....I suppose ". I looked doubtful, I felt doubtful ..Each day that passed, my old life seemed more and more desirable.

" Only you can decide what you really want . Just try not to let others persuade you. Including me . " Anita chuckled.

" Do you think that sometimes circumstances push us into certain decisions? "

" Yes, they do sometimes. But remember these are not always the right decisions. "

We finished our snack and realised it was time to go. I had parked my car near Park Place, whereas Anita's was in the large multi story connected to St David's Centre, which was in the opposite direction.
Therefore , we left the cafe and emerged in the arcade. We hugged in Anita's ' big hug ' style, and said " Goodbye" , promising to phone in a day or two.

I walked slowly to my parked car. I had a lot to think about.

●●●

I opened the door to my mothers house and immediately she appeared in the hallway, just like an apparition.

" Where've you been? What did you do ? " she asked cheerfully.

" I told you mam . I met Anita and we did some shopping "

" Dd you buy anything? "

" Yes, a salmon pink jumper "

" Oh lovely. Do you want a cup of tea? I've got some fish for our dinner tonight. "

" I'll just go upstairs, try on my new jumper and get freshened up "

" OK. I'll make a pot of tea and cut some of the carrot cake I made. "

" Thanks mam "

I climbed the stairs wearily. I loved my mother to pieces , but I'd lived on my own, before my marriage , for five years. Not including my time in university ..which was another three.

Eight years living alone, thinking only of myself and doing as I pleased ...had this caused some of the problems between me and Josh?

In the bedroom, I took out my new top and my other purchases. I tried the jumper on. I was already wearing jeans , and it looked really good with them. As I thought, it suited my colouring. I took it back off and hung it in the wardrobe with the few meagre clothes I had brought with me.

I took off the rest of my clothes and put on a track suit bottom and tee shirt. I didn't want to get the clothes that looked half decent dirty, and it was comfy to hang around in ' slouchy ' clothes.

I picked up my other ' buys ' and went into the bathroom.

No Refuge

The bubble bath I placed on the shelf next to mam's " smellies". Her favourite was Radox herbal ...."Rosemary " scent . I preferred the more musky " Beautiful" and had also bought the body lotion.

My third purchase was still left in my hand ....I opened the box and read the instructions. My hand was shaking. " shall I or shan't I ? " I asked myself. I considered waiting until bedtime.
Perhaps that would be more convenient?

Pulling myself together, I pulled down my trousers and panties and sat on the toilet . I put the stick from the box under myself ......and peed on it.
After I had finished, I balanced the stick on the side of the wash hand basin, wiped myself, dressed and washed my hands.

I left the bathroom and the stick , exactly as instructed. I had to wait 1 to 2 minutes. Those minutes felt like a lifetime. My heart was beating as if it would burst out of my chest, my palms were sweaty and clammy ....I felt faint. My God , that little stick held my future, could change it beyond all belief. Wait...wait ..wait, the hands of the clock ticked slowly.

" Jodie ! " shouted my mother " Your tea and cake is ready "

I nearly jumped out of my skin ...talk about timing.
" I won't be long mam " I called down the stairs. I think my voice sounded normal.

" Hurry up ! "

" Yes, mam "

I looked at my watch ...one and a half minutes. Is that long enough ?

Slowly I walked into the bathroom, deeply thankful that my mother hadn't decided to go to the toilet.

Mrs Thea M Hartley

I picked up the stick gingerly, closing my eyes.

I peeked, first one eye then the other. There were two faint blue lines... as I looked at them , they became darker, more defined. I checked with the instructions ....I was pregnant

CHAPTER TWENTY FIVE

"Honey "

Val walked into Honey's house, where her sister was sitting on the sofa with a cup of tea enjoying a few minutes peace.

Val had taken the twins to school, and she was going with Honey to the hospital today to see Dr Carstairs. . Val wanted to volunteer her bone marrow as a donor for Honey.

" You mustn't do that Val " Honey had protested. "It's quite a painful procedure and you have to stay in overnight. "

" Honey Bunny, we've been estranged for so long, and now I get this chance to do something really good for you. I didn't realise how miserable your life had been theses past years. "

" I can't have a transplant anyhow . Who'd look after the kids? I'd have to be in hospital in a sterile unit for a week to get rid of my bone marrow , then another week or so to see if the new bone marrow has taken"

" I will look after them. We'd only need help for the short time they're harvesting mine. If that lazy no good husband of yours won't look after his kids for a night. .... Then , we' ll find someone else. "

This morning however, Val was on a different mission .

" Where's Glen? " she asked Honey

" He's in bed of course . Where else would he be this time of morning ?"

" When will he be getting up? "

" I dunno, why? "

" Because today's the day you tell him about your illness, and all it's repercussions . "

" Ohhh " Honey looked down, shamefaced. How the hell did Val know? She'd promised her a week ago that she would tell him, but still hadn't broached the subject.

" I'm not stupid Honey. I've seen you ...and him, most days, and I was talking to Natalie this morning , by the school . You have been pretending that you are still working and that's why you've " popped down " my house some nights. My bet is you haven't told him about your illness either, have you ?"

" No , I'm too scared "

" Why Hon? are you scared he'll hit you or do something terrible to you and the kids? "

" Not really, he's not been really violent to us, just to objects ...he'll lose his temper. Break up my favourite things ;rip my clothes up. Make sure I never have any money ....he'll take my debit cards off me. He threw the books I had into the fire. "

Val looked visibly shocked

"I don't know what else .....Any little cruelty he can think of . The kids toys might be chucked away, and he won't let me buy them shoes ......but

No Refuge

worse of all......he will go on and on and on , stopping me sleeping ....making me exhausted .

I can't bear it Val. I'm too tired, too worn . I'd rather not tell him. " she looked at her sister with large, pleading eyes.

" He's brainwashed you. For years he's made you obey him and you've become brainwashed. You've got to break out of it. Stand up for yourself. Don't let him do those things . "

" And how do you propose I do that? I can't fight him . He's a hell of a lot stronger than me. I've tried...in the past. Now, with the illness as well, I haven't the energy to even try "

" We'll I'm going to then! If he doesn't like it ....he can lump it or leave. If not, you and the twins can come and stay with me . "

Honey's eyes lit up with the first bit of hope in years. She had made this a good home for them, but if it meant getting Glen out of her life, she'd live in a coal shed.

Val's place was far from that. She lived on a small holding in Abercanaid with a three bedroom house attached to fields ....and animal pens........where she kept her horse and a small number of livestock.

The twins loved it already, especially when Aunty Val had promised to teach them to ride. If they had to stay there for a while, it would be no hardship. Of course, the best outcome would be for Glen to leave, what with the twins school and proximity to the hospital.

Honey looked at her sister, thanking Jodie in her heart for contacting her. She was becoming her saviour ....in more ways than one.

Glen woke up, he could hear the nattering of women downstairs. ' don't say she's got that bloody sister of hers here again' he thought ' they've only met up a week or so ago after years of not speaking , and now she seems to be here every bloody day'

This put Glen in a right mood. 'It's about time I sorted Honey out again,' he considered. 'She's been getting a bit big for her boots recently , going out and about as she feels like , taking shifts off work.

I'm not going to stand for it any longer. I'll tell her exactly what she can and can't do ....or I'll find some way of punishing her and the kids. ....

I might smash the television up this time. It doesn't bother me, fucking square box in the corner. I can always go out . But she likes them soaps and the kids like children's telly....they'll play hell if we haven't got one .' He smiled and ribbed his hands together, anticipating the upset he would cause.

'It'll take her bloody ages to save for a new one......that"ll teach her . "

He chuckled and sniffed as he cane downstairs.

" Huh, you're here again are you? " Glen looked at Val, his eyes narrowing.

" Yes , I've come to visit my sister " replied Val evenly.

" Don't bother with her or the little uns for years...and then you're hanging about the place like a bad smell "

Ignoring him, Val turned to see Honey handing Glen a cup of coffee and some toast. Inwardly, Val groaned.

" Honey " called Val quietly , " Tell him "

Glen heard Val's whisper

"What you got to tell me? " Glen demanded. Honey, nervous, felt her mouth go dry. She was unable to speak. ..... " Tell me ......FUCKING TELL ME " screamed Glen.

No Refuge

Honey jumped, then automatically cowed.
Glen gave a smirk as if to say ' see , I can control her .....'

Val nudged Honey, both of them were sitting on the sofa. Honey started to speak.......
"Glen....I've got something to tell you ... "
"What could you possibly have to tell me " he sneered.

" Glen, I've got a serious illness . I have to have intensive treatment , and I need a bone marrow transplant ." She said it very quickly

" What d'ya mean? You've only got a bit of anaemia "

" No, I've got a disease called ' Aplastic Anaemia' and it's serious, "

" That's anaemia ain't it? What's the difference ? "

" She could die ". Butted in Val

" Die ? From anaemia ? "

" Yes, Glen, it's like blood cancer " explained Jodie, it was the only way she could get through to him.

He looked gob smacked. His mouth opened and closed like a goldfish. It was the first time something had shut him up.

Seizing on the advantage , Honey blurted out
" I can't work anymore either. I have to rest, and keep away from crowds and people."

" Can't work ? Die? I can't believe it " muttered Glen
" I'm having chemotherapy at the moment, that may help, but a bone marrow transplant is the answer . Val's going to be tested to see if she's suitable. "

" What we going to do for money? " asked Glen, his colour pale, a fearful expression on hi s face

" You'll have to get a proper job. One that can provide for us all " suggested Honey

" You mean, YOU'LL have to stop spending so much. No more new clothes and shoes for the kids...go to OxFam.
Shut off the gas and electric most of the time... You're always fucking wasting it. AND
NO more luxuries for you lot. I'd better not see the kids with chocolates and sweets or catch you with a fag. All this squandering MUST STOP. "

Honey started shaking with fright. Val could see the state on her. Whatever the reason , this nasty little bastard frightened the shit out of her.

Honey was crying now :
" B.b.but Glen. I'm weak, the treatment makes me cold. I need warmth to get better ...to use the gas and electric. The kids need stuff ...they can't go to school looking like scruffs "
She was trying to reason with him. To defeat his argument with logic, pointing out what was needed and that he should be the one to provide it.

Val realised that this was useless. There was no way you could reason with him. All he cared about was himself . He didn't care what happened to Honey as long as he was OK.

" You may as well save your breath Honey " said Val " You can't educate pork, and he's the thickest piece of pork I've ever come across "

Glen gave them both a look of distain
" Well you needn't think you'll get a penny off me " he said " what I can get I need for myself "

He helped himself to another piece of toast from a plate on the table.

No Refuge

" Glennnn? Please? " pleaded Honey

This was obviously some type of dance that the couple choreographed . Val was disgusted, but unsure whether or not to interfere.

Glen looked at Honey then at Val " get her outta here ," he said indicating Val ,
" Then you can do I few things for me which might persuade me to hand over some of my hard earned dosh to you .....if you're good.....really good " He chuckled, a leering look on his face It was obvious what he meant . His face showed a variety of expressions......lust, power and vanity.

He was so certain he could get what he wanted and that he had Honey exactly where he wanted her.

Honey looked at Val " Shall I leave ? " Val asked " I can call back later, pick the kids up for you ? "

There was no mistaking the look of glee on Glen's face now. Val wanted to smash it ...into millions of little pieces .

Honey's eyes grew wider. She was used to this game.

She pleaded, he asked for sex, she did it and if he was pleased he might give her a fiver. How far would that go?

Now she no longer worked she could envisage a future at Glen's hands where she obeyed his every whim, including sexual favours , in order to obtain any money for food and rent. However Ill, however weak she felt .....it wouldn't matter a fuck to Glen ....his wants would always come first.
No, she was too tired for this ....she'd rather die .
The only thing which was keeping her going was the twins.

She stood up , pulled her shoulders back , looked at her sister . She was sick of prostituting herself.

" Stay Val " said Honey . " I'll just sort this put, won't take a mo "

Turning to Glen, she said
" No, I'm not going to to " nice" to you so you can throw me a pittance. I'd rather beg in the street.
The only person you love Glen, is yourself.
I'm not pleading anymore.......Fuck off ! And never, ever come back "

Glen was dumbfounded. . He had never heard Honey speak like that before. What the fuck had happened to her ? Was it that sister? He gave Val an evil look, which made her want to recoil, although she wouldn't give him the satisfaction.

" Now, now, Honey ...love ..don't be like that " he tried to wheedle

" Glen, I've said my piece now...fuck off "

" I'm going.....but you'll be sorry " he pushed his face into hers so that they were almost touching.

Then he picked up a fleece , and marched out , slamming the door.

" Your clothes will be in black bags for you outside the front door. Call back at 2.30 pm and pick them up ". Shouted Honey after him . Then SHE shut the door .

Honey sat down , shaking. Val put an arm around her shoulder " that was very brave of you Honey. I'm so proud " praised Val.

" But what will he do now? I wouldn't put anything past him "

" Honey , there's nothing he can do . If he tries to chuck you out, he can't ...you've got the children . The law is on your side! Tell you what ...I'll stay here with you for a while. I have to go and check on the animals, but that's all . I'll make sure Glen leaves you alone . "

No Refuge

" Oh Val. You're wonderful. Why or why didn't I try and get in touch with you before? "

" Why or why didn't I find you ? We were both too bloody stubborn. ...it's a family trait"

" Too true ! But from now on we'll stick together . Do you know, even though I'm Ill , in some ways I'm happier than I have been for years "

They both smiled at one another.

CHAPTER TWENTY SIX

"Betty"

Betty finished laying the table and looked admiringly at the two place settings on the crisp, white tablecloth.

This reminded her of the meals they would have when Ray returned from a tour. The last few years it had mainly been only the two of them for food, as the children left home , or were out with friends.

She always laid a "lovely " table , Ray would remark, and take her in his arms and kiss her until she could scarcely breathe . ' dear God...how she still missed him ' .

Now she had laid a lovely table for her and her only daughter to enjoy a dinner of fresh plaice and home made chips. Ray and Jodie always shared a love of plaice and both enjoyed her cooking.

" Jodie ! " Betty called , placing bread and butter on the side plates " Dinners ready. ". Jodie had gone upstairs to have a lie down after sharing a cup of tea with her mother, a hour or so ago . Betty wondered if she was coming down with anything. There was that flu still doing the rounds as well as the 'Nova 'virus or whatever it was called . She certainly looked a bit pale.

Jodie appeared at the table and took her seat. " Sorry I was so long mam. I was fast asleep " she said

" Are you feeling alright ? " enquired Betty

" Yes, tired that's all. "

" You look worse now than before you went for your lie down "

" Thanks mam...you know how to make a girl feel good "

" Perhaps you should go and see a doctor. My GP is Doctor Clements , she's ever so good "

"No need , It's probably to do with all the upset over Josh "

" Yes....I agree.....but perhaps it would be worth checking out that there's nothing else . "

Betty set out the fish and chips and they both started eating.

" Beautiful fish mam ....you've always been a great cook " complimented Jodie

" Knew it was your favourite. It was your dad's favourite too. "

" Yes mam, I remember "

They continued eating in silence. Betty enjoyed her meal , happy with the brownness of the chips and the thick white meat of her fish. Jodie however, picked at her food, moving it around on her plate.

" Jodie, I know you're upset over Josh, but I've a feeling there's something else ....call it mother" s instinct " commented Betty.

It was the word "mother", that did it .
" Mam. I'm pregnant "

No Refuge

Betty was so surprised that she nearly fell off her chair, and chocked on her meal. For a few moments she just looked at Jodie and said nothing . Then:

" That's wonderful! A grandchild ...a baby . It will be the makings of you! " a large beaming smile spread across her face , her eyes twinkled with joy .

" Oh Jodie , I'm so pleased "

" Are you?,are you really ? I don't know how I feel"
tears sprang to Jodie's eyes.

" Jodie, having a baby is always a cause for joy ...whatever the circumstances. " said Betty firmly

" Do you really think so ? Said Jodie hopefully

" Yes, love . I do , but how do you feel about it? "

" I really wanted a baby , and we were trying for one. But since all that has happened I feel very confused "

" Yes, you are bound to, is there anyway you and Josh could make another go of it? "

Jodie looked really sad, and some other emotion crossed her face, but Betty couldn't place it.

" I don't think so mam. To tell you the truth I'll have to really think about it . I know that I'll have to tell him. "

"I can't believe you'd ever think anything different."

" Oh I did consider not telling him "

" Whatever's gone on between you, that wouldn't be fair on the baby.

I remember when I told Ray I was expecting you. He was over the moon. He was so proud I thought he would burst! When you were born, he fell in love with you straight away. You were daddy's little girl , he spoiled you more than the boys , and you were so much alike ....enjoyed th same things ! He was so proud of you "

" Yes, I remember waiting for him to come home from one tour or another, and he'd swing me up in his arms and swirl me around. He used to take me fishing ...just me and him, the boys weren't interested. "

" Strangely , the boys are more like me. But they adored their father too. Jodie a child needs a father " stated Betty resolutely. " You must contact Josh and see if you can work things out.

He gave a good reason for getting upset , you know. He was worried sick, and although that horrible man had taken you ....well, what was he to think when he found out you'd been for a meal with him? It didn't sound like much of a kidnapping did it? I know he over reacted and shouldn't have called you those names and accused you of things. But I'm sure he's really sorry. "

" Is he mam? I wish I was as sure as you "

" Yes, he told me he is. At least talk to him and find out how he feels. How you both feel. There's a baby to consider now "

It was obvious what Betty thought, but she didn't know the full extent of Josh's behaviour , and Jodie wasn't going to tell her.

• • •

"Jodie "

I didn't know if I was on my head or my heels.

No Refuge

I told my mother that I was pregnant and she was over the moon. The trouble is, she thinks I should go back to Josh, that our " tiffs" were misunderstandings, which Josh is sorry about.

She gave me examples regarding my father and me . How we had bonded pretty much as soon as I was born. How it is so important for a child to have a father. I remember the times I had with my dad , how he would play with me and swing me about. We always seemed to have a special bond, and I would hate my child to miss out on that.

But my life , my pregnancy l was so much more complicated than my mothers had been. Also there was so much she didn't know, so much I haven't told her. I'm not even sure if I love my baby's father. So what good would it be to live resentfully together as our child grows up? Surely that would be no atmosphere in which to give a baby a good start in life?

All I can do is wonder and worry and sob my heart out .

What will happen next? What will I do?

CHAPTER TWENTY SEVEN

"Josh "

Josh sat on an old wooden frame chair with a red velour seat. He was aware of the lumps and bumps of the broken padding, through his jeans, making him move about to get comfortable. The booth he was seated in was large enough for two people maximum. The walls were made from plasterboard , and only gave an illusion of privacy. If someone made a noise on the one side, it would be heard loudly on the other. There was almost total darkness, the only light allowed in was through the viewing window . His feet were placed on the old carpeted floor which was very sticky with unmentionable fluid emissions. Although surprisingly there was no rancid odour but rather a sweet smell. Abundant use of ' Febreze' he thought .

His whole sensory system was heightened as he peered through this viewing box in " The Club" where he was watching some "girl on girl " action. Two females were writhing about on a mattress in a smallish room. Around the walls were other " viewing boxes" where voyeurs could watch them in " an exciting Lesbian love session " as it was labelled.

The girls -one blonde, one brunette , were both on the slim side of voluptuous and adept at the use of sex toys. Their faces tried to express ecstasy and sexual pleasure, with much moaning and groaning.

Although, on occasion, boredom swept across their features.

Josh was trying yet another sexual experience to try and get rid of his erectile dysfunction. He had resorted to getting a fellow GP to prescribe him

Viagra, much to his embarrassment. He blamed his problems on stress and tried masturbating after taking the little blue pill. He was pleased to note that he managed a strong erection, so wasn't totally impotent. However, after a few minutes it deflated, and failed to perform. This made Josh angry and he had taken him self off to " The Club ", to watch the live show ...and swallow another tablet.

The two girls writhed and squirmed. Sucked, licked and bit. They used dildos and double ended dildos ...which made them look as if they were on a complicated, naked see-saw. Unfortunately, Josh's cock refused to stay erect. He looked at the complimentary box of tissues with contempt. There was no way he would need them.

He put his head in his hands, not knowing what to do, with his sexual prowess being part of his personae, this was worse for him than men with ' normal ' sexual proclivities......or so he thought, anyway.

The only remedy Josh could think of was Jodie. He firmly believed that his impotence was related to her "abandoning " him and that if he could woo her back to his bed, he would be cured.

Josh decided to leave and try phoning Jodie again and begging her to see him.

The two girls were still performing sexual acrobatics and getting into the most unimaginable positions, when he left the booth and made his way down the corridor to the exit.

On his way out, Josh noticed Vincent talking to Stan, near the entrance into the pole dancing room. Even just glimpsing his large frame made Josh shiver. He hated the man, especially since his ' kidnap' of Jodie. " Bet he never has any problems getting it up " thought Josh, giving Vincent's back an evil look. Both Stan and Vincent were unaware of Josh's presence. They had important matters to discuss relating to the clubs premises which had been brought to a head this morning.

No Refuge

In his car, Josh dialled Betty's home number. Recently, Jodie had stopped answering her mobile....obviously avoiding speaking to him . Maybe she would answer the house phone and he would shock her into a conversation.

" Hello, whose speaking? " to Josh's dismay it was Betty's voice which answered the phone

" Hi Betty, it's me, Josh. Is Jodie about ? "

" Oh hi , Josh " He was surprised by the warmth in her voice. " Jodie's having a lie down, she's not very well "

" Oh no ! What's wrong with her? "

" A migraine mostly, so I'm leaving her alone in a dark room. "

" Yes, that's probably the best. Has she taken her medication ? "

" Oh yes . " Betty didn't want to tell him that Jodie hadn't for fear of it affecting the baby. It was up to Jodie to give him that information.

" Josh, why don't you come down and see her later ? " Betty urged, much to Josh's delight and shock. " I think you should both have a good talk. You can't leave things like this . "

" I don't want to. I want to see her. I miss her so desperately Betty, and I want her back. I realise I haven't been a good husband up until now. "

" That's good to hear Josh , very good. Come around 7pm . Oh ! And bring her a present , maybe a large bunch of flowers? "

" Yes, yes of course Betty, of course. See you later " Josh rang off, delighted.

He practically scampered out of his car and into the town centre. Jodie would see him, she would forgive him and come home, everything would be alright . He would never take out his anger on her again, and he would control his sadistic urges.

Reaching the shopping centre, Josh entered the jewellers shop and asked to see some opal necklaces. Jodie's birthday was in October and he knew she loved the stone. He was shown several different pieces, but finally chose a large, single opal in the shape of a teardrop set in gold, with a fine gold chain. The jeweller gift wrapped it for him, and he placed the package in his pocket.

Josh then went to the nearest florist and bought an enormous bouquet of white roses, white lilies and yellow freesias, arranged with gypsophila . He took his purchases, and placed the flowers carefully on the back seat of the car , and drove home to freshen up for the drive to Cardiff.

• • •

At 7 o'clock, practically on the dot. Josh rang the bell on Betty's white front door. The bell resembled an old fashioned brass servants bell, polished to within an inch of its life , an advertisement for Betty's love of cleaning.

It was Betty who opened the door. She hadn't said anything about Josh's impending visit to Jodie, thinking that surprise was probably the best course of action. The unpredictability of Jodie recently may have lead to her going out if she had even an inkling...if the mood took her.

" Well, hello Josh....what a surprise!!! " cried Betty, overacting a little " Come on in ! Jodie's in the kitchen ! "

Betty went ahead into the room at the back of the house, with Josh trailing behind her. " Look who's here " she cried merrily , to Jodie , who was sitting at the table .

The room looked the same as it always did. A somewhat old fashioned kitchen with a sideboard and a large cupboard set into the corners rather than

No Refuge

fitted units. It was really a sort of kitchen/diner. The area where Betty cooked had modern fitted units in grey and white. The fridge, washing machine and dish washer were hidden behind matching unit doors, the split level cooker and hob were also integrated , and the units included the sink. The other end of the room however, was where the table and chairs were placed with the wooden carved cupboard and matching sideboard. It was cosier there, and the whole effect was of an integration between modern and traditional.

Josh entered the room gingerly, with the large bunch of flowers held in front of him, as if he was holding a shield ....he proffered them to Jodie. She looked up as he stood near her. He could see that her face was pale and that she had purple smudges beneath her eyes. He wanted to hold her tight and comfort her.

" Josh" she said, her voice slightly tremulous " what are you doing here? "

" I wanted to see you . I want to apologise. We need to talk. " again, he offered the flowers. This time Jodie took them out of his hands and held them to her nose, breathing in their evocative scent
" They're lovely Josh..my favourites, thank you " still her voice held no emotion , just that slight tremble .

" Jodie, please talk to me . REALLY talk, I mean. I don't want a divorce. I love you " he sat down next to Jodie . She was only a breath away from him.

" You treated me abominably , you know you did "

" Yes, I know " he looked shamefaced, and couldn't meet her eyes .

" I'm scared of you Josh. Of what you'll say or do next . "

" I'm sorry. I won't do anything to frighten you ever. Please Jodie come home. I promise I'll never behave in that way again. I'll never hurt you in any way. Whatever you want me to do I will . Whatever you want me to be I can be, "

" Words are fine Josh. It's actual deeds that matter. I've got a job now. Temporary English Lecturer in the University ...and I intend to keep it. "

" Good. Well done Jodie. Keep your job. I promise I won't try to stop you . You can work, join clubs, see friends, do anything you want and I'll support you 100 percent. I promise ". Josh was sure he could see a change, a subtle shift in her attitude.

" I am not a supervisor for the builders or a practice manager either Josh. You can afford more administrative support in the Practice now , and you can sort the builders out yourself. "

Josh could sense that she was definitely weakening, coming around to the idea of a reconciliation.

" Yes, I'll put an ad in the paper . You'll be surprised how much the builders have completed. It's time to choose the appliances and colour schemes "
He smiled at her, and caught her eye, tentatively , she smiled back.

" It's not just us we need to think about Josh " Jodie stated.

" Oh I know, there's your mother and our friends, the patients..... "

" No, I don't mean them " Jodie cried " I mean a baby ....I'm pregnant . "

" What ? when" How? "

" I thought you were a doctor Josh, I thought you knew the answers to those questions " she chuckled, feeling a return to the way they used to be, remembering how easy they were in each others company. Laughing and joking , enjoying just being together.

" Yes , I do. But.... Never mind , When do you think he'll be born ? "

No Refuge

" Around October, I guess, but I'll know more when I go and see my gynaecologist . What's this about " HE' ?

" He, she it doesn't matter ! I just meant baby ....October ! That's fantastic . Look I bought you this ". Josh took the present out of his pocket

Jodie unwrapped it carefully, then she placed the navy leather jewellery box with gold filigree pattern , onto the table " It's beautiful " she muttered " You haven't seen what's inside yet ...open it " urged Josh. Jodie lifted the lid " Oh my goodness..it's so lovely she cried " Opal , my birthday ...and the baby's "

Josh took it from the box and placed it around her neck, it fitted beautifully. He got up and brought a mirror over from the side board and placed it in front of her, so she could see how it looked.

Jodie admired it from every angle. The myriad colours in the opal sparkled in the light and bounced on her skin, contrasting against its creamy tone.
" Josh it's lovely ....absolutely gorgeous ". Jodie beamed and reached up to kiss his cheek . However, he manoeuvred himself and it landed on his lips. he kissed her gently, but with passion, and was overjoyed when she responded.

A few minutes later , they were sitting down in the kitchen , talking avidly, hands clasped together. Betty came in, and at the sight of the couple , smiled to herself.

Josh turned towards his mother in law " Betty, we've had a long talk, and we're going to try again. Jodie's coming home tomorrow . I want her to have a good nights sleep here tonight, considering her condition ". He beamed " Doctors orders. "

" Oh I'm so glad " cried Betty hugging them both . " And congratulations "

They all smiled at one another . Josh thought " everything's going to be alright …..I'm going to be a wonderful dad " He swept Jodie into his arms , and held her tightly for a few moments

" I'll leave you now " said Josh " I've got to go and get the house ready. Come home as soon as you can tomorrow darling…..but no rushing . Remember you've got an important passenger now "

" I'm off to bed " said Josie , trying to stifle a large yawn." Pregnancy doesn't half make you tired. "

Josh left Betty's house happier than he had been in a long time. He was resolute that from now on they would have the perfect marriage.

Jodie climbed the stairs wearily to bed. She undressed with a smile on her face for the first time in ages, ' perhaps things will work out ok ' she thought as she lifted the duvet and got into bed.

Her mobile phone rang, she picked it up, thinking it was probably Josh saying good night

" Hello pretty lady " came a voice.

CHAPTER TWENTY EIGHT

"Honey"

Val left Honey lying down on the sofa whilst she left to collect the twins from school.

It had been several days since Glen left the premises, and thankfully, there had been no word off him . Honey was beginning to wonder if she ought to try and find out where he was and arrange for him to have some contact with the children. At the end of the day, he was their father, and although things had gone wrong between them , he was still entitled to a relationship with Sam and Sally. In fact, Sam had only asked last night why they never seemed to see daddy anymore.

The tablets which Honey was taking had caused a minor itchy rash on her arms. Although not a serious side effect, it was enough to keep her awake itching and Val had got her some cream from the chemist which she slathered on. The other problem was this constant fatigue. Some days Honey could barely drag herself out of bed and put one foot in front of the other. Other days she was able to take the twins to the park and play with them for a couple of hours. Doctor Carstairs had told her to expect all these effects...and more .

They were still waiting to hear the results of Val's blood and bone marrow . Honey knew now for certain , that this was her greatest hope of a cure and a future with her family. Sometimes she was so scared she felt like running away from her own body, her veins turned icy cold and she could swear that a hand squeezed her heart.

Honey was dozing when suddenly Val burst in through he front door " Honey" she shouted " Glens taken the kids ! "

Honey alarmed , sat up, woken with a start, she shook her head to clear it . " What do you mean Val? " she cried.
" I went to collect them from the school and they said that their father had collected them about half an hour ago to take them to the dentist "

" Oh no ! Where's he taken them? Why did he take them? "

Honey got to her feet and ran into the street. She realised that the car, her car , had gone. Her old maroon Renault 5 had been driven off....Glen had obviously taken it, and most likely picked the kids up in it.

But where had he gone? Where was he staying?
Honey racked her brains trying to think where he was. Th first thing she did was phone his mobile. It wen straight to answer phone " Glen " she said steadily, no need to upset him. " I believe you've taken the kids from school. There was no need to do that , we could have arranged times for you to see them. Just phone to let mr know where you all are, and what time you'll be back" she thought the more pleasant the message she left, the more likely she was to have a positive response. The last thing she wanted was to put his back up and trigger his temper.

Honey and Val sat together on the sofa trying to keep calm, and drinking tea. Every so often,Honey would ring Glens phone ...which was still off. They kept telling each other " It will be alright " " He'll bring them back soon" and similar platitudes.

The time ticked by. At six o clock Honey telephoned the police, she just couldn't stand anymore .

No Refuge

" Can I help you? " came a strong female voice, when Honey had eventually got through to someone who might be able to help. " Detective Sargent Marsh here "

" My husband has taken the children without my permission "

" Can you explain a little more ...missus mmmm? "

" Mrs Sullivan. My husband and I are separated and he collected the children early from school without my knowledge. He's taken my car from outside the house, so I assume he's using that and his mobile phone is switched off. I have no idea where he could possibly have taken them "

" Do you have an injunction against him? "

" No "

" Have you been awarded sole custody ?"

" No ...we've only recently separated "

" Have you reason to believe he might harm the children ? "

" No........he's been very nasty , verbally in the past, but no physical violence"

" The car you mention....is it solely in your name? "

"No, it's the family car really. It's just that I
normally use it for work "

" So he's allowed to use it? "

" Yes, he's on the insurance "

" I'm afraid Mrs Sullivan that there's nothing we can do. He hasn't done anything wrong. If we chased ever estranged husband who took his kids out we would be doing nothing else. He has as much right to those children as you have."

" But he didn't tell me! "

" He doesn't have to tell you. He has full parental rights. I do understand your concern but I'm afraid I can do nothing about it . "

The conversation ended. Honey was so frustrated she flung the phone down onto the table. " I can't just sit here !" She cried " I've got to do something"

Honey phoned Glen's closet friend Bryn . " Bryn, " she said " Do you know where Glens been staying?" " Yes, Honey , he's been here with me and Molly. I told him today though that he'd have to find somewhere else because we haven't got enough room. Is he back with you? "

" No, he's taken the kids from school, an I 've no idea where he's gone"

" He said he'd see them today, then find somewhere to go "

" Where ? Bryn , have you any idea? "

" Not a clue. He seemed quite certain , mind "

Honey slumped back , it was hopeless. She thanked Bryn and rang off.

Just then, her phone rang . " Hello Honey is Glen there? " it was Stan's voice . " No, didn't you know we've split up .....a few days back,? but today he took the kids from school and I don't know where he's gone " her voice broke, as a sob escaped.

" No, I didn't know. He was supposed to serve behind the bar tonight. I was ringing to find out why he hadn't turned up, "

No Refuge

" No idea Stan. I'm worried sick , I'm going out to look for them. No one else will "

" What car's he got? "

" Mine, you know the old maroon Renault 5 "

" I'll go and have a bit of a gander as well..... and alert some of the boys "

" Oh thanks Stan, thanks. "

They rung off.

Honey and Val put their coats on. It was a cold night . " I hope the children are warm " whispered Honey " Oh I expect they are . He's never been cruel or violent to them as he ? " asked Val
" No, he just tries to do anything he can to torment me. He's probably taken them to the pictures or something ...just trying to upset me ....and he's bloody succeeded . " "Yes, I bet they're fine " said Val comfortingly " he's only trying to get at you. "

Just then there was a knock on the door. It wa Natalie from next door.
" I could see something was up, especially with you here and your car gone. Is there anything I can do? " she asked, after Val had filled her in on the circumstances.
" Could you stay here, In case they come back? " asked Val . They hadn't thought of that , yet Honey wouldn't stay at home Val knew, and she wasn't well enough to drive around on her own leaving Val behind.
" Yes, fine" said Natalie, " I'll just go and tell Colin. She left the house and ran back to her own , returning with some blankets for the women to take with them in the car " just in case" .

They got into Val's large four by four and Val pulled out carefully onto the main road. One of the advantages of this vehicle was that they could drive 'off road' if necessary....although neither of them mentioned that, not wanting to verbalise the thought.

As they reached the roundabout at Penydarren, Honey's phone rang. She snatched it up " Hello? Hello? " she cried "Ah ha it s Honey the whore " came Glens voice, he sounded drunk . Honey ignored the insult " Glen! Where are you ? " she cried " are the kids Ok? "

" Yes ..they wiv me..their Dad " he mumbled " jus, wanna tell you ...... you'll never see them agin "
" Glen, Glen, whatever do you mean? Don't be silly now, bring them home ...we can have a talk...work things out ". She'd promise him anything to get them back, safe, in her arms.
" I don't FUCKING believe you !!!!!" He cried angrily.
" Yes, honest Glen " Honey was sobbing now " We'll sort everything out . Have a new start. You ,me and the kids. We'll even move if you want to "

" Huh ! I don't fucking want you anyhow...you slag . I just want you to suffer. You will suffer without your precious twins won't you? Won't you? "

"Ye...es . Don't Glen, don't hurt the twins ....please don't hurt my babies... please........ I beg of you .....Glen ! "
Honey was weeping, she was so frightened. Where was he ? What was he doing? Where were the kids? Were they alright ?

" Glen, where are you ? Please tell me . Il come to you . You can do what you like with me ...I'll give the twins to Val .... Sally....Sam!!!!!" She screamed

" No. I don't want to physically hurt you . That will only make you feel justified. I want to tear you up inside ...take the most precious things off you . That'll devastate you ...more than you can bear "

Glen ... Glen.... Sam!!! Sally !!!! Please " she cried down the phone .

No Refuge

"Say goodbye to mammy " Glen's voice came over the phone " Goodbye Mammy.....Goodbye Mammy " came the sweet little voices of Sam and Sally. Then the phone went dead.

Honey screamed ...she sounded like a banshee with a wail of pure grief. "Awwwwww Owwwww"

Val stopped the car, they were at Dowlais top. High up above sea level.

For a few moments, Val let Honey weep. Then she said " At this moment, they are fine . So lets bloody find them! "

Immediately, Honey sat up and pulled herself together . " Right Val, lets look at all the mountain lay byes " she said determinedly.

Val and Honey drove from Dowlais top to Pontsarn -covering out of the way areas and crossing onto off road paths. It was now dark. Val put the headlights on full beam and Honey clasped a torch in her hand, ready to jump out and investigate further if they spotted any parked vehicles. They were surprised at how many parked vehicles they spotted. Mostly, they could identify them without approaching the vehicle because it was the wrong make and colour. Occasionally, Honey investigated a likely looking car and disturbed some smooching lovers in compromising situations.

Neither of them voiced what was in the back of their minds or why they were searching for the car in these particular spots. Yet they knew.....oh yes, ... they undoubtedly knew, what this deep dark act was that they suspected Glen of attempting to carry out.

Honey had managed to phone Stan and briefly describe what Glen had said. He and some of e other boys had already started looking but now were doing the same as the women, and concentrating on out go the way spots and lay byes. They could all be wrong, but prayed to God hey would find the location and get there in time.

In the event, Stan and Vince, who had gone out ltogether, spotted a car tucked away in a hidden gully on the Rhigos mountain . The end of the car was slightly sticking out from its enclosure and the headlights of Stan's car spotted a reflection of silver .....off the bumper.

The two men got out using torches, and could see that the car was a maroon Renault 5 . Stan recognised it as Honeys. Vince spotted the exhaust pipe leading from the car exhaust into the back of the car through a window, which had then been sealed with cling film. The engine was running as the car obviously filled up with poisonous carbon monoxide fumes.

Stan tried to open the doors ...but they were locked, so he wrapped his hand in an old cloth, took a heavy stone and smashed the back window .
There were two children lying still on the back seat, and a man slumped in the front.

Stan and Vince got the children out quickly and lay them on the grass. Stan rang for an ambulance, as Vince pulled out Glen from the front. Glen made a slight noise.

The children made no sounds

Vince placed Glen in the recovery position on the grass and went over to look at the children. He asked Stan to bring some blankets from the car. Their bodies were warm due to he heat from the car heater, but they would very quickly cool.

Vince could not tell if they were breathing. He tried to find a pulse but could not, so he commenced CPR on Sally, whilst Stan did the same to Sam. They had both trained in first aid, and used child CPR ...covering mouth and nose simultaneously for three breaths then five chest compressions.

They continued until the ambulance arrived . Two paramedics in yellow fluorescent jackets jumped out and immediately took over the children's care, they continued the CPR and lifted them gently onto stretchers and into the ambulance. The paramedics told Vince that the children were being taken to Prince Charles Hospital, and for them to follow by car. Glen was put on

No Refuge

a stretcher , taken in the ambulance ,and given oxygen. He appeared to be regaining consciousness and opened his eyes slightly before the ambulance doors were shut, and Stan could see no more of the passenger inside

Stan telephoned Honey, told her that they had found the children and Glen and that they had been taken to PCH . He said he would meet her there. He did not give Honey any other information, he thought it would be best to do that when they met at the hospital and knew more about the children"s condition.

Honey screamed with joy when she was told that they had been found. she then became deadly serious to have her worse fears confirmed as to Glen's intentions and the fact that they had been rushed to hospital. Stan hadn't indicated anything about the children's health, which Honey took as a bad sign. She was sure he would have told her immediately if they were fine...awake and talking.

The fact that he just said to meet in the hospital meant that the news wasn't good , that the were probably unconscious ...or worse. However, this was no time to breakdown . She and Val would go immediately to PCH and then act accordingly. She just prayed to God that her babies would survive.

Vince and Stan arrived at Prince Charles Hospital minutes after the ambulance. They gave the names of the children and their father to the duty nurse, and asked about their condition . They were informed that it was too soon for any news as they two children were in resuscitation , and Glen had been taken to intensive care. The two men took a seat in the waiting area.

They had barely sat down when Honey and Vak came running in. Their curly hair was wild ...sticking out in all directions , Val was red in the face whilst honey was as pale as alabaster with a red feverish patch on each cheek. She looked extremely ill as well as worried. It was also obvious that these two women were sisters.

" Where are they! What's their condition ? " cried Honey to Stan. Val smiled tentatively at the two men. If she was surprised to see two very large, muscular men ....one white and one black, dressed in impeccable dark suits , sitting in the hospital, looking concerned and obvious friends of Honey, she didn't show it. Instead she hugged them and thanked them for finding her niece and nephew.

Stan put his arm around Honey " The twins are in resuscitation at the moment and we were told to wait here " " Where is it? " she asked . Stan indicated the double doors at the end of the corridor. Immediately Honey took off, before she could be stopped and ran through the doors.

As she burst in a voice said " You can't come in here! Will you please leave "

" No. I want to see my children " cried Honey and approached the two tables where the twins were lying, eyes closed , drips in their arms and oxygen masks obscuring their faces.

A kindly nurse, led her away and assured her that she would be told as soon as there was anything to tell. " The good thing is that they both have pulses. Weak, but regular . Now we need to get oxygen into their lungs and work on them. Sit with your friends and have a hot drink . We'll let you know as soon as possible . "

Sitting back with the others , Honey slumped in the waiting room chair. " They will be alright wont they Val? " she asked her sister , piteously " they are doing all they can " was Val's reply.

Vince had found the vending machine, and after scrounging change from various people , he bought them a hot chocolate drink for each of them . " This is the only palatable liquid from any of these machines " he mumbled as he handed them out.

Val sipped hers gratefully. Honey sipped without seemingly aware of what she was doing, her eyes looked glazed and Stan fancied that her breathing was a little rapid .

Time was in a vacuum, after what Honey thought was half an hour, she asked how long since she had burst into the resuscitation room . " About five minutes " replied someone. Much to Honeys consternation. She seemed oblivious of time or space.

No Refuge

A doctor approached them . They all sat up, alert. " Mr Sullivan has regained consciousness and is receiving oxygen therapy. We believe that he has a good chance of a full recovery " this enraged Honey. " Mr Sullivan can rot in hell for all I care " cried Honey " Go and tell someone who gives a shit! ". One of the men explained the situation to the doctor, who then turned red with embarrassment. He said he would look in his records and find out if he had anyone else recorded as a relative. " Try his bloody sister " cried Honey " Cheryl Smith .....her numbers in his phone " the medic quickly left in the direction of Intensive care.

After what seemed like hours, but was, in fact thirty minutes , another doctor approached them.
" I'm pleased to tell you the twins are out of immediate danger, we are gong to transfer them to children's intensive care for oxygen therapy. We are really monitoring them carefully, and they will need nursing for quite a long time. However, we are optimistic that they will recover "

Honeys eyes lit up as If a lamp had been turned on inside her. " My babies will be alright! She cried " Thank you, thank you, thank you " She moved her mouth into a smile ....and promptly collapsed .

Val bent down beside her sister and tried to waken her up, bring her back to consciousness. However, she remained still, unresponsive. The medics carried her into a cubicle and placed her on a trolley. She continued to be unconscious despite their immediate efforts.

" She's under doctor Carstairs care, " said Val " suffering from Aplastic Anaemia . ". The emergency doctor got in touch with Dr Carstairs team and his registrar admitted Honey into ward 12.

After an examination and some tests, Honey had briefly re-gained consciousness, but then seemed to fall into a heavy sleep. The doctor explained to Val that her body had taken on board so much shock, and , that because of her compromised immune system , she had used up too much of the vitamins, protein and blood , that she needs.

This had resulted in her collapse and he was going to treat her with antibiotics and a blood transfusion.

" It will probably take a few hours before she becomes more alert " he explained. " With Aplastic Anaemia, the blood cells can't replenish themselves "

Val felt that her emotions had been on a very fast roundabout . It was now only 9 pm and she felt as if she had lived a week in the past three hours. Her curls hung about her face in disarray, and she would have liked to have joined Honey in a deep sleep.

Whilst Stan sat by Honey's bedside, his dark hand clutching her porcelain white one , with a concerned look in his deep brown eyes, Val and Vince visited the twins in intensive care.

Val was delighted when Sam managed to smile at her and speak ." Aunty Val, where's Mammy ? " " She's having a little sleep in a bed at the moment , sweetie" Val replied " In a few hours after you and Sally have had a good sleep , well all go and get her "

This seemed to satisfy Sam, and he fell into a natural sleep with a little smile on his lips. A few minutes later, Val had a similar conversation with Sally , who insisted on a " big cwtch" from her Aunty Val. Val willingly obliged, holding the little girl close to her heart, only then realising how they could have lost her and her brother.

The night passed slowly for Val and the two men. Yet none of them left the hospital, each taking turns to sit by Honey or the twins. It was not until dawn had broken, and the sunlight played on their faces that the doctors reassured them that all three patients would recover.

Val, Stan and Vince , an incongruous trio, left the hospital for their own beds, promising to meet back there that afternoon. They didn't want to miss Honey and the twins reconciliation.

CHAPTER TWENTY NINE

"Jodie"

I had decided to try again with Josh. Whether this was the right thing to do I wasn't sure. My mother was all for it. She was so pleased when we told her we were getting back together, even though it was mostly to do with the baby.

He turned up a few days ago, with a puppy dog expression and his hair flopping over his eye, just as I like it. He brought me an enormous bunch of flowers and a gorgeous opal necklace ...in the shape of a teardrop ....significant or what? When I told him about the baby , well , he was overjoyed .

He promised that he would never act towards me badly again. Never do or say any of those terrible things again. What could I do ? I'm having a baby and the baby needs a father . Hopefully we can regain the relationship we had on our wedding day , and make the future together I had always dreamed of .

I have been here a few days now, and so far so good. When I spoke to Vince the night before I returned, he didn't think it was a very good idea to return to Josh. He set off all the doubts in my mind again and made me suspect there was something about Josh he wasn't telling me. I didn't tell Vince I was pregnant, I wonder what he would say if he knew? "

I was totally shocked to hear what had happened to Honey. My God how awful.....on top of her illness as well ! That Glen is a right bastard, even if he did try to kill himself.

Mrs Thea M Hartley

My thoughts were all about Honey as I turned into her street to visit her now that she and the twins had returned from hospital.

It was a fine day for a change. Hopefully March would fulfil its promise of Spring. Today was St David's day, and it was lovely to see the little girls in their welsh costumes walking to school . They chattered away to each other, the tall black hats bouncing up and down, as they tried to keep their white aprons spotless ....at least until after the mini Eisteddford they would have at school. The boys either wore rugby shirts and elbowed their way past one another, dreaming of scoring "try's "for Wales' or they dressed as miners ; in dai caps and scarves and carrying mock " Davy lamps " as their Grandfathers would have done years ago , going to work underground cutting the 'black diamonds ' of coal.

I had loved the Eisteddford when we'd lived in Cardiff . Each class would sing a Welsh song, some pupils would recite poetry , others would sing solo . The Welsh emblems of leeks and daffodils would be everywhere, in vases, pictures on the wall and pinned to the teachers shirts or tops. It was a day of celebration and I looked forward to the day my child took part.

As I walked up to Honeys door , I wondered if Sally and Sam would be dressed up today or if they would still be ill after their ordeal,

I knocked the door , and was soon rewarded with the excited voices of children, indicating that they were far from tired . Honeys sister Val opened the door and beckoned me in.

Honey was lying on the sofa. She looked pale, but I have seen her worse. The twins had dressed up and couldn't wait to show off their costumes.

Sally twirled like a model, whilst Sam had a rugby ball which he tried to kick . I complimented them on the outfits then they ran upstairs to continue playing some game they were in the middle of.

No Refuge

" Honey, I suppose it would be stupid to ask you how you are , but how are things going ? " I asked

" The twins appear to be fine ...as you can see, thank God . Glens been seen by the police and a psychiatrist and they've sent him to a mental hospital pending trial. He's been charged with endangering the lives of the children and attempted murder, but I think he'll be unfit to plea , so they'll probably send him to Park lane, a secure mental institution "

" I hope they keep him in forever! "

" I'm taking out every injunction and legal order that I can , in case they do free him . I still can't believe he would do that just to hurt me. "

"There's been lots of similar cases "

" Yes, I suppose. All this worry has Los made my condition worsen and they've up the drugs. We're waiting for Val's results and hopefully I 'll be able to have a bone marrow transplant ."

" That's bad and good news . Bad you're worse, good if you can have the transplant. I've got a bit of news too........ I'm pregnant"

" Oh fantastic " said Honey " Congratulations " piped in Val . They both beamed. It made me feel so good that people loved my news.

" Is that why you came back? " asked Honey tentatively .

" Mmmm yes, I suppose . Although I can't really say what I would have done otherwise. I've got a temporary job in the University ....and I'm not giving it up "

" Good for you. How do you feel about Josh ? "

" I don't really know. Part of me still loves him ...always has. But to be honest, some of that love was destroyed by the way he treated me ...and I find I'm still wary of him . I'm very confused ..in many ways "

" You don't have to stay with him you know. Lots of people are single parents ..I am now anyway "

" I know.......but ...? "

" You don't have to explain, I know how you feel " Honey reassured me.

I stayed for a cuppa and a chat, we talked bout more everyday things. Honey told me that Stan had been very good. It was he and Vince who had found the twins and stayed all night in the hospital.

Since then, Stan had called in to see them a few times.

Since my meeting with Stan he had gone up in my estimation , and I was glad that he was looking out for Honey. I should imagine this would also make her feel safer, knowing she could call on his help

CHAPTER THIRTY

"Josh"

There was a myriad of emotions going through Josh's brain. As he sat in his consulting room on a bright sunny morning, he was filled with confusion as one feeling after another chased around inside him.

He felt anger, frustration, misery, pride, happiness at becoming a father, loss and goodness knows what else.

He was very concerned by his lack of sexual prowess. Sexuality had always been an important part of his life. He had shagged hundreds of women ...all types, shapes and sizes. Respectable ones and whores. In all those encounters he had never failed ...until recently. Now he couldn't even shag his wife.

Sadism had always turned him on...given sex that extra dimension, but even that had failed in an encounter with one of the girls in " The Club", he remembered with embarrassment.

He had tried every remedy for erectile dysfunction that he knew of...except one. This one sexual practice that had actually been used for centuries to cure men of impotence, was his last resort. He was aware however that he needed to do it safely, so he was going to the club this afternoon, to try it with one of the girls. He just prayed that it would work.

In the meantime, he sat in his room, waiting for patients. Josh looked at the beams of sunlight playing on his desk, illuminating the dust motes in their rays. The sun mocked him in its radiance , when all he could see was an impending darkness, right into his soul.

Mr Mahoney came in the room and took a seat. He caught a glimpse of Josh's face which looked solemn and dour. Mr Mahoney was here for test results and now expected the worse. The doctor obviously had bad news for him .

Josh looked up at the man sitting opposite " Good morning Mr Mahoney " he said. The patient started to tremble with anxiety.
" I'm pleased to tell you that all you are suffering from is a vitamin deficiency. I will write you up a prescription and after around a month or so you will feel a new man"

Mr Mahoney was delighted . He stood up and shock hands with the doctor. " Thank you, thank you. I was expecting bad news ". " Why on earth was that? Asked Josh, puzzled. " it's just when I came in you looked so..... " he shrugged. Perhaps better not to turn attention to it . " well thanks doctor " " Bye, Mr Mahoney, glad to be of help " dismissed Josh, still looking confused.

The rest of the morning followed in much the same way. Josh had very expressive features, his emotions tended to play across his face, making his patients " read" him . In this case wrongly . Mrs Harris expected good news on her blood test , meeting a buoyant Josh . However, she had to go to see a specialist for further investigations.

Josh , as well as his patients, were glad to see the end of morning surgery. He called Sheila at reception to tell her he had to go to a meeting . It was clinics only this afternoon run by nurses, so he had no bookings for patients. Sheila was to telephone him if there was an emergency. Josh realised that the time had come to try and get another GP to buy in to the practice. I'll sort that out, once this issue is over, he thought.

Arriving at the club, Josh sought out Stan.

No Refuge

" Stan, " he enquired" have you a girl who could take me through auto-erotic asphyxiation .?"

" Didn't think it was your bag, Josh " Stan replied.

" No, never tried it before. Confidentiality, I've been having some 'problems ', if you know what I mean? "
Stan nodded.

" I've tried everything. Extra porn and sadism, live shows ..the lot . I've even taken Viagra . Jodie's come back to me ...and I can't even perform with her "

" This is a risky way to solve it "

' I know...but it'd my last hope. That's why I came here ...because its safe with someone there . "

" Well you should know..you're the doctor " chuckled Stan. " Lottie's done a fair bit of this, she's in this afternoon, and she could do with the money...it's 'specials 'rates ...OK? "

"Ok . I've also got a bit of good news ....Jodie's pregnant...I'm going to be a dad. I want to sort out this sex thing so we can have more " he joked

" Oh, so we're not going to have your custom anymore are we ? You a respectable Dad and all . "

" I expect there'll still be the odd occasion when I need the old S & M "

" Missus not into it is she? "

" No, she doesn't even know I like it "

" Mmmmm bit of a dilemma that . But I suppose that's what we're here for "

" Can I get on with it Stan? I've got Jodie coming home from her new job around five . "

" Oh alright , come this way and I'll get Lottie . All the equipment is already there ...room 7 "

Josh and Stan made their way through the concealed door into the cellar . Private room 7 was empty except for a chest, a single bed and a chair. It actually reminded Josh of his consulting room. He sat on the chair to await Lottie . Stan left he had plenty to do.

Josh looked around his sparse surroundings. He supposed it was a bit tacky, and Jodie would be appalled if she could see him . He started to remove his clothes until he was fully naked and he put on a dressing gown which was hanging on a peg at the back of the door.

Lottie came in. She was a leggy brunette who Josh recognised from the pole dancing arena. She was well toned...better than most of the girls and you could see that beneath the heavy make up, she was a naturally pretty girl. She wore a negligee which see removed to reveal a leather bondage outfit which covered her like a bathing costume, but with holes in strategic places.

" You don't really need me to dress like this " said Lottie " because what you are indulging in is self masturbation, but it doesn't hurt to give an extra bit of frisson "

Josh nodded his agreement .
Lottie bent down into the chest and took out a long rope , some capsules and an eye mask .

" Do you want it with or without amyl nitrate and do you want an orange segment? " she asked.

" I'm not sure, this is new to me ...what's the advantages.? "

No Refuge

" Some people say amyl nitrate poppers give a better experience and use the orange to oppose their bitter taste. Other people , with or without amyl nitrate have a segment of orange to bite on to help them regain consciousness. You don't need to have an orange at all though. "

" I'll pass on the amyl nitrate, I want to see if I can do it myself , if you get me? " she nodded " But I'll try the piece of orange. "

" Ok ...do you want an eye mask or not ?. Some people like to see what they're doing, others like to just concentrate on the feeling. "

" Difficult one that . No, no eye mask . How does the hanging happen? "

" Again, you can have the rope over the door and pull on it until you are nearly unconscious . You pull the rope with one hand and masturbate with the other. Just as you feel intense orgasm and nearing ejaculation and/or just about to pass out, you bite on the orange and let go of the rope.

Some people like to have the rope around their neck and then fixed to their ankles . You tie it with your knees bent and your ankles near to you . Then you make it tighter by straightening your legs. At the penultimate moment , you pull your knees and ankles up to release the rope. You can do this one lying down if you like , or sitting. The other method is usually standing up.

But people find loads of different ways. Many people practice this a lot, they find the best position for themselves. As you no doubt know, doing this is usually on your own and that's the danger of actually hanging yourself , although to some, this adds to the excitement. Recent figures suggest that between 500 - 1000 men a year die accidentally like this. Only a few women do it , but it works for women too. "

Josh felt very surreal. Here he was receiving a well researched lecture by a woman dressed in leather, displaying her nipples and genitals, talking about autoerotic asphyxiation!

Josh decided on the neck to ankles rope position, and a piece of orange.

Lottie made a professional looking hangman s knot on the noose and placed it over his head whilst his ankles and knees were pulled up to his chest. She then tied the rope length around his ankles . She asked him to try straightening his legs slowly and made sure that if he pulled his legs back up, the rope would loosen immediately around his neck. His hands were free, so he could immediately free himself . She gave him a piece of orange and said:

" Bite on this as soon as you feel you're going to become unconscious and it will shock your senses into normality and you will draw your legs up. Don't worry, I will be here if you start to pass out and will cut and release the rope."

She had a pair of heavy duty scissors at the ready.

Josh nodded and smiled . He held his penis in his hand and started masturbating, simultaneously straightening his legs . He was lying on the bed.

His free arm was by his side, but it comforted him that at anytime he could use it to release himself.

Within seconds his penis hardened and became engorged, Josh felt spaced out and the lack of oxygen from the strangulation gave him a feeling of euphoria and orgasmic pleasure. He started to black out, bit the orange, pulled up his legs and ejaculated! He pulled off the noose and stared at Lottie , only one minute had passed.

" Wow that was awesome " exclaimed Josh .

Lottie put the rope away, and stripped the sperm stained sheet off the bed.

" Thanks " said Josh " that's been a great new experience for me.

No Refuge

He dressed and gave Lottie an extra twenty pound tip. She smiled in delight ' this was money for old rope ' she chuckled to herself at the witticism.

Josh practically bounced out of the cellar . This proved that he could still do it and now he'd broken the barrier , he was sure he would be able to do it without asphyxiation .

•••

Stan and Vince were sitting in Stan's office.

" Doctor Josh is here " said Stan

" No-one ill I hope? "

" No , he's here for a trick with Lottie "

" With Lottie! " Vince was surprised " What trick?"

" AEA"

" That doesn't seem his thing "

" He's been having 'problems' with his hard on. Nothing else has worked , not even Viagra"

" Oh ...he could always use a splint" Vince laughed

" Ha ha ....Jodie's back with him ...and he can't perform with her. "

" What? Jodie's actually gone back . She did do it"

" Yes....and what's more, she's pregnant "

Vince's face fell ...he looked totally gob smacked ...and upset.

" What's the matter with you? " asked Stan

" She's pregnant ....that's what the fucking matter is " he sounded angry.

" Oh well. It's not really our concern is it ? " stated Stan .

Vince didn't reply.

•••

An exuberant Josh left the club. He popped into the nearest florist shop and bought Jodie a large bouquet of mixed roses.

Everything 's going o be fine now he thought. Jodie's back, I'm going to be a dad , the practice is doing well and the house is looking good...........and what's more my sexual prowess has returned.

All in all Josh felt very self satisfied.

CHAPTER THIRTY ONE

"Jodie "

I was enjoying my job in the university ....loving it in fact. How could I have gone so long without teaching?

I walked down the corridors, covered in wooden panels, the smell of age and knowledge in my nostrils. These hallowed halls had such atmosphere it was difficult to deny the air of privilege. To imagine Lecturers with mortar boards on their heads and flowing black cloaks, students with books under their arms walking quickly to lectures.

The reality nowadays , was somewhat different. The lecturers wore casual clothes, often jeans and sloppy tops . They only dressed in cap and gown for degree ceremonies and the like.

The students seemed to be scruffier than ever. In the last few years the fashion for 'Goth' looks, piercings and tattoos had led to a plethora of bizarre looking individuals with thick make up (male and female) sitting in lectures. Still, the surroundings were good.

In fairness, the students actual work could be as inspirational as ever. I had given a lecture comparing 19th century literature with today's and asked students to choose two books ; One a classic and one a contemporary book , which they consider as having the same, or similar stories and themes . The assignment was to identify these features and provide evidence for their answer via quotes from the novels . The students were also asked about what made these novels interesting to their audience /readers.

I was very pleased to get some really good assignments in, with the students using excellent references and original ideas . One of the students had made a very good attempt at comparing "Svengali" with " 50 shades of Grey" , and used a very interesting argument' together with quotes and evidence, much to the delight of their seminar group.

Finishing my final lecture of the day, I switched my mobile phone back on. I had five missed calls from Vince. ' What on earth could he want ? " I wondered Before I reached the car park, my phone sprang into life ..Vince again. " Hi " I said " What's up ? " " I've been trying to contact you all afternoon "

" I've been teaching. I turned off my phone "

" I think we need to talk "

" Why? There's really no point "

" I think there is. You went back to him .....after all"

" I told you I was going to, he's my husband "

" Yes, well I still want to talk to you, "

" Ohh OK "I sighed . " Where and when? "

" The sooner the better "

" This evening? "

" Yes, where are you now ? "

" Cardiff , just leaving college "

" How about the 'oriental garden 'just off the A470 , on your way home? "

No Refuge

" Ok, in about 45 minutes "

" Fine...see you then"

He put the phone down . I now had to phone Josh to tell him I'd be late! That wasn't going to please him in his present mood , but he'd have to put up with it.

I dialled Josh on my mobile " Hi Josh! "

" Hello Jodie....can't wait to see you ...what time will you be home?"

He sounds happy I thought, surprised

" Oh that's the problem. They've called a meeting at work for the new staff. To bring us up to date with all the procedures etc , and them the others have suggested we all go for a bite in the refectory , get to know one another a bit...you know ? "

" Oh, yes...I understand. I was just hoping we could have our own little celebration " he sounded disappointed.

" I'll be home as soon as I can ..a few hours ...ok?"

" Ok love. .....see you then , Bye"

He rang off. I wondered what had changed his mood from the sullenness of last night. All I had to do now was see what Vince wanted , then I could relax .

I turned the car out of the university car park and headed for the A470. Wondering what on earth was the matter with Vince that he had been so insistent on seeing me.

I arrived at the " Oriental Garden. " and was lucky to find a parking space. I walked around to the main entrance and stood by the waiters desk .

I had expected this to be a Japanese restaurant with oriental deco. However , it was laid out as a sort of olde worlde barn , with lots of beams and cubbyholes for separate dining. In the centre, it was more open plan with several tables , but had moveable screens if people wanted some privacy.

I suppose the screens were vaguely oriental but everything else was more " country living. "

There was a long bar which took food and wine orders and an area just for drinker, which had a plain wooden floor, rather than the thick patterned carpet which covered the rest of the restaurant.

It was a mush mash of styles I suppose , but strangely it worked and gave an overall ambience of comfort and bonhomie

" Have you a reservation, madam " asked the waiter

" Umm I'm not sure. I'm meeting someone here a Vincent Saunders ? " I rose my voice up at the end questioningly, so that the waiter would look at his list .

" Ah yes madam, he has already arrived. Table 23" follow me ".

He picked up some menus and set off down the main area. I followed him.

He showed me into a small booth where Vince was already ensconced . I slid in opposite him . We smiled at each other and took the menus.

The waiter left us after asking if we required anything to drink;

" I'll have an orange juice " I told him " Pint of Lager ..Stella for me please " said Vince. He shuttled away, leaving us on our own.

" Well then Vince " I immediately said " What did you want to see me about.? "

No Refuge

" Lets order first " he replied looking deep into my eyes with his midnight blue ones . I found I couldn't read his expression. Whatever he wanted he for, he wasn't letting on yet.

I looked at the menu and decided to have a salmon salad . This was a light choice and had nothing potentially harmful to the baby in it.

Vince ordered sirloin steak with all the trimmings. This was beginning to remind me of the meal we had together when he " kidnapped" me.

" How is the house coming on? " asked Vince as if he was some polite friend catching up on news .

" Fine. The builders had completed a lot in the weeks I was away . Nearly every room is completed in terms of building work. It's just painting and decorating to be done now ......and furnishing of course "

" That's good. . It's a large house...great potential "

" Yes, you've never told me where you live ? "

" Pontsarn Close . I bought a house there some years back. I've just had it redecorated actually "

" Lovely spot. In the country, but near the town "

This small talk continued until our meals arrived. I ate slowly , I found that I was getting a lot of heart burn recently . Vince , on the other hand, got stuck into his steak with relish.

It was not until coffee, that Vince agreed to tell me what our meeting was about .

I was drinking a cup of tea, instead of coffee and Vince commented on the fact that I hadn't had a glass of wine, or any alcohol.

" Not drinking tonight ? " He asked

" No...I've got the car "

" Sure that's all it is? "

" What do you mean? "

" C'mon Jodie, I've heard that you're pregnant "

" Who..o told you that ? "

" It doesn't matter who, does it? The point is, is it true? "

" Yes, yes, I'm having a baby "

" Congratulations...when's it due? "

" October "

" Oh, is that why you went back to Josh ? "

" Partially, I suppose. A baby needs a father "

" Yes, but a good, kind father . One who's good to its mother "

" Josh has promised he's changed. He'll never become violent again...he said he'll look after me and the baby . He's my husband "

Vince took hold of both my hands, and clasped them tightly in his . His large palms covered mine easily, they seemed to disappear within his grasp.
He looked deeply into my eyes again, his eyes seemed to bore into my soul, they were like dark whirlpools.

" Are you sure it's his baby ? " he asked

No Refuge

I didn't reply. My thoughts went back to that day that Honey had first had her results and Vince had kissed me in the car park , before I left for my mothers house in Cardiff.

I had pushed him off and told him that I wasn't interested.

(One month ago.)
...........Later that night , there was a knock on my mother' s front door. I knew who it would be. I passed my mothers bedroom and looked in at her through the slightly open door.

She was sleeping deeply, her gentle snores blowing the folds of the floral quilt on her bed . I quickly shut her door tightly.

Downstairs I opened the front door and there stood Vince

"You said next time I was watching the house, to give a knock and you'd make me a cup of tea " he said.

" Yes, I did , didn't I . " I replied smiling at him. He looked like a roguish little boy , standing there , his dark hair gleaming in the light of a street lamp.
I stood aside to let him in.

I showed Vince into the kitchen and put the kettle on. Then I rummaged in a cupboard for some biscuits, found chocolate digestives and put them on a plate.

" Milk? Sugar? " I asked " Yes, please, both " he replied.

We sat at the kitchen table drinking the tea and eating the biscuits.

Vince took my hand. His hand was large, but gentle , he caressed the back of my hand with his thumb....in soft, slow circles, it was incredibly erotic.

He looked into my eyes, his midnight blue ones seemed to lighten with sparks of brilliance in them .

I could see the look of desire on his face. I stared back at him, holding his gaze. My heart had started beating faster, and I felt my stomach contract. He leaned over the table and kissed me gently on the lips as he had this afternoon. This time I responded , he stood up and came around to my side of the table.

Vince's arms went around me . I was aware of how tall, and broad and strong he was, but he held me so gently, as if I were a piece of fragile china.

His kisses became more passionate, as did mine , and he ran his fingers through my hair, then gently caressed my cheek.

I knew I wanted him ....I knew I shouldn't have him . But Josh had always been so hard and rough . Vince was so gentle and soft.

I enjoyed this feeling of being cared for, of being wrapped in a soft cocoon. I took him by the hand and lead him up the stairs to my room.

He undressed me , oh so slowly . He touched me and tantalised me . Every touch was feather light , yet exciting ....I helped to undress him until we were both naked .

Vince picked me up as if I was weightless. He laid me down on the bed and towered over me . Yet I felt no fear as I had with Josh. I felt safe and protected ....and loved .

We kissed passionately and touched each other tenderly , we probed and explored each others bodies and Vince rained kisses all over my flesh...each one burning my skin with desire .

Finally, when I could stand no more ...he entered me. Even his first penetration was gentle, ensuring that he didn't hurt me in anyway. it wasn't until I cried out in passion for him to thrust harder that he did.

He looked at me all the time with those midnight eyes and I looked back at him, drowning in their depths. Our desire matched each others, and our

No Refuge

movements became stronger and more passionate , yet he held back until I reached the pinnacle of pleasure and orgasmed stronger than ever before in my life .

It was only then he allowed himself the release he craved and shuddered with ecstasy . We had lain there for a while , just holding each other. I had truly never experienced love making like it. Never believed it could be so passionate, yet so gentle. I actually yearned for him again , despite all rational thought.

We had to be quiet because the last thing I wanted was my mother to find us. Did I know what I was doing? Don't ask me . All I knew was what I was feeling.

Shortly before dawn, we crept downstairs. Vince kissed me passionately , before he left....................

....

This was the first time I had seen him in person since that night. We had spoken on the phone and I had told him I was returning to Josh . He had been upset. He would probably be more upset and perhaps angry , now I thought.

" We'll, " prompted Vince " are you sure it's his? "

" No, no, I'm not sure Vince " I said " But he's my husband and we were trying for a baby . "

Vince put his hands in his head .
" I want you Jodie. I want you and the baby ...whether its mine or not . Please, please leave him ...come and live with me. "

" Sorry Vince " I said " I married him, I made vows. My mother and the rest of my family would disown me. Josh would go mad ...he'd kill us "

" Don't you think I could handle Josh.? He's not the man you think he is anyway. "

" What do you mean? "

" Oh nothing...just being jealous , I suppose "

" He's over the moon I'm pregnant. I think this time our marriage will be as I expected. I have to give it a try. I have to believe the baby is his...and it probably is . Don't you see? "

" No, I don't really. All I know is, I would never, ever hurt you . I would love you and the baby with all my heart. That's all I know. However, you must do as you see fit. I can't stop you , I wouldn't try. You see, I'm nothing like Josh "

Vince looked heartbroken. He got up and left the " Oriental Garden " He even looked bereft from behind. He didn't turn around . Just carried walking out the door.

I sat there for a few moments , then I also left and got in my car to drive home.

I knew I had hurt Vince, but I wanted to protect him too. I knew that without a doubt , if Josh found out about us , he would kill Vince . I truly believed that. I also believed that I had to try and make a good marriage, as my vows had promised, and bring my baby up with a mother and father.

As for the babies true parentage ....'that was something I had to live with.

I was nearing North Street. I pulled my shoulders back and plastered a big smile on my face ready to greet my loving husband.....Josh

CHAPTER THIRTY TWO

"Jodie"

I was going for my first scan today . It was exciting, yet terrifying. I just hoped everything would be alright. I had seen women clutching those hazy black and white images of little blobs , even proudly showing them off.

To be honest,in the past, I always thought they all looked the same and how could you be attached to a globulous shape.? People would invariably say " Ooooo he's well endowed " and the proud parent would explain " that's the babies arm ". This always seemed a bit silly to me. However, now, I couldn't wait until I had my own little black and white Polaroid.

Anita had even bought me a silver picture frame to put it in .....a double one, with scan one engraved underneath the first and Scan two under the second.

Josh was coming with me at 2pm. I had just directed the delivery of the final pieces of furniture into the living room, and, if I say so myself, It was looking beautifully stylish and comfortable.

A large plasma TV set was on the wall above the modern sideboard. The red sofa had been joined by a cream one, and an oversized cream and red chair. We had natural woot side/lamp tables jotted about the room , some with enormous silver lamps with cream shades placed upon them.

The blinds had been fitted and the cream curtains put up on the large bay window. The old, renovated, fireplace had been fitted with a "real flame" gas fire which added warmth to the room, as well as a focal point. I loved it all . It had been my first attempt at home decor and I was pleased that it had turned out so well.

I thought I would visit Honey this morning to find out if they had finished testing Val, and what the outcome was. The first set of tests had looked extremely positive, with a strong possibility that Val would be a match as a bone marrow donor. She had now undergone a more invasive biopsy in order to be certain as to the quality and match of her blood and marrow so that there would be nothing left to chance.

Josh had become quite buoyant for a while. He had seemed particularly happy and I though it was to do with the baby. However, this was a few weeks ago, and hadn't lasted. He had lapsed back into a dismal mood finding fault in everything and everybody.

I hadn't been intimate with him since that failed attempt and I think this frustrated him. I pleaded tiredness, sickness or some other pregnancy induced condition. The truth was, I couldn't bare him touching me. I knew I had to get over this ...he was my husband, and we were having a baby together. Just at the moment , the morning, (afternoon and evening) , sickness was taking its toll and I couldn't be bothered to rouse myself to passion. In fairness to him, he had held back his frustration and suppressed any anger he might have felt . I hoped this would last and that nothing would set him off. I still felt as if I was walking on eggshells at times.

" Hi ya it's me !" I called , slightly opening Honeys door.

" Come in Jodie , Come in ". She cried.

I walked into the living room ,and saw Val there, reading today's newspaper. I was also surprised to see Stan in a chair , his large frame apparently filling the room. " Hi Stan " I greeted him " I haven't seen you since coming down "The Club" about 8 weeks ago.."

No Refuge

" Oh Hello...it's Jodie isn't it . Yes I just called in to see how Honey and the kids were getting on. I'm so glad Sam and Sally have recovered from their ordeal "

" They looked so cute in their outfits for St David's day " I said

" Yes, they're great little kids " he smiled, and there was real affection in his voice.

" I came to see if you had heard anything about Val's test ? "

" Yes, yes, " beamed Honey " She's a match...as near as perfect as can be! I'm going in next week to have my own bone marrow radiated and then I'll have Val's donor marrow, "

" Yes, " confirmed Val " I'll look after the children whilst she's in . It may take a couple of weeks. During that time Honey will be isolated in a sterile room because she'll have no immune system. "

" And ...I'll lose all my hair " said Honey, pulling a face

" Don't worry" I said. " I'll get lots and lots of colourful bandanas and we'll have fun trying them on. I'll wear them as well...and Val. We'll be the 'Bandana Trio' " I flung my arms out dramatically and they all laughed.
" I'm going for my first scan this afternoon" I continued " Josh is coming with me "

" Congratulations " said Stan " I didn't know you were pregnant ! You are, aren't you? " he asked with a worried look .

" Yes Stan I am ...due in October " I assured him.

" I won't be able to see you when I'm in isolation " explained Honey "because Ill be radioactive and you're pregnant "

" Oh that's shame " I said " But I'll phone you . Will you glow in the dark ? " I teased . She threw a cushion at me, and we all laughed.

I really wished life could be like this all the time. I don't mean Honey having radiotherapy treatment. But having a laugh with friends, Josh was so bloody miserable and we never saw anyone else. I suddenly realised that we had no mutual friends at all. Josh seemed to go out to see " the boys " once or twice a week, but he never introduced them to me, let alone their partners or wives.

Josh wasn't keen on Anita, and went ape shit when he found out I was friends with Honey , said she 'wasn't our sort' . He couldn't stop me seeing them, but he moaned about it every time. I had suggested we go out with Anita and her partner, but Josh baulked at the idea and refused to go.

Most nights we sat in and watched television or read in silence . Sometimes I'd stay late and go to the pub with colleagues from work, but that and visiting my friends was the only social life I had. I hoped to meet some other mums in ante-natal classes , and perhaps there would be some couples we could get to know. I really was trying at this marriage, but it was very difficult.

"How's Vince these days ?" I asked Stan . Taking a risk at what he and the others might think.

" I don't really know " he replied " He's like a bear with a sore head most of the time. Finds fault with everything. At other times he just sits about moping . I think he's got women trouble "

" Oh , has he got a girlfriend ? "

" Not that I know of. But I'm sure there was someone he was fond of a couple of months back ..I think they must have split , and that's what's wrong with him . He's had a rough deal with women".

" What do you mean? " against my will, my heart was beating faster .

No Refuge

" Vince was married. tragic business it was. "

" What do you mean? "

" He was married for about a year and his wife was pregnant. I've. Never seen Vince look so happy. He was really chuffed, couldn't wait for the baby.

Then , a couple of months before the baby was due, his wife, Maura , her name was, started having headaches and flashing lights. They thought it was migraine. However, it kept persisting, so Vince took her to the hospital and it turned out she had something called pre enclampsia .

She was very I'll, because she'd had no treatment . They admitted her, and gave her an emergency Caesarian . Sadly it was too late . Maura died.

Vince had a little girl , he called her Carla , and sat by her incubator hour after hour . She was very small and her lungs were under developed. She died four days after her mother. "

" Oh my God . Poor Vince" I cried, my voice cracking . If anyone noticed, they didn't let on.

" Yes, that was four, five, years ago now. He found it very hard to get over. The only time I've seen him happy since was a couple of months ago , as I said , but now I think that's ended too "

We all looked sympathetic, and sorry for Vince. but I think my colour had gone. I still had palpitations and was afraid to get up in case I was dizzy. ' Poor, poor Vince ' I thought . He must be suffering more than I imagined. It must be worse for him because I'm pregnant ! . I felt so guilty ......what had I done to him? Yet there was nothing I could do about it .

I waited for my heart and breath to get back to normal, then said :
" I must go now and meet Josh , the scans in half an hour. I'll bring the photo to show you . "

" Bye " said Honey and Val, giving me a hug " Good luck " said Stan and waved his hand at me .

I walked out into the fresh air and took a deep breath. I hoped this scan was Ok, that my baby was fine. I couldn't help but think of Vince after what Stan had told me.' He probably feels he might be losing another child' I thought, guilt filling me. But Josh is my husband ......there's nothing I can do.

CHAPTER THIRTY THREE

"Jodie"

I was lying on an examination couch in the radiography room waiting for my scan. There was a machine by the side of me which looked very technical, attached to which was what looked like a TV monitor. Josh sat at the other side of me.

In the waiting room there had been lots of other mums to be at various stages of pregnancy. I was amazed at the age range. Some looked as if they were young school girls and others looked as old as my mother.

Everyone had someone with them , mostly their partner, but some had their mam's with them,and others had a friend. The air in the room was full of expectation. Totally different from Josh's waiting room, with all his ill patients. These women were not sick , they were bringing a new person into the world ....what could be better than that? It was obvious we were all looking forward to meeting our son or daughter. The posters on the wall were all about nutrition, breast feeding and other aspects of baby care. Colourful advertisements for baby products jostled for place.

I was going to the NCT meetings later in my pregnancy to learn about natural labour, breast feeding and post natal care. Then, armed with the knowledge of how to breathe correctly, relaxation techniques and the way to have a fully medication free delivery , I would probably ask for all the drugs available when in labour . What I really hoped for was to make some friends .

The room we were now in was full of trolleys and other equipment. The posters on the plain cream walls to my left were of embryos and foetuses in various stages of development . From the tiny four week blobs to the fully formed and developed 36 week foetus. I was totally fascinated by them all.

The radiographer came in and greeted me and Josh. She was young, in her early twenties, wearing a white uniform of trousers and overall. Her blonde hair was tied back off her face into a tight ponytail. Looking at her list, she said " Mrs and Doctor Harrison? " we both said yes, simultaneously.

" Lie back Mrs Harrison , and put your head on this pillow " she placed a pillow behind my head . She was so close I could read her name badge ' Miriam Collins ' I read. ' well Miriam I thought, 'you can be the first to show me my baby. '

Miriam rubbed gel over my , ever so slightly , rounded belly. It was cold. I was surprised at that . Then she picked up what looked like a sort of microphone and placed it firmly on my abdomen.
She moved the probe around and pressed harder , whilst studying the monitor which was faced away from me. I felt nervous ' oh dear God , I hope the baby's Ok ' I thought.

Then I noticed a smile stretch across her face and she turned the monitor so that both Josh and I could see it .

There was the baby! A small blob waving arms and legs as if greeting us. I was overwhelmed. I couldn't speak as the emotion I felt choked me.

Josh was also speechless as he just stared at the image of the foetus on the screen. " Gosh it's so small " he said, sounding astounded.

Miriam looked at my notes " It says here that you are 12 weeks? " she formed it as a question " Yes, ,that's right " I replied still watching the monitor . " The scan indicates around 10 weeks + 6 days " said Miriam. " Could you have your dates slightly wrong? "

No Refuge

" I'm pretty sure I gave the correct date of my last period " I said " Does it make a difference ? "

" Not that much , but it could mean the foetus is small and we'll have to keep an eye on its development.. The date we take as correct is the scan one... they're so accurate these days ...and you could have conceived a week later than you thought. " she gave a bright, reassuring smile. I felt an icy fist clench my heart.

Josh was still staring at the screen and I took a sideways glance at him. It was only visible to me, but I could tell his teeth were clenched and his eyes slightly narrowed. A shiver of fear ran down my body.

" But if I'm absolutely certain of the date , it could still be right couldn't it? " I asked

" Ummm yes, if its a small foetus , like I said , we will have to keep an eye on that to chart it's development ....but don't worry it's probably nothing to worry about ......and I bet you'll realise you could have conceived later " she said with a bright reassuring smile and a twinkle in her eye .

' Shut up stupid woman ' I thought ' couldn't you just have agreed with me , not tried to make out that we have such a rampant sex life I could've conceived on a different date ' .

Miriam wiped the gel off my belly and I pulled my leggings and panties back up. She bent over to the bottom of the ultrasonic machine and asked how many copies of the scan picture we wanted " Two please " I said and got the money from my handbag to pay for them . She took the money and handed me the pictures in an envelope . Josh had not muttered a word during this exchange.

" Goodbye " I said

" Bye ...see you next time " said Miriam cheerily.

We left the room and the department.

Walking through the hospital , to the main doors of the maternity unit , we didn't speak. My mind was swirling, but I was very practiced at not showing what I really felt.

We got in the car, Josh drove . " Oh that was wonderful wasn't it ? " I said, in the brightest voice I could manage

" Yes, it sure was " said Josh in a monotone . I wondered if it would be better if I addressed this apparent discrepancy or kept quiet.

" I hope everything's ok with the baby . I'm worried that its too small " I said, as normally as possible.

" You heard what she said…your dates may be wrong " replied Josh.

" No, no my dates are right " I protested.

" Sometimes babies can be small to start with but catch up later on…don't worry " I felt relief at Josh's comment.

"Yes, that'll be it " I agreed , sighing with relief.

We travelled the rest of the way home talking about the house and the nursery. Gradually, I could feel myself relaxing. I wasn't going to say anything about the scan to Vince, I was just going to put it to the back of my mind and forget about it . This was Josh's baby …..and that was that.

We had cottage pie for dinner followed by a sugar free trifle …it was delicious if I say so myself. I cleared away and happily put the dishes in the dish washer…how great it was to have modern appliances.

I stood there admiring the built in machine, and the wooden door that encased it . The washing machine and dryer were also integrated . The only free standing appliance was the large American fridge with its gleaming matt silver body and the drinks and ice dispenser at the front ...what luxury. I have never appreciated household gadgets so much. A side effect of being without them for months.

We sat together in the living rom once I had finished clearing up . Josh sat next to me on the sofa and put his arm around me. He was sipping a brandy and I was hoping he wasn't going to overdo the alcohol.

The soaps were on the TV , which Josh hated , so he insisted we watch the new DVD of the latest Bond film. I agreed, because I had heard that it was good, and not the ' usual Bond' . Josh put the DVD player on and I brought some pop corn in a bowl from the kitchen. We settled ourselves , I tucked my feet underneath me and relaxed into the story.

When the film ended I made my way to bed. I Checked the doors were locked, whilst Josh checked the lights and switches. I took a glass of milk from the fridge , and checked that everything in the kitchen was in its proper place. The new staircase was slightly winding, made of real oak and carpeted in thick sand coloured pile. I held on to the bannister as I made my way up. My only concern was , that Josh had had quite a lot to drink and that sometimes this made him irritable and in a bad nood .

The bedroom was totally different from its original shape and style . It was spacious, with a high ceiling , a large bay window , with a fitted window seat upholstered in a suede type of fabric in cream with gold and cream cushions which matched the bedding and curtains.

The bed itself was a deep polished wood, in a kingsize , quite high with fitted bedroom furniture surrounding it. The furniture was palest grey and beautifully made and fitted by "Sharps" . A whole wall of fitted wardrobes . ..four double wardrobes with the two central ones having glass doors. My dressing table and stool was beautiful and the rest of the units and drawers placed perfectly in nooks and crannies. We had also had an ensuite included with a double shower and wood floor . It was a luxurious extra which I truly appreciated.

I undressed, washed and got ready for bed, pulling on a long, sleep tee shirt. I got in between the new sheets and stretched out enjoying the comfort of the bed, it's softness enveloping me.

I heard Josh climbing the stairs, hitting his legs against the bannisters and swearing "fuck", as he hurt himself. He'd obviously had too much to drink. My heart sank. Best thing to do was turn on my side and ignore him.

He managed to get in the bedroom, . I could hear him hoping about on one foot trying to take off his socks " fucking socks...ouch ....where'd that bed come from? .....where's my old tee shirt? ....fucking don't fit ....bugger ". A shirt flew through the air.

Eventually he managed to get into bed.....I lay statue like on my side.

His arm crept around my waist and his other hand got to the neck of my tee shirt and tried to pull it down , choking me. " Arrugh " I squealed " Oh you are awake then " he said in a sarcastic voice. " get that...that..thing off then" he pulled at the tee shirt now, it ripped slightly at the neck.

" No, I'll be cold " I replied

" Cold? It's bloody boiling here ...we've got brand new expensive central heating ...remember? "
Again, he pulled at my tee. I took it off to avoid anymore damage.

" Ahh that's better " declared Josh " Let the dog see the rabbit......or should I say bitch? "

" Go to sleep Josh, you've had too much to drink "

" Go to sleep! GO TO FUCKING SLEEP. You'd like me to be asleep all the fucking time,,,,wouldn't you ? ....wouldn't you? ". His voice rose

No Refuge

" No, no, " I said placatingly " it's just that you must be tired... You've drunk quite a bit "

" I am not drunk " he stated, word by careful word.

" Ok " I agreed with him.

" I'll show you I'm not fucking drunk "

He was naked, and tried to swing his cock around. It was semi erect. he sort of plunged it at me.

" Please Josh, stop messing. I'm tired, I'm going to sleep "
I turned my back on him.

" You're not going to sleep until I've had a shag "

" Honest, I'm worn out ...I've got baby sickness all the time ...I'm totally wreaked "

" I'm totally wreaked " he mimicked me, using a squeaky voice. " You're always totally wreaked. We haven had sex since you came back "

" It's because I'm pregnant . Hormones and sickness ...it will pass. "
I realised he was right, and thought perhaps I ought to try.

" The last time I shagged you was the night before you left me " his fuddled brain was now trying to think, he sat up and looked deep in thought " ....and you were on. There was all blood on me .....lots of it ". He continued to ponder, and moved to sit on the side of the bed.

I lay very still , wondering where this was leading.

" ....yes, you were having a period. I don't usually like that...too messy ...but that night was after you were 'kidnapped' "

" You were horrible to me Josh "

" Shut up!.... I'm working this out ...."

He sat in silence for a moment then turned to face me.

" That's not my baby is it? IS IT? " he screamed

" Yes it is Josh ....it is " I protested

He slapped me across the face, my cheek stung so painfully that tears sprung to my eyes.

" It is yours Josh " I repeated .

" No it isn't ! ..... I listened to the radiographer about the scan. She said the baby was about 10 and a half weeks ...not 12. She said you must have conceived a little later than you thought . DIDN'T SHE? ". I nodded , biting my lip .

" We'll you couldn't have ....not with me anyhow ...because we didn't have sex after that night . We still haven't had sex. "

" She said it could be that the foetus is small for its weeks ...and to watch its development " I said

" Possibly....POSSIBLY .....but you were fucking ON, menstruating , having a period , bleeding ..whatever. I'm a doctor , and I know that it's rarer than winning the lottery than conceiving during mensuration. "

" Yes, but it does happen .....and it must have happened to us ! "

" Oh yes, of course ....the foetus is small for 12 weeks, which is rare AND you were on, which is even rarer ! Too much coincidence I believe . You'll be telling me it's the immaculate conception next ! "

No Refuge

" It is yours " I said despondently, almost whispering.

"LIKE FUCK IT IS "

He hit me across the other side of my face, my teeth rattled. My cheek stung.

I was terrified now. Josh was towering above me, I was cowering in the bed. I was aware of his power, how much stronger than me he was .

He punched me ...full on the nose, I felt an almighty blow and blood tasted in my mouth . I think my lip was also cut. I remember worrying that he would knock out my front teeth.

I don't know what sort of mode I went into. I would say survival mode, only what I did made things worse in terms of escaping injury . Was it anger? Why did I fight back?

I tried to get out of bed. He pushed me back on to the sheets, the lovely new sheets which I had not long ago luxuriated in. He held down my arms, pressing his thumbs into the fleshy part causing pinching and bruising . I kicked him. Over and over, as quickly as possible, I tried to rain kicks on any part of him that I could.....mostly I missed....he moved out of reach. Josh laughed...... 'he was enjoying it?' I wondered. To stop my kicking, he kneeled on my legs, hurting the flesh and bone. I cried out in pain, but he took no notice, in fact it seemed to spur him on.

" We'll I'm going to fuck you now, you dirty slag " he said .

He held both my hands in his one, and forced my legs apart. I resisted him and twisted and turned. I tried to kick or keep my legs together....but he persisted and struck me in the face again. By now , one eye had swollen up. He forced his way inside me . He was actually erect , and as I twisted to get away for him , he ejaculated.

He turned over after raping me, allowing me to get out of the bed. I put on a dressing gown, realising that my whole body, especially my face, was throbbing with pain. Josh just lay there.

I was so glad it was all over. I would wash myself and dress, get out and drive to the hospital. Then I would phone my mother and this time tell her the truth about my injuries and the violence Josh had perpetrated. I would stay there and think about the future later.

in the bathroom, I dabbed at my face, but it was too painful. The only clothes I could find were a pair of old tracksuit bottoms and a loose tee shirt I had been using for decorating. . Those would be ok I thought, too scared to re-enter the bedroom to take my underwear or find more appropriate clothing.

I made my way down the stairs. I would take nothing with me, except my handbag and mobile phone, I just wanted to get out. Anything else could wait . The pain was throbbing, worse and worse with every step.

Then.....suddenly.....I felt a blow to my head and fell down the remaining stairs . I had been hit by something, some object. It turned out to be a Christmas tree which had been stored on the top shelf of the airing cupboard, which was located on the landing.

I was literally stunned, my head spinning and black and white flashes obscuring my vision. I landed on the wooden hall floor with a bump. Hurting my left leg and side. A figure towered above me. Josh holding the Christmas tree.

" You think you're getting away that easily ? " he snarled and swung his leg and kicked me on my right hip. " I'll kick that fucking baby out of you " he threatened.

I put my arms around my belly as he aimed his kicks in that region. He managed to connect with my pubic bone and the pain seared through me. . Finally, I lay still and he stopped his barrage of blows.

No Refuge

Blood was seeping into one eye, but through the other I could see that he had dressed. . He gave one final kick and said " I'm out of here to find some pleasanter company " . With that, he stormed out the door slamming it behind him.

I couldn't move, I lay there for a don't know how long, bleeding from cuts and wounds.

Finally I pulled myself to the kitchen and managed to reach my handbag. Inside was a mobile phone.

I rang Vince " Vince, please come to the house . I've been beaten up " I said, and promptly lost consciousness.

CHAPTER THIRTY FOUR

"Jodie"

The next thing I was aware of was a loud crashing sound, then Vince by my side, quickly followed by people in fluorescent yellow jackets. These were obviously paramedics, who lifted me gently onto a stretcher and took me off in an ambulance.

I kept drifting in and out of sleep, waves of pain waking me, injections soothing me . I could hear the "Dah...Dah...dah...dah " of the sirens as the ambulance rushed through the roads and lanes to the hospital. Eventually, some medics examined me and washed me. I was bandaged and tested. I kept asking " is my baby alright? " and received soothing noises in return, but no solid " Yes" .

I couldn't be x-rayed because of the early stage of pregnancy......so other signs were observed. There was a great deal of bruising; one bruise melting into another , a great map of the world appearing over my torso. My head, nose and mouth bled, I was attached to a drip and given painkillers. Some parts of my limbs were swollen, sore , broken? I cried in pain. My head hurt, it throbbed then felt as if it was being crushed . I was hot, cold, in agony , I drifted in and out of consciousness. My baby? My baby? "wait and see, " said the nurses, " wait and see " . I slept, I dreamed, I woke up and saw faces ...Vince, Mam, Val, Stan , my brothers ...looking concerned, Aunty Joyce and Sharon .....looking tattooed.

They all frowned, then smiled. ....I tried to smile back, I said their names, then I drifted again, in and out, dreams of Josh. Josh happy, Josh mad , Josh hitting me .... I screamed , someone held me .....I went back to sleep. Time passed....

I was aware of pain, but not so intense, not so wrenching. I opened my eyes and realised that I was in a bed , in a hospital room. The walls were painted pink and cream. There was a window where sunlight flowed in, it's beams playing on my duvet, making patterns on the cover . The bed was an " S" shaped hospital bed controlled by a hand held remote , placed at my rIght hand side . The curtains, which pulled around my bed ,and the duvet ,were patterned with a green and white logo. It reminded me of visiting Honey and hoping for her recovery, little knowing I would end up in here .

There were get well cards on my locker together with plastic implements for drinking , and a jug of water. I lay back gingerly on my pillows , looking at the drip I was attached to in my swollen and bandaged left arm . There didn't appear to be any broken bones as far as I could tell. There was no plaster on any joints , and I could wriggle my toes and fingers, my torso and back were sore, but that was probably bruising.There was, I realised , a bandage around my head . ' just as long as the baby's Ok ' I thought ' that was the most important thing . '

A nurse entered the room. " Oh , good , you're awake "she said " How is the pain? " " Sore, " I replied " But less than it was." She poured me a drink, and helped me hold it to my mouth. Then she started doing all my observations and recorded them on various sheets which she placed in a file in a holder at the bottom of the bed.... temperature, Blood Pressure, breathing rate...... I realised I had a catheter in my bladder. The nurse emptied the bag. " is my baby alright? " I asked her.

." Mr Graham , the gynaecologist is on his way to see you. He'll explain everything . " she said with a professional voice and smile.

No Refuge

After that , she tidied me up and sorted out the bedding, checked the drip, and busied herself tidying the room before leaving.

She had struck fear into my heart. ' what was wrong? What was the specialist going to tell me? ' I worried myself into a state of extreme anxiety.

A few fearful moments later, Mr Graham appeared. He was in his fifties, with receding hair, a gentle , paternal face with twinkly blue eyes behind half moon glasses. He wore a shirt with a pink stripe, a maroon tie , grey trousers and the obligatory white coat. He had a stethoscope around his neck, and pens in his breast pocket....which I noticed had leaked leaving a dark blue stain spreading beneath it....... He was of medium height and build , the tufts of hair which remained were brown with grey streaks. He gave an air of benevolence .

" Hello Mrs Harrison " he said, smiling at me, and putting his hands together at chest level " It's good to see you 'compus mentis ' . You suffered a great deal of pain and bleeding from your injuries.The neurologist was extremely concerned about the damage to your skull. You are lucky to be talking to me, or anyone. "

" Yes, but it's not so bad now ....tell me about the baby " I rushed the words anxiously.

He sat on the chair , which he had pulled up to the side of the bed . " First of all, your baby is fine at the moment , and we hope to keep things that way " he said.

I sighed with relief

" However, you did suffer a great deal of bruising, spraining and some lacerations. We couldn't X ray you because of your pregnancy, but an ultrasound indicates that your bodily injuries appear to all be external and will heal. We cannot see any evidence of major fractures, but will keep an eye on things. The greatest concern is your pubic bone, which appears to be injured, and may have a small fracture. A C T scan suggests this, so we have made the area stable and you must continue to rest and mobilise slowly. This is why you have a catheter. Once that is removed, you must have daily physiotherapy and gently start to walk. Any pain or bleeding and you go back to resting. This normally takes about 6 weeks, but due to your pregnancy , it may be longer. There is also the danger of an early birth due to the pressure of the baby on the pubis, also it may cause it to re-fracture. Probably you will have to have a Caesarian delivery. "

I sat for a moment, taking this in .

" What do I have to do to help my baby? " I asked

" Stay in until its safe to remove the catheter. Rest totally at home except for the daily physiotherapy and start walking when the Physio agrees. Return to hospital if you have any pain or bleeding and arrange a Caesarian birth, " he summed up.

" Ok , Then that's what I'll do " I said firmly.

" I believe your husbands a doctor. Do you want me to explain it to him. ? "

" No, no . I'll do that, I fully understand, thank you. "

" Very well, Mrs Harrison. I'll let you rest until your visiting starts . I'll see you tomorrow "

" Thank you Mr Graham " I replied

" Mr Nesbit, the neurologist , will be around to see you in the morning "
I had a lot to think about. It was obvious that the medical team had no idea how I had sustained these injuries . They talked of ' My husband, the Doctor " I wondered how this had come about. Did anyone know ? Surely Vince and my friends had guessed?

No Refuge

Had Josh been here ? There were lots of questions I needed answered and I had a lot of planning I needed to do. The bastard was going to pay for this, there was no way he would put my baby's life at stake and get away with it . Oh no, I would get my just revenge.

Val was my first visitor. It was early afternoon, way before visiting time , when she popped her head around the door. I had been dozing, filled with pain killers .

" Hi" she said " Are you OK to see me for a few minutes ? "
" Yes, yes, come in "
" Oh it's so good to see you conscious. You've even got a bit of colour "
" Thanks Val..I vaguely remember seeing you before "
" Yes, I've tried to pop in when possible...but you've been so out of it "
" For how long? "

" six days "

I gasped with shock , I only thought it had happened about 24 hours ago !

" My God, I never realised "

" Yes, it's been terrible. Vince found you in your house , somehow you phoned him. No one knows why or how "

" What do you mean? "

" Josh told us how someone had broken in when you were in bed and he was out. He was after the jewellery, and when you discovered him you tried to get your jewellery back. The burglar beat you up, and left via the back door ...which was wide open. Then, trying to alert someone, you apparently fell down the stairs ! "

" Why did I phone Vince? "

" The police think it was the last number in your contacts list and that you just pushed it. "

" Police? ". ' stranger and stranger ' I thought

" Of course. Josh called them . All your jewellery s gone . I'm afraid . The burglar also broke something's of yours I believe "

"Oh, I see....who's visited me ? "

" Me, of course " Val gave a beautiful smile " Vince has come to see you most nights.... late" I think he feels responsibility because he found you " she whispered conspiratorially . " Your mother, Aunty, brothers , cousin .....oh , and Stan's popped in now and then, after seeing Honey "

" What about Josh? "

" Oh yes. He comes at visiting times with the others ....but you've been refusing to see him and getting upset. You seemed to mistake him for the burglar . He's been very upset Jodie. When they thought you weren't going to make it ...he was devastated "

I felt as if I was ' Alice in Wonderland ' or living in a parallel universe. Josh had nearly killed me and the baby , and here he was, smelling of fucking roses.

" I feel rather confused Val . " I said

" Oh you are bound to be love . The injury to your head was life threatening . "

" How's Honey? "

No Refuge

" She's had the transplant. She'll be out of isolation in a couple of days .. and will come and see you . You can recuperate together . " Val was so happy , and I was overjoyed for Honey ......an idea was starting to take seed in my mind.

" That's wonderful Val, and I can't wait to see her. We've got so much catching up to do . "

" Thank God you're both on the mend "

" Yes Val...the best is yet to come "

I smiled a tired smile at her , as she got up to leave .
" Bye for now love....I'll call in tomorrow. "

With that , she left the room as I closed my eyes and fell back to sleep.

When I awoke again, I had a headache, I touched the bandage around my head and winced. I pressed a buzzer and a nurse came in and brought me some pain killers . Through the window , I could see It was becoming dusk, which meant that visiting time was soon. What was I going to do ? If I accused Josh of being responsible for my battered state , it would probably be dismissed as confusion, due to my head injuries ....no -one would believe me ..... I had to be careful and clever.

Visiting time arrived and in came Josh and my mother. Josh bent over to kiss me and I shrunk away from him. " No ! No " I cried " He's come to get me .... mam , mam " I looked at my mother with fear , she put her arms around me.

" Now now dear " she said " That's Josh, your husband ".

" No it's not ....it's my attacker ...he' s not my husband ."

She held me close to her. I could see out of the corner of my eye, Josh and my mother exchanging looks of disappointment. ' The bastard 'I thought,' I bet inside he's dancing with glee. He thinks I've lost my memory. '

Mam calmed me down, and gave me a drink of squash. I still stared at Josh with terror in my eyes (this was not difficult to portray). I could actually make out a small smirk on his lips ....what a fucking bastard he was.

" Have you seen the doctor today? " asked my mother

" Yes, the gynaecologist saw me. He said I'm getting better except for the pubic fracture, and the baby's OK at the moment. I have to rest, and do what the Physio tells me. I will probably have to have a Caesarean birth "

" Oh, that's very good news " said Josh, jovially.

" Fuck off " I said " Mam, what's HE doing here "

" Sorry Josh " she said, looking at him. " You'd better go. She still thinks you're the attacker. Perhaps you should have a word with the neurologist? "

Josh gave me a look. I couldn't tell the real meaning of it .....somewhere between fear and hatred I'd say. He left the room.

" Mam " I said, when we were alone " Can I come and stay with you when I'm discharged. I can't stand the thought of the house where I was attacked and I don't know where Josh is? "

" Of course you can love " she said, her eyes filling with tears. " But that was Josh, who was just here with us "

" No, it wasn't. That was my attacker " I insisted

No Refuge

My Mother just looked very sad. 'Poor mam' I thought ,' she'll be so shocked when she learns the real truth ' . .

We talked for a few more minutes, mostly about the baby. This cheered my mother up no end. She recounted stories about me and my brothers when we were little . The old story of when I ran off with my youngest brother, Eddie , in his pushchair and gave him away to the woman next door because he ' was crying all the time ' . My mother laughed so much she couldn't drink from her bottle of water.

The bell sounded for the end of visiting,. Josh hadn't returned , for which I was glad. My mother gave me a gentle kiss, so as not to hurt any of my wounds . " See you tomorrow " she said, touching my arm.

" Yes mam, goodnight "

I was really exhausted now. Today was the first day I had really been aware of where I was and what was happening. I closed my eyes , ready to fall back asleep.

I suddenly became aware of footsteps in my room . My body tensed, but I kept my eyes shut . The person approached the bed. They bent down to my ear " You had better not remember the real story ....or next time I will definitely finish the job and make sure you are dead. ". Whispered Josh ....then crept away again.

I shivered ' you'll never get the chance 'I thought 'because I will get you first . And that's a promise.

CHAPTER THIRTY FIVE

"Jodie"

I had fallen into a restless sleep after Josh's whispered threat. I tossed and turned for about an hour or two when the nurse came into my room.

" You've got an extra visitor " she said " Are you up to seeing him? "

" Who is it? " I asked

" Vincent Saunders "

" Yes, yes, ok . Send him in "

A few minutes later Vince entered the room.

" Hi Vince " I said, smiling at him .

" How are you Jodie? " he asked tentatively

" Much better apparently "

" Oh thank God! " ...He said this with so much feeling that he put his head in his hands " Thank God !!"

I looked at him in shock, I didn't expect such a reaction from him, from anyone .

" Oh Jodie for days you've been so confused . I've held you when you screamed. You've been in so much pain, and at first the doctors were very worried. You had swelling and bleeding on the brain. They didn't know if you'd survive, if you'd have brain damage or what! "

" I think my brains OK, even if the things people tell me are confused . what happened after I phoned you? "

" Oh you know you phoned me ? The police said it was the last number on your contacts, so was the first you pressed ....not knowing who it was "

" That's another thing ....what's all this about police and a burglary ? I definitely phoned YOU on purpose, and as far as I know there was no burglar"

Vince was the one who now looked shocked .

" Josh said....... " he began

" Fuck Josh .....he's the one who did this to me. "

" I thought that when I broke in and found you . I was going to tell the plods . But they came to see me saying it was a burglar who harmed you . Stole jewellery and broke expensive belongings . They were pretty certain. What could I do? How could I know the truth with you out of it ? "

" You couldn't " I said meekly. "What happened when you found me? "

" I broke down your front door , and there you were lying in the hall, bleeding from all over as far as I could tell. I called an ambulance, didn't move you, just held your hand. I came in the ambulance with you and phoned Stan to pick up my car and follow on to the hospital. When we got here you were

No Refuge

taken off into resuscitation and they put me in the relatives room. There I was again, the same place as we had sat waiting for news of Honey'stwins.

Stan arrived , so we waited together. He was very surprised that you had phoned me .....I said it was just as much a shock to me. The medics came in after a while to tell me you'd been taken to intensive care . Thankfully, they thought I was your partner so they told me the baby was ok . Stan knew you were pregnant because he'd seen you earlier in Honey's house. I sat with you there , in Intensive Care....you were totally unconscious . After about a couple of hours Josh arrived , he appeared devastated. He ignored me , and kept asking the doctors if you were going to die. The police arrived and Josh told them about the robbery, and what he thought might have happened. I left then. He thanked me for bringing you in, and sort of dismissed me . I had no way of knowing what had happened, although I suspected him from the first. "

" What happened after that? When did you come back? "

" I came to see you the following day, only Josh had stopped all visitors except you mother. I know people here in the hospital, particularly the night staff, so I started visiting you after hours. You clung to me when you were in pain or upset and the staff told me that you wouldn't let Josh near you , that you thought he was your attacker. "

" Yes" I snorted " that's because he is "

" What really happened Jodie? " Vince asked holding my hand, I didn't pull away.

I told Vince about that night. How Josh had started abusing me, accusing me of having an affair. How he punched and raped me . Then, when I dressed and washed he crept behind me and battered me with the Christmas tree. When I was lying in the passage he had said that he would kick the baby out of me and kicked me in my stomach , hips and pubic bone, fracturing it, even though I had my hands and arms wrapped around me. Then I lost consciousness....after phoning him , Vince .

With each word I said , Vince became paler and paler. His brows knitted and his mouth became stern, hard. I could see his nostrils flaring . He was like a cache of dynamite just about to blow.

" I will kill the fucking bastard . With my bare hands I will kill him " he exploded.

" No, no Vince " I put my hand on his arm. "We have to plan. There has to be a better way of punishing him, of getting my revenge. I want to see the bastard suffer, and I want to be the one to administrate it. I also don't want to go to jail or for anyone else to. "

" Ok , what do you suggest ? " asked Vince.

" I have to talk to some of the others first, and then put the plan together. Once that's done, I'll tell you all. In the meantime, I'm pretending I can't remember what happened , but I think Josh is still the attacker. That way , I can stay with my mother for the time being. "

"You can come and stay with me.......please....I'll look after you " his voice and his face were pleading. "

I can't . If I did people would suspect . Everything must appear as Josh as explained ....just for now. Don't worry the truth will come out soon. "

" Ok, I'll go along with you, pretty lady, but only for a while "

" It won't be too long Vince, I promise "

He looked at me with those midnight blue eyes that drew me into his soul.

" I wasn't going to tell you , but things are different now " I said, "Judging by the scan results, the baby is more likely to be yours than Josh's . There's no certainty mind. We will have a proper DNA test when it's born, but the dates seem to verify that. "

Vince's face burst into a large beaming smile " that's a miracle " he said , " a miracle " and he leaned over and kissed me .

" Jodie, I just can't believe it . I'll look after you both. I'll love you and never hurt you , whether the baby's mine or not it doesn't matter. Please Jodie, when things are sorted out with Josh ......please come and live with me ? "

" Vince , you are a lovely man. You are strong yet gentle , but I can't think that far ahead . I have to get through these next few months. I have to recover, ensure I keep this baby safe, sort out what I'm going to do about Josh. I can't give you any promises until after that . We' ll just have to wait and see . "

Vince's face dropped, he looked so disappointed.

I couldn't make any promises. I had made a big mistake marrying Josh. I needed to get over that before entering into another relationship.

I wasn't at all sure about my feelings for Vince. I couldn't honestly say I loved him , I didn't know how I felt about him . He had been there for me when Josh had abused me and he had made me feel safe and cared for, but I couldn't say I was in love with him.,however much he wanted it ....not yet.

" We won't talk anymore about us for now " said Vince " there's plenty of time . I'll be here for you in the meantime "
glad of that, I really am " I held his hand and we sat for a while peacefully, just settling quietly with each other.

Vince started talking about the baby . Making plans for him or her . I could sense the excitement bubbling in him , but tried to change the subject. I didn't want to hurt Vince , but nothing yet was secure, nothing was on safe ground.

I started to talk about the club , asking him about the various activities which went on there. I knew about the pole dancing, but the rest of it was still shrouded in mystery.

Now it was his turn to avoid talking.He hummed and ahh..ed , said there were things I didn't need to know. This annoyed me , but I didn't push it... not yet. He had once said that Josh wasn't the man I thought he was ...but would say no more .

This, and Josh's involvement in the club had made me suspicious and I wanted to know everything . It would help me to build up my case against the cruel bastard. I decided I wouldn't push Vince at the moment . There were others who could help me . Others who Josh couldn't accuse me of being involved with .....the seeds of my plan were starting to grow.

We talked for a little longer, I was getting tired, and although I enjoyed his company, I realised that I had to go to sleep . Even when talking of everyday things, I could sense Vince's emotions bubbling beneath the surface, he had a glow about him I had never seen before and a sparkle in his eyes . I hoped I would not be the one to hurt him or take that away.

Vince could see me falling to sleep , so he said he'd better leave. " Goodnight pretty lady" he said " I'll see you tomorrow " and kissed me gently on the lips.

• • •

I slept more naturally that night than I had since I had been admitted . My dreams were not as disturbing as the dark images which had haunted me for days. Even Josh's threat had been neutralised by Vince's visit. I smiled at the fact that Vince , who had originally ' kidnapped' me, made me feel so safe.

Mr Nesbit , the neurologist , came to see me that morning. He was the opposite of Mr Graham in looks. He was young, in his thirties, tall and slim with a blue shirt and casual navy chinos beneath his white coat. He had the air of a man on a mission, and frequently pushed back his thick fair hair. I noticed that he had an Irish accent and a twinkle in his eye.

" Ah ..ah Jodie...a good morning to you " he said cheerily , smiling and twinkling away, his brogue adding to his attraction .

" Hello Mr Graham " I said , reminiscent of school registration.

" How would you be feeling today? " he asked me

" Much better "

" I'll just take a bit of a look at you "

He then carried out a batch of neurological tests on me . He shone a light into my eyes, asked me to squeeze my eyes tightly shut, clench my jaw and move my eyebrows. He had me making tight fists with my hands, then push against his palms......then pull his wrists as strongly as I could.. I had to try and lift my legs as he pushed them down, and he used a tuning fork on various parts of my body asking if I could feel the vibrations. He checked my reflexes , and scraped a pointed instrument across the soles of my feet. . All the time muttering " Good....marvellous.....well done ".

When he had finished , he turned to me " I am very happy, if not amazed by your recovery " he said
" You had a head trauma, including a small subarachnoid haematoma , a bleed . I am very pleased to say that you have recovered all use of your physical neurological functions . The only problem there seems to be is some memory loss....which the staff have reported to me. "

" Yes, I am much better, but I can't remember the attack, and this man who came to see me last night I feel is my attacker, yet he and others tell me he is my husband. "

" Yes, the nurses reported that. I wouldn't worry too much about it, it is extremely common for this type of amnesia after a blow on the head. You will find that it may return soon, or perhaps you will never remember the exact incident, but you will start to recognise your husband again. "

" Thank goodness ....I feel much better after you telling me that " I hoped my acting ability was good enough.

" So now you have recovered consciousness, and your signs are good , I will just liaise with the other medics and you can be discharged. "

I beamed at him " I'm going to stay with my mother...she'll look after me, make sure I stick to my tablets and Physio regime . "

" Aye, mothers are good at that... and by the way, good luck with being a mother yourself "

I smiled at him.

He left with his entourage of medical students nd nurses and I lay back on my pillows.

An auxiliary came around with cups of tea , and I tried a cup , sipping it tentatively after only drinking water. It was hot and refreshing . I really started to feel that I was on the mend.

One of the nurses removed my catheter, which I was pleased about, despite the discomfort. Shortly afterwards, the Physiotherapist came to treat me.

" You have to learn to walk and use the toilet much more carefully than before. You must not put any pressure at all on the pubic bone or pelvic area. No long walks, no running , no lifting OK? "

" Yes"

" What's very important is that when you go to the toilet, you don't strain or push,AT A LL . This means taking diuretics if necessary and constantly

No Refuge

taking laxatives. Any pain in that area , and you rest. If the pain continues then you have to come back into the hospital "

I agreed to all she said. Then she helped me get out of bed to use a walking frame. I looked at it thinking ' well I won't need that ...I'll look like an old granny using it' .

I put one foot on to the floor then another. The pain shot up my body through my centre. I gasped , my eyes filled with tears of pain, and I held the frame.

Lucy, the Physio, showed me how to hold on to the frame in order to switch the weight on to my arms. When I put the pressure on the handle, the pain subsided and I could tale a step. I continued doing this for a few steps , then Lucy got the chair to take me to the toilet. I sat on the toilet and just did nothing allowing a stream of urine to come . I realised how difficult this was going to be , and cursed Josh for what he had done to me . I swore I would get revenge on him .....I would soon be able to put my plan into action.

CHAPTER THIRTY SIX

"Jodie"

I had been in hospital for a fortnight, and was just about ready for discharge. The Physiotherapist had been working hard with me, and I had been putting in a tremendous effort.

Today, the senior OT had tested me to see if I could manage to go home . I managed to go to the toilet on my own with crutches, made a cup of tea in the small kitchen and managed to walk up and down a few stairs in the way shown to me ....sideways , with a handrail and crutch.

The OTs had also visited my mother's house to make sure she had the rails I needed, a special toilet and equipment for the bath . Horray ! I was on my way. Tomorrow hopefully, I would go home to my mothers house.

Honey was also well on the mend and she would soon be discharged . Val had promised she would bring her to see me this afternoon. I was so looking forward to it, not just to see Honey and catch up , but to ask her to help me with my plan. The plan I had to wreak my revenge on Josh. Talking of which, he still kept visiting me , I still wouldn't speak to him, pretending I had amnesia but he seemed resigned to the fact I was going to stay with my mother and had stopped trying to persuade the doctors I would be better off going back home with him. No doubt he had some other plan for me

Just after lunch , Val came into the room pushing Honey in a wheelchair. My eyes lit up to see her, it seemed ages since we were in her living room and I told her I was going for my scan. It was only just over 14 days ago, yet we had both been through such a lot of pain and treatment since then. Hopefully we were both on the road to recovery. I had also reached an epiphany relating to my feelings and future .

We hugged each other gingerly. Honey was mere skin and bone , but her face had a slight colour to it, showing that the transplant was doing its job. Her head had a multi coloured bandana wrapped around it in a turban style ...the first of the " Bandana girls ". My greasy locks would probably look better under one at the moment anyway. She seemed afraid to press against my injuries. The bruising had turned to yellow and red shades, my eye was less swollen , and of course, my pubic bone was sore but healing. I must have still looked quite a sight to anyone who hadn't seen me or a while.

After we'd talked generally ,skirting any serious issues........it seemed that a lot of our chat related to the tastiness or not, of hospital food..........I pulled a "this is important" look.

Honey and Val picked me up on it and asked why I was looking so serious.

" Honey". I began " I want revenge on Josh "

" I don't bloody blame you " replied Honey " " Id like to string him up by his fucking balls "

" Yes, me to, but unfortunately I'm not strong enough "

" There's people who'd do it for you , you know "

" Yes, but I want to get my OWN revenge on him and I don't want anyone to get into trouble over that bastard on my account. "

" They won't ...the boys are too clever for that "

No Refuge

" I know, but if I don't face up to him , I'll always feel he has some type of control over me. God knows what he'll plan to do when the baby's born! "

"Yes he's a tricky bastard and no mistake. So how can I help love ? "

" First of all, and don't worry about upsetting me or anything, please tell me the truth about Josh ....all the things he's got up to in the club.? I know he's been doing stuff, I've had enough hints off people. "

Honey and Val looked down at their feet. Honey seemed reticent, as you do when you've got something embarrassing to tell a friend ..something they didn't know about.

" Jodie......do you really need to know? " asked Honey , her voice soft .

" Yes, I do ....it's part of my plan "

" Ok.....here goes. There may be more mind, that I don't know about, Ok ? ". I nodded

" He's been coming to the club for years. When he was in Cardiff he'd come there at least once a week, but since living in Merthyr, it's been more frequent. "

I was surprised at this, thinking it had been a recent activity, but I suppose if you've got a certain type of personality ......then......?

" Ok Honey ...so what's he interested in? "

Honey seemed to squirm a little , as if uneasy about telling me ....But I HAD to know

" He watched the pole dancing ....that's how I recognised him. The girls said that sometimes he went into the lap dancing booths "

She looked down again, reddening. I wouldn't have thought that Honey, so streetwise and with her experience would feel embarrassed .

" What's wrong love? " I asked gently

" It's just ...I don't want to hurt you "

" You couldn't ...not after what he's done to me. It will make me more angry..and motivated! "

" OK then......if you're sure? "
I nodded once more.

" Well sometimes in the lap dancing he'd have 'extras' ......that's sexual acts of some kind up to intercourse "

I remained impassive. I knew if I expressed any emotion, Honey would stop telling me.

" Then, he started in the viewing booths " she continued " this is watching a girl strip off and masturbate, or a couple having sex , sometimes a threesome . Lesbian and gay acts as well."

She was looking at me for a reaction, I still stayed cool. " Anything else? " I asked .

"Yes, Josh was a platinum member so he could use the cellar."

" What's the cellar? "

" BDSM. ...do you know what that is ? "

" Yes, but what was his thing? "

" Sadism . He liked bondage and inflicting pain , then sex . He liked being bound sometimes, but in a resistant way. He was very controlling "

No Refuge

" Good! " I exclaimed

" What do you mean? "

" This is evidence of his nature. Why he's behaved like he has to me. "

" Yes that's true" pondered Honey, " strangely " she continued " Stan said that recently he's been into AEA "

" What's that? "

" Auto Erotic Asphyxiation ."

" Oh I know , like that Steven Milligan and Michael Hutchence....deprive yourself of oxygen by suffocation until the last moment ? "

" Yes, that's it. Dangerous it is. "

" I know why he tried that ....he had problems getting hard "

" Or he was finding it difficult to find anything to arouse him...you know....getting jaded "

We both looked at each other,I was thinking about the power sex had over men, how important it often seemed to be to them, to define their masculinity. I shook my head back and fro.

" You OK? " asked Honey

" Fine " I replied " Just trying to see how I can use this against him. "

" What's your plan? "

" I need some help. Are any of these things Josh has been involved in recorded? Filmed? "

" Well, some are because the customers want them. CCTV is used everywhere for the protection of the girls ....in case someone goes too far, you know, but this is destroyed daily if there's no need to keep it. "

"Could he be filmed if he goes there from now on then?

" Yes, I'm sure Stan could and would sort that out. "

" Oh, that would be great ! do you think one of the girls would come to he house and lure him into bondage games ? I'd pay her of course. "

" Yes, I'm sure that could be arranged "

" I want as much evidence as I can against him , not just for the divorce , but to destroy his career I want to send it to the BMA . I want photos, DVDs the lot. I won't get the club into trouble I promise. "

" Don't worry " Honey was now smiling " There's lots we can get . I'm sure Stan and Vince will help "

" I want to keep Vince out of this. I don't even want him to know . You must tell Stan this . Get him to promise hell keep it from Vince"

" Why? Vince is very discreet and he can find documents and stuff. He was great finding my twins . Much nicer than I realised . He helped out a lot. "

" I just want him kept out of it " I mumbled, I could feel myself blushing

I also felt Honey and Val's eyes boring into me.

" What's between you and Vince? " asked Honey, still staring at me , a puzzled look on her face.

No Refuge

" Well…Umm…ummm " It was my turn to look at the floor in embarrassment . I trust these two I thought , they're my friends . " Vince and I ……ah .. um….Vince might be the father to my baby " I blurted out.

" What! " Honey and Val chorused together, " You dark horse. How can that be? "

" How do you think? ….usual way ". I laughed.

They were still sitting there open mouthed, silent.

" It was after I left Josh the last time ….the day of your results Honey? I went to see Stan remember and he gave me that money for you . Well , I bumped into Vince , we talked and he walked me to my car . Just as I was going, he kissed me. that's all, and I went home ….to my mothers .

That night , when I was in bed there was a knock on the door. It was Vince. I had told him that next time he was watching me, to knock the door and I'd give him a cup of tea. So he did."

"….but he had more than tea". Finished Honey, laughing . We all giggled . It felt good.

" Does Josh know this ? "

" No, but he did accuse me of an affair, he has no idea about Vince though"

" How do you feel about Vince?" Asked Honey, curiosity getting the better of her .

" To be honest I don't know at the moment . I like him and he's so different from Josh. He's not controlling and he's surprisingly gentle, but I have so much to sort out . I have to get better, get Josh out of my life , and make sure the baby's alright before I can think about Vince or the future. "

" I can understand that. I promise we will do all we can to help you nail Josh . Stan will help I'm sure he's shown me a side to him I never knew existed "

" What about you and him? " I asked , this time I was getting my own back.

" He's just a good friend. Like you I want to recover and look after my kids before I can think about anything else. "

We all agreed ...including Val , who had seen many relationships go wrong. She declared that she preferred her own company, that of her sister and friends and her menagerie of animals to any romantic liaison. I must say , I could see the attraction in that myself. Perhaps that was the way to go in the future?

" I'm being discharged tomorrow and going to my mothers ....here's her number " I handed Honey a price of paper " and you've got my mobile. Keep ringing. I want to know how things are going and perhaps you can ask Stan to start getting things sorted ? I suppose in order for him to keep quiet you'll have to tell him about me and Vince . "

" Don't worry . We will sort our end out. I'm going home tomorrow as well. Val's still staying with me, but come the school holidays, me and the kids are going to her's for a while......but we're still in the area. "

She looked up at the clock on the pink wall. "I'd better get back to my ward now ....tablet time! Yipee ! " Honey pulled a face . I pulled the same one, in sympathy.

Val pushed Honey back out of my room , leaving me feeling so glad to have such good friends . I couldn't believe I had only known them a short time. The only fun I had enjoyed in the past few months had been with these women, despite all our difficulties.

No Refuge

Visiting time my mother arrived first. We spent about ten minutes or more discussing how I'd manage in her house, and where I'd have the baby's birth. I decided to talk to my specialist before I left about transferring my care to Cardiff and having the baby there. It was going to be difficult for my mother to take me to and from appointments as it was. I realised I was going to be a big burden on her, which she didn't need at her age.

She told me that my cousin Sharon had offered to help. I didn't know whether to laugh or cry. Apparently , since my attack she had decided her future career (until she was discovered) was working with adults suffering physical trauma . " What's her plan....to make them worse? " I asked cattily " Now, Jodie " my mother reprimanded me " she means well . Poor girl can't help how she is . "
My mother had a kind heart. I personally felt Sharon could do a lot more to help herself.

Because of the difficulty with my crutches and the size of my mothers car, the staff nurse had arranged for an ambulance to take me to my mothers house in the morning. She decided to take most of my belongings with her that night to save problems . So we were reasonably sorted and ready to go.

It was about halfway through visiting time when Josh turned up. I put on my amnesia act again, and he looked irritated by it. I now knew a lot more about him, since my talk with Honey, and he disgusted me. I felt repulsed when I looked at his blonde hair, his light , faded, blue eyes, and his lips which now looked too fleshy, too perverted. I could imagine him carrying out those acts with various women and I felt physically sick.

I dreaded telling my mother everything, but knew that I must in order for us to live honestly together . Otherwise she might start trying to persuade me to return to Josh again. I hated the way she interacted with Josh now.

" How nice of you to visit " she said, sickening me .
Who did she think he was ...fucking royalty?

" She's still my wife Betty " he replied in a condescending manner.

" How are you feeling Jodie? " he turned to me " I wish you'd come home, I really miss you "

' Urgggh arghhh I want the sick bowl ' I thought . 'You false bastard you want to rape and kill me, I know . '

" Why is he here ? " I said, out loud " Get him away from me ...he attacked me....he's not my husband, "
I buried my face in the pillow " Don't let him near the house mam... please " I begged.

Josh looked at me with loathing . My mother didn't notice, but I did . Straight to my face and my mothers, he pretended to look hurt and sad .

" I'm sorry you feel like that Jodie " he said " I hope you'll soon feel differently ". Never in a million years I thought.

My mother and Josh talked about me going home to her and she told Josh she had no idea what time it would be and that the medics had insisted on an ambulance. He agreed with this, but said that he would be down to visit . My stomach churned once more. By now I was pretending to sleep in order to avoid him. After what seemed like eons, he left.

My mother tenderly stroked my hair, it must be difficult for her I thought, and she doesn't know the half of it. Oh I wish it was all finished with and Josh was out of my life and I could start again with my baby.

Not long after mam left , Vince arrived. He was glad that I was well enough to go home, but worried about my protection.

" I'm just on the end of the phone " he said " and I'll be down to see you everyday "

No Refuge

" Wait until I've told my mother the truth about Josh "
" Why? I could just be a friend? "

" I'll tell her as soon as the opportunity arises. "

" Ok, tell you what. You phone me when you want to see me . I don't want you to think I'm like your ex forcing myself upon you "

I smiled. This was what I liked about him. He understood.

" I' d take you home tomorrow only that would lead to a lot of questions, so you'd better use the ambulance " he continued.

" Thanks Vince, thanks for understanding. I don't know when I'll get the courage to tell my mam about you and the possibility that you're my baby's father "
"You'll know when it's right and you'll do it. I have total confidence in you ." he kissed me gently " and it IS my baby "

I laughed at his 'certainty' , but loved him for it . I knew that Vince would be there whatever happened in terms of a relationship or not. One thing I did know was that I could rely on him ...and that was a big thing to know.

Since Honey had told me about the activities in the club that Josh had been involved in, I had had many thoughts rolling about in my head. There were some things I wanted to ask Vince ....things I might not like the answer to.

" Vince, you know all the activities which go on in " The Club" , are you personally involved in any of them? "

" In what way? I make sure the club is safe. I do checks on the customers , I manage most of the finances in conjunction with the accountant and I report to the board. I do most of the Management tasks except for personnel which is Stan's bag "

" Ummm I sort of meant take part in them, use them? I mean you're single it's up to you what you do ". I knew I was going red.

" Ha ha ha ...are you jealous pretty lady? "

" No....not jealous ....sort of curious "

" Pity, I liked the idea of you being a bit jealous about me........ But the answer to your question is no , I don't take part in the so called ' activities ' . I've seen things as I go around making sure everything's ok. The pole dancers ....some like Honey are good dancers, the lap dancers I see briefly . The other activities as you call them I very seldom see anything let alone take part . Stan arranges the girls, but he doesn't hang around.
Strictly management that's me. To be honest none of it would even turn me on. It's a job, simple as.
Believe me or not, the activity I like is making love to the woman I love ....and there's a big difference in that. "

He looked right into my eyes. I could see desire there , I felt my heart beating too fast and returned his look. We kissed gently once more.

" Thanks for answering me Vince . I shouldn't really have put you on the spot. "

" No problem , pretty lady, you have a right to know. "

I didn't respond to that , I didn't want to go down that particular road at the moment . Technically I had no right to know anything . I knew Vince hoped for us to end up together, but my mind was too mixed up right now. I just held his hand and we sat quietly , then talked about mundane matters until he had to leave.

CHAPTER THIRTY SEVEN

"Jodie"

I had arrived home to my mothers yesterday. It was as if I had run a marathon with a backpack on. All I had done was come home from hospital.....but I was soooo tired. I managed to get upstairs to my room , with the crutch/ rail action and get into bed.

I slept for hours, a deep dreamless sleep in which I felt cocooned from pain. It was very different from the interrupted sections of sleep in hospital , when the noises or procedures woke you periodically .This was an uninterrupted rest , which my battered body badly craved.

I woke in the morning , feeling better than I had for weeks. I still felt sore and stiff, but the fog in my brain had started to clear. My mother brought my breakfast and a cup of tea up to my room . She had cooked a boiled egg exactly how I'd liked it as a child with toast soldiers.

" Thanks mam" I said " but I'm going to try and get downstairs in future. A bit longer every day . I want to get as strong as possible before the baby's born . I have to go to the Heath Hospital on Thursday, for a check up. They've transferred my care down here "

" Oh, that will be easier " said My mother, " Josh called last night, he wanted to come down to see you. I told him you were deeply sleeping and it would be best to leave it until tonight. "

" I don't want to see him at all mam . Not at all. Josh is to be banned from this house. "

" What do you mean? He's your husband ...he didn't attack you, you've got things mixed up "

" Mam, please listen to me....Sit in that chair " I pointed to a bedroom chair that was near my bed . She did as I asked and leaned forward to listen .

" What is it? What is it love? " she asked in a soft tone.

" I haven't got anything mixed up. Josh is my husband and Josh attacked me . "

" No, Jodie, a burglar attacked you " she spoke to me as if I was a retarded five year old.

" No, mam , Josh did " I stated this firmly .

" What on earth do you mean? "

" There's a lot I haven't told you. I'm afraid you are going to be a bit shocked. I didn't want to upset you, that's why I haven't said anything before.
"

" Jodie...you're worrying me now ....what have you kept from me? "

I took a deep breath before starting :
" The first time I left Josh and came here remember? "

" Yes". She nodded

" Well that time he had got annoyed because I had a makeover and a new dress. I looked a bit glamorous I suppose. Josh went berserk . We didn't just argue . He called me all sorts of names, ripped the dress off me and

No Refuge

raped me ...violently. He hurt me mam, I was sore. I left the house and came down here and told you we'd had a row. "

" Why didn't you tell me all this ? " her eyes were moist, her face stricken . he'd violated her little girl

" I didn't want to admit it I suppose. Then you said he'd explained, it was a misunderstanding, and Josh came down here full of apologies and said it wouldn't happen again. He had never been like it before , and I thought it must be a one off. "

" Oh Jodie, I would never have encouraged you to go back if you'd told me...I never expected ..Josh is so, so, believable "

" I know mam. That's why I went back. I tried to be the wife he wanted. He didn't want me to work , so I didn't. I watched the builders, helped in the surgery , made him meals , but still things were not right and then he became insanely jealous ...for no reason "

I decided not to explain about the club and Josh's involvement at the moment , she had enough to take in as it was.

" What happened then? "

" He hit me mam, hit me . Called me names again and got drunk. He was violent and forced me to have sex. As soon as he fell asleep I cleaned up and came down here again "

" Oh My God ! " Mam put her hands to her mouth. Her face was red and tears were streaming down her cheeks " Jodie, Jodie you've been through so much , on your own. You should have told me. I'd have stood up to the evil bugger . I could ring his bloody neck "

" Well you know what happened next. I stayed here for a while, and discovered I was pregnant. I really didn't know what to do. You thought I should make up with Josh and try and make a go of the marriage...especially with a baby. "

My mother was sobbing by now. She felt guilty that she had inadvertently sent me back to hell.

" There there mam" I comforted her " it's not your fault, I didn't tell you . "

" Oh Jodie, you should have. You really should have. . "

" Anyway, you can see what he did next" I indicated my body. " This was because the scan showed that the baby is small for 12 weeks and the radiographer thought perhaps my dates were wrong. He accused me of being unfaithful, hit me, raped me and pushed me down the stairs. Then he kicked me ...he was trying to kick the baby out of me " by now I was crying too. I sobbed when I remembered how he wanted to make me miscarry.

We both cried for a while, holding each other. I don't know who was comforting who. " Oh Jodie, I feel awful that you went through all that hell.. and I never knew. If you had told me ...."

" If I had, what could you have done mam? "

" I could have got your brothers to have given him a good hiding, for a start. You would have stayed here from the beginning and divorced the bugger.
"

I could see mam was now getting angry .

" Why haven't you told the police all this Jodie? "
she asked

" When I came to from the latest beating , he had concocted that burglary story and convinced the police and everyone that it w the truth. They would never have believed me, thinking I w suffering from amnesia., and confused. Also, he's a doctor. Doctors don't do things like that ." I snorted

" I'll never let him in here, or listen to him on the phone. " said mam. ." he is totally, totally persona non gratis . ....but you'll have to do something . Not only divorce him, but expose him . You don't want him having access to the baby , if he's capable of this. .....Somehow you will have to get legal action against him. "

" I have a plan, and I have some friends who are willing to help me. I also plan to expose all his violence in the divorce petition, and there may be some way I can take legal action .. I don't know yet. But I'm going to get my revenge ....one way or another. "

" If there's anyway I can help with your plan I will "

"I'll let you know . Thanks mam" we hugged one another. My mother was still very emotional and slumped in the chair , for a few moments.

I dressed and went downstairs, settling my self on the sofa . Day time TV for me, for the foreseeable future, I thought. I didn't mind a taste of Phillip and Holly, but Jeremy Kyle got on my nerves after a couple of days....all that shouting at each other !

I picked up my mobile and phoned Vince (couldn't I keep away from him?) He answered immediately and told me that he was at work sorting out the new mirrors which had been delivered. The idea was to make the dance room where the lap dancing took place into a hall of mirrors, with the dancers reflected from every angle. It sounded quite artistic to be honest, and would give the illusion of more dancers than there really was.

" How are you pretty lady and my pretty baby ? " asked Vince (I chuckled at the ' my baby ' reference)

" Better for a good nights sleep in a proper bed, without the hospital sounds. "

" Good, glad to hear it. I wish I was there with you . "

"I've told my mother about Josh. She's truly mortified, crying because she'd encouraged me to go back to him. "

" But she had no idea , you didn't tell her "

" I know but she feels she should have known some how . She wants to string him up "

" I'd give her a hand with that " Vince chuckled.

" I bet ! Anyway, why don't you come down here tonight . I can introduce you to my mam . You won't be able to stay mind , I haven't told her anything about us or the baby yet. One shock at a time "

" Don't worry I will be the height of propriety "

" What's happened to you? Swallowed a dictionary? "

" I knows 'ow t' talk proper when I wants "

We both burst out laughing . " See you later " I said, putting the phone down.

I told my mother a friend would be calling in later to see me and she seemed a bit happier after that.

In the meantime, I had a lot of phone calls :

Honey rang me. After some general chit chat, we started discussing 'the plan.' She had talked things over with Stan who was only too happy to help.

No Refuge

He had nothing but loathing for Josh and was extremely pleased for me and Vince . Although I don't know exactly what Honey told him, or if she exaggerated.

Stan's role was to get photographs and video evidence of Josh's proclivities. He managed to get some old footage from somewhere, and, as Josh was using the club on a daily basis at the moment , it was easy to get photographs etc.

I was told by Honey to write down all the things he'd done to me and his stupid, so called reasons. I had made rough notes and was going to ask my solicitor for more advice.

Lottie had agreed to lure Josh back to our house by promising him delights which he couldn't sample in the club. She was sure she could do it if she appealed to his vanity. Then, she would take bondage and other equipment with her and would get in him a position which would make it impossible for him to move .....then I would arrive and tell him exactly what I was going to do.

I was not yet sure of all the places I was targeting with the evidence of Josh"s perversions and cruelty. All I knew was that I wanted him struck off from practising and shamed within the community. I knew how much status and appearances mattered to Josh....so this is where I wanted to hit him .... right where it hurt.

My next contact was my solicitor. I had been in school with Linda Meredith, and she was bloody Good at her job. She told me to get all the evidence together and bring it in to her. She suggested sending it to the GMC, as many patients on his list as possible, the golf club , and to see the police and present it to them.

Even though Josh had convinced them over the burglar story, I might be able to persuade them differently, and they could certainly take my statements regarding the earlier incidents. In all cases of domestic abuse, proof was the most difficult thing to get. However, by showing his liking for cruelty, the police may decide there's enough evidence to bring a case against him. She thought it was definitely worth a try.

After all these conversations I was worn out and went back to bed for a rest. I slept soundly , dreaming of little babies floating on clouds whilst I watched as their hair changed from fair to dark. I remember in the dream feeling so relieved as the babies hair colour got darker and their eyes were midnight blue.

The next thing I knew was hearing my mothers voice, " Jodi, Jodi, Vince is here to see you. " I levered myself out of the bed and donned my best dressing gown. I managed to brush my hair which was now past my chin in length. And brushed it under into a bob. I put on a pale pink lipstick - goodness knows why . Taking my crutch I manoeuvred the stairs with the crutch/ handrail technique and hobbled into the living room .

There sat Vince with a cup of tea in his hand reclining on the sofa. My mother in the chair opposite smiling at him with shining eyes, and flushed cheeks . what had been happening?

" Josh called, said he was on his way down" mam addressed me " I gave him what for . You would've been proud of me ! " she bristled " told him he was a no good son of a bitch " I was very surprised at this turn of phrase " How come you said that mam? " I asked " That's what the goodies say to the baddies on those American programmes "she answered. I had to chuckle.

Vince had stood up by now, and helped me to sit beside him. He looked at a picture of my father that my mother always kept on the lamp table at the side of the sofa . It was one of him in full dress uniform looking strong and handsome.

"It was a big loss when Captain Traynor was killed " said Vince, picking up the portrait. " He was a true leader among men, and well respected "

No Refuge

My mouth flew open with surprise.

" You knew my father? " I asked

" Yes, I was in his regiment. That's where I first met Stan. Stan left about six years ago now, and I was discharged a year later, not long after your father died. I learned all my military and management skills from Captain Traynor. I had risen through the ranks and he recommended me for a commission. We saw some action together, in some of the worse hell holes in the world. "

" Why did you leave the army? "

" I had a personal tragedy, and went off the rails after that. Left the forces, felt they had nothing to offer me anymore, I felt life had nothing to offer me.

Stan saved me two years ago by getting me a job in the club. By then I knew all the villains, all their tricks. That and my military training made me ideal for the job "

" I am totally astounded. I had no idea. "

" I realised who you were when Umm.. Ahh ....someone mentioned your maiden name " Vince caught himself just in time. He was going to say " When I spent the night here. " but that was not for my mother's ears.

" I remember Ray talking about you. Lieutenant Vincent Saunders " said mam " Didn't you get some medal for bravery under fire ? "

" Ummm Yes....I did " replied Vince blushing with embarrassment.

" Must have been a good soldier to impress my Ray " stated Mam.

Vince surprised me more and more by the minute. Perhaps it was the qualities which reminded me of my father that attracted me to him.

Mam had made a chicken pie and invited Vince to eat with us. He enjoyed the meal, regaling Mam with stories of my father which were humorous or light hearted. I am sure, that by the dark, intense look that sometimes crossed his face, that he had plenty of other, far more unpalatable and gruesome tales in his repertoire . They had been through several bloody conflicts together. As my father had always said; ' it does things to a man'.

I was getting really tired , trying not to fall to sleep on the sofa, when Vince announced that he had to go.

My mother insisted on making him a cup of coffee before he went and discreetly absented herself into the kitchen. I wondered what vibes she had picked up ?

" I wish I could stay, just to hold you and protect you all night long " said Vince, gazing at me with those mesmerising eyes.

" I wish you could too. Don't worry , it will happen ...one day " I reassured him .

" I can't help being impatient . I want you now. I haven't felt like this for a very, very long time. "
I silenced him by putting a finger over his lips. I didn't want to hear anymore at the moment .

He pulled me gently into his arms, making sure he didn't hurt any of my injuries , and kissed me deeply. I could se those clouds of dark haired babies from my dreams.

Eventually we pulled apart, due to the loud noise my mother was making bringing in the coffee. It sounded as if she had a pair of cymbals with her.

We drank the coffee, talking of the minutiae of the day. Vince drained his cup and bid my mother good night, with a kiss on the cheek , which made her go coy and bashful again.

No Refuge

He kissed me with a peck on the lips and left. I wanted to accompany him to the door, but he wouldn't hear of it with my crutches and the pain I was in.

He left, pulling the door too, with a gentle slam .

" Seems a really nice fella " said Mam .

" Yes, I replied. really nice, "

CHAPTER THIRTY EIGHT

"Honey"

It had been a few weeks now since Honey and Jodie had been discharged from hospital.

Thankfully, both of them were recovering and had met up a couple of times.

Val had driven Honey and the kids to Cardiff, to see Jodie at her mothers, and Val and Betty had found a lot in common and become firm friends. They were both very protective and always alert for any pain or tiredness in the two younger women. It was like seeing two mother hens clucking over their chicks. Considering all they had been through in the last few months, Jodie and Honey found this very amusing, to suddenly be treated as children. They found it rather comforting, also, to be honest.

Stan had come with them once, to help finalise the plans for Jodie's " revenge" . He swore that he hadn't told Vince a thing , but warned them all:

" Don't underestimate Vincent. He's like a bloody Oracle , he finds out things you think he couldn't possibly know " .

Honey was pleased at how her relationship with Stan had developed. There was no romance, just a great friendship. After Glen, she was very , very wary of men. She had also decided that she didn't want to return to lap dancing at the club. Stan fully understood that . It would be too tiring and arduous for her now, considering her condition.

She was in remission, but no one knew what the future held, and in all likelihood she would always be on a cocktail of drugs.

Stan had obtained some old footage of Josh in bondage situations and recent photographs and DVDs of him carrying out sadistic acts on a few different girls. He also had a few pictures of his latest fad of Auto Erotic Asphixiation , and some limited film from the CCTV camera.

Jodie had met with Linda Meredith, the solicitor , and made statements regarding Josh's brutal attacks on her, including the last one. She had signed affidavits on Linda's recommendation , swearing that everything she had told was the truth. These statements stood a much stronger chance of precipitating a criminal case.

Copies had been made of all this evidence and were in padded envelopes ready to be sent to the GMC , the Practice Patient Group, The Golf Club and The Local Health Board.

Jodie had abandoned the plan for Lottie to persuade Josh into some sort of bondage at the surgery house. She decided this after a sleepless night, worrying about her own involvement. Was this being childish? She wanted a mature end to her marriage, and not to be brought don to his level.

" I am worth more than that " said Jodie " sorry everyone, I don't blame any of you making money out of it. It's just that it's not ME . I am going to arrange to meet Josh in the house alone.
No tricks, no smoke or mirrors, just me and him. I am going to end this marriage on my terms , legally and respectably , not as part of his perversions or absurdities"

" Fair enough " agreed Honey " but we won't leave you alone with him.. We'll all be outside , in case he tries to attack you...and you are taking a rape alarm with you and giving me a spare key. "

No Refuge

Honey thought that Josh deserved more of a punishment than public humiliation and loss of status. However Jodie assured her that this would be devastating to Josh. He was her husband and it was her plan. They would all support her.

•••

"Jodie"

I telephoned Josh and asked if we could meet.
" Oh, suddenly you want to meet up with me do you? " he sneered " I thought you and your witch of a mother loathed me " .

" I think that now I'm feeling a bit better, we need to finalise some things "

" Finalise what? ….the only thing I want is for you to get back here, where you're supposed to be, and we prepare for the baby "
At his words, my blood grew cold. A shiver went through me .

" I am never coming back Josh. you had better get your head around that . However, we do need to talk about finances, property and some other issues. I also need to collect some of my things "

" If you are not coming back, you'll get fuck all off me "

" We still need to talk. I'll come to the house at 6 pm on Tuesday , because surgery finishes early that day. "

" OK. But unless you return, it's fucking pointless "

•••

Tuesday evening , mam and myself arrived at Honey's around 5pm.

We sat drinking tea and talking. I was rubbing my hands together, they were clammy and I could feel perspiration on my brow. This was not something that I was looking forward to, but it was something which had to be done

" I feel nervous , just seeing Josh . Let alone presenting him with my revenge . He's an evil, cruel bastard you know " I explained to the others.

" You don't have to go at all you know " said Honey " We could all come with you as a group . Alternatively, you could send out all the stuff and just sit back and see what happens "

" No. I want him to know what I've discovered about him and what I'm going to do about it . Together with the divorce papers and my affidavits on his cruelty to me. I have to do it for my own courage and self esteem "

Just then , there was a knock on the door. " I'll get it. It will be Stan " cried Honey getting up to open it.

However, she returned with Stan and Vince. " I thought you hadn't told him about it ?" I accused Stan

" I didn' t " he replied " somehow he knew ". He muttered darkly.

" I knew something was up by the way you were all acting " Vince looked at me and my mother. " You'd be hopeless secret agents ha ha "

" OK. you're here now. I'm going to see Josh, show him all the evidence I've got against him , serve him the divorce papers and make sure he knows he' ll pay for all he's done to me ! " I said.

" You can't go and see him on your own! " Vince objected " He's a nut case. He'll attack you ..and you're still using a crutch "

No Refuge

" I've got plenty of back up " I indicated everyone in the room " and Honey's got a spare door key, and I've got a rape alarm " I held it up to show him

" I'm still not happy " pouted Vince

" Well wait right outside the door "

" Don't worry I will "

" You two are bickering like an old married couple " said my mother. We both shut up and stared at one another.

I picked up my jacket, got the bundle of papers together and asked " Who's giving me a lift? "

Everyone seemed to speak at once. I ended up with Stan and Vince, obviously . Val, my mother and Honey following in Val' s 4 x4 . Natalie stayed with the twins. Our convoy got to the surgery in less than ten minutes. we parked out of sight around the waste land at the side of the building.

I clambered out of the car, levering myself with my crutch on one side, Vince on the other. Then I hobbled around the wall to the front of the building .
I placed my key in the lock and opened the door.
' At least he hasn't changed the locks ' I thought.

I looked in the living room.....no sign of Josh . the new modern kitchen ....not there. I shouted his name " Josh, Josh ...I'm here .....it's Jodie " Nothing. This was strange. I was certain Josh would be here for our meeting. Then aI heard a noise from upstairs , " Mmmm.......mmmm....bang bang " . I called up the stairs " Josh..are you there? " I heard some more humming noises.

Bravely, I decided to investigate and made my way up the stairs. I was getting quite fast with my crutch/ rail manoeuvre now.

..The door to the master bedroom was open. There was Josh, spread eagled on the bed, naked and handcuffed to the bedrails by his hands and feet. A large piece of duct tape was placed over his mouth.

I gasped in astonishment ....then laughed . , He looked so funny , with his pale skin and knobbly knees exposed to the world and his very flaccid penis almost invisible. . " M...Mmmm.mm. .....mm.m " he said , moving his head back and fore. I still laughed . .., Finally I removed the duct tape, in one swift movement.

"Fucking bastard ! " he said

" I hope you don't mean me " I replied

" No, that fucking whore! "
I was uninterested as to what whore he was on about.

" I think I'll sit down and we can have our talk "

" Get these fucking things off me! " he roared

" No.....We talk first.....then I'll find the keys"

Josh shouted and performed for a while longer whilst I took no notice of him. I found a note and some keys at the far end of the room , on the dressing table in the bay window. The note read:

" Couldn't leave you to an unrestrained Josh .....whatever you said . Here's the keys for when you finish. Just unlock his hands and go before he can get free. ". Love Lottie & the gang xxx"

Once Josh had stopped ranting and raving,and was out of breath , I started again.

" We are going to talk, as I intended, and when we have finished I will unlock you and go . Agree to this, or I am off now.....with the keys "

No Refuge

Eventually, he nodded his head in agreement " Ok I've got no choice I suppose "

" In here Josh " I began, holding up a large envelope. " I have photographs and film of you carrying out many perverted sexual practices .... especially sadistic, cruel actions. All our married life you used and abused other women "

" No, no, that's not true " he argued

" Yes it is Josh ....I have proof " I spewed out the photographs of him fucking and whipping women in bondage gear,over the bed so he could see the images

" That wasn't enough for you, though was it? " I continued " You had to abuse me, rape me, and cause me such terrible injuries that I nearly lost ny baby. "

" You've got it wrong, you hurt me by your behaviour, you weren't a proper wife "

" Rubbish....you didn't want a wife. You wanted your own personal " sub" as they call it in BDSM circles ...and you should know. You were totally prolific in that area.... You cruel, conniving, bastard. I don't know what you were subjected to in childhood to make you such an evil man. That's for the psychiatrists to work out not me . "

" Look Jodie, let me out of these manacles. lets talk properly. I'll make it up to you. I promise. Well be happy again "

" I have never heard such bloody bullshit. Sometimes I think you even believe yourself. I have made statements about every attack and every rape you have perpetrated on me. I have signed affidavits, sworn in a court on the bible, to this effect. ....and do you know what else I have dome ? "

" No, no, ...what ? "

" I have copied everything. every picture, CCTV image, film, every statement ....the lot . And who do you think I have sent them to? ......ah ah...it gets funnier and funnier .....the GMC, The golf Club, Your patients and the local health board. Oh yes, I nearly forgot...........and to the police ! "

" No, you're having me on. You wouldn't do that. I'll be ruined. I'll have no job ...I'll be humiliated . I might even be prosecuted . ...how the fuck did you find out? "

" That's for me to know ....and you to worry about."

"Please don't do this Jodie, please........remember what we had! "

" We had fuck all...that's what we had....fuck all. "

I got up and unlocked one hand..... quickly I moved back out of his reach .... and put the key for the handcuffs balancing on the edge of the bed, where, if he pulled his freed arm right over to the left, he would be able to grip them.

I walked to the door as he scrabbled for that key , still holding onto the key for the feet manacles. As I got to the door, I threw them, and they fell on the floor near the bed. It would take him a while to shift and pick them up. He couldn't catch me...I'd be well gone by the time he was free and he would be stiff and numb , as well as naked.

I made my way downstairs, out of the front door ....and straight into the arms of Vince.

He helped me into his car, and we made our way back to Honey's house. Everyone was still congregated there, ready for the post mortem.

No Refuge

I told them all what had happened, and considering Josh's volatile nature, I had been glad of the fact that he was secured. It had also made him look ridiculous, which had calmed my nerves.

" That was my idea " said Honey " I know you had decided to confront him in an adult to adult conversation, but I don't trust him as far as I could throw him. I persuaded Lottie to turn up at 5pm and persuade him into some " games", then leave him there, trussed up like a chicken. "

" I got her note. Thanks Honey " I said, giving her a hug around the shoulders.

" Well, now he knows what's what " said my mother

" He's going to suffer a great deal of backlash, when those folders are received. "

" Yes, and you should have a good divorce settlement " pointed out Val.

" I'll just have to wait and see " I said " What I do know is that I feel a lot better for having confronted him. I feel more empowered than I ever have and finally feel that he no longer has any control over me. "

" That's the most important thing " agreed Vince.
" But what about the baby? ". His face furrowed, he looked really anxious

" My solicitor said that with all the evidence I have of his nature, she can get an injunction to stop him seeing the baby and a court would only allow him supervised access in a designated centre. "

My mother and Vince looked somewhat relieved. However, I would tell Vince, when we were alone that if the baby proves to be his, not Josh's, then we would put his name on the birth certificate, and Josh would have no rights whatsoever.

" I ' m really weary now " I said " I'll soon be making my way home. This will seem like a different life one day ...and Josh become just a memory. Are you ready to go back to Cardiff ? Mam "

" Yes" replied my mother readily " I feel pretty worn out myself.....lets get going ".

She handed me my coat, Vince helped me on with it, as she put on her jacket.

" Let me come home with you " whispered Vince .

" No, it's OK , my mothers driving and she'd prefer me in the car with her. I'll see you tomorrow."

" I 'll come with you...Stan can take the car. I want to make sure you're safe. Don't worry, I'll sleep on the sofa. I bet your mother wouldn't object "

" No, I expect she wouldn't " I laughed " proper little charmer you are .... Lieutenant. However, the answer is no . I just want to think and process stuff on my own . you do understand don't you ? "

" Yeh, OK . I suppose so " he shrugged , grimacing.

We said our goodbyes , promising to ring everyone tomorrow, and to keep an eye out for the inevitable fall out ....news ....whatever.

Mam and I got in her little car and sped off home to Cardiff.

" Interesting night " commented mam, whilst we had a cup of tea before making our way to bed .

" Yes, it was. I just hope that my relationship with Josh will soon become a thing of the past "

No Refuge

" Let's hope so love, let's hope so ………… Vince seems to think a lot of you . "

My mother was on a fishing expedition.

" Yes, we've become quite friendly "

" I've seen the way you look at each other. ……..Especially the way he looks at you "

" Mmmm. I don't want to talk about it at the moment Mam. I've got enough to think about . We'll discuss it again, right ? "

" OK , I've got all the time in the world "

I gave her a peck on the cheek, and a quick hug . Then made my way wearily to bed with my now skilled crutch/rail action.

Undressing , slowly , I felt as if I had been through an obstacle race. The strange confrontation with Josh, the planning of it all, the discussions , meetings and compiling of evidence had taken its toll. I had become a stronger, empowered woman, in charge of her own life . However, at the moment I had no idea where this new life was going to take me, and I was too tired to think about it.

' Best to leave all decisions until tomorrow ' I thought, as I crawled into bed, pulled the duvet over me and put out the light.

CHAPTER THIRTY NINE

"Jodie"

I slept deeply for a while before the edges of slumber lifted.

I was aware that something had awoken me , but not what it was.

I felt cold…..there was a draft coming from the window. ' surely I shut that when I came to bed ?' I thought.

Every morning I open the window before going downstairs , to freshen the room. However, in the night I shut it due to the cold at this time of year. Now, it was at least a little open and making me shiver…….perhaps I hadn't shut it properly?

I lay there and slowly became aware of a presence in the room.

I knew someone was there, I could hear a slight movement " Mam, is that you? " I called …there was no answer. I was certain I could detect someone or something …..a slight rustle and a creak….my heart began to beat faster. I didn't believe in ghosts …but what the hell was this?

Then a louder movement " Vince ? " I whispered. No answer…." Vince, is that you? " I held my breath ….nothing. …..something dropped on the floor…I jumped, and started to shiver…who's there?

Suddenly …I felt a body drop onto the bed. I breathed in heavily " What the fuck do you mean ….Vince? I was right all along " Oh my God it was Josh ! How the hell did he get in here ? I remembered the window! My window was allocated directly above the roof of the porch….he had climbed onto the porch and got in through the window.

No sooner did I realise this ….than I felt my pillow being put over my face….I squirmed and moved my head, I took in a deep breath of air. He pressed down harder " You fucking cunt. Did you think I'd let you get away with what you did to me? I'll make sure you never get up to something else again…..I'm going to finish you off …and with a bit of luck Ill get away with it. I know how to make your death look natural, and if not, they'll never prove a thing . "

He kept pushing the pillow down. I moved my head from side to side….I.tried to kick but pain from my fracture swept through my body.

He was still trying to smother me as my hands flailed and I tried to get at his face …I caught his skin with my right hand and tried to stick my thumb in his eye…. all I managed was to scratch his cheek …I caught the ends of the pillow….and tried to pul it off…he grabbed both my hands with one of his , and leaned across the pillow with his other arm and pressed down on me forcing my face to be in direct contact with the cotton material of the pillow case he was pushing…pushing……pushing . I was losing oxygen…..everything was swirling….. it was becoming black …….

Suddenly the pressure stopped and my hands were freed …I threw off the pillow……I gasped for breath and kept gasping. My lungs burned . I realised that I had been holding my breath to try and survive as long as possible . My breath came out in painful gasps .

The lights went on ……….there was a startling tableaux of Josh on the floor his nose bleeding, Vince holding him in an arm lock and my mother standing in the door way.

" Phone the police Betty " said Vince, looking at my mother who appeared to have become petrified with shock. She turned to look for the phone. I continued to take in deep breaths . Looking at Josh and Vince in disbelief .

The police arrived promptly . A male and female officer who introduced themselves as Sergeant Phillips and Constable Delaney . They asked what had happened and Vince quickly filled them in.

No Refuge

I nodded when they asked me if his account was accurate, but my throat was too sore to speak. They told me they would be back in a day or two to take a statement off me. Vince was very much in control, Josh didn't even speak except to mutter " she has ruined me, ruined me " they handcuffed him and took him off . ' Not his usual use of handcuffs ' I thought.

I was still sitting up in bed in the same position as when Vince had saved me. My lungs and throat hurt and although I wanted to cry, I found that I couldn't . My eyes felt dry and scratchy, with an emotional pain behind them, but a worn out tear duct. I had gone through so much I was empty....empty of emotion.

Mam sat on the bed by the side of me it was now 4 am and she looked so very tired. All this worry over me had aged her , I felt guilty for putting her through so much anguish.

" Are you OK love ? " she asked , pushing my hair back off my face. I nodded , and pointed to my throat to indicate difficulty in talking. " alright " I croaked, in a whisper. " go back to bed " .

She did as I told her ,too weary to argue, so glad to lie down.

This left me and Vince alone.

" How we're you here? " I whispered hoarsely

" By taking no notice of you again " he replied

" I have had men like Josh working for me. Basically, they are psychopaths . Although handy in warfare, they need keeping on a tight lead. There was no way Josh would take all that off you All that humiliation and exposure , then to be let physically free ....he was bound to explode ......they don't think .... not like normal people..........I knew he'd want revenge ....Only question was.... when? He might have bided his time ...days, weeks , months , but luckily he was so het up he reacted as quickly as possible . "

" luckily? " I croaked

" Yes, otherwise I would have had no sleep for months maybe. Anyhow, I got here just in time , noticed the window ajar……got in through the back door and caught him, trying to suffocate you …the slimy bastard. Well, he's in jail for now , and with luck , if they charge him with attempted murder he'll be remanded in custody " .

" Vince, will he ever leave me alone ? "

" Hopefully he will be in jail for a long time pretty lady . Don't worry . Try and get some sleep . Move over I want to hug you "

I moved over gingerly, trying not to set off the pain again. Vince lay down next to me and put his arms around me. He looked at me and once again, I was lost in his eyes . He gave me a deep loving kiss, then nursed me back to sleep until the morning light was bright in the sky .

The next day , my throat and lungs felt better , and I insisted that Vince go to work and my mother go out with Aunty Joyce as she had previously arranged. I was fed up of people changing the routine of their lives to fit around me.

In any case Anita rang me and. Had a long chat as I gave her the news about Josh and the " revenge I had taken followed by his subsequent attack. She had visited me in hospital, but I hadn't seen her since being discharged. She was shocked by all my news and said she had never met anyone else with such an eventful life .

I rested, had a snack whilst waiting for Mam to return , when who should turn up but Honey and Val. They had heard about last night and wanted to see how I was.

" I can't believe it said Honey, I thought you had sorted him out . "

" So did I " I sighed " I'm worried that I 'll never be rid of him. "

No Refuge

They both reassured me that now he'd actually been arrested, he'd be sent away to jail. They were convinced that this would sort the matter ......I wasn't
. There was still the divorce to go through, my belongings, finances and , of course, the baby. The truth was....the baby could be Josh's ...however hopeful Vince acted.

They were still there when the phone rang. It was my solicitor, Linda.

" Hi Jodie " she began

" Hi Linda "

" Bit of bad news I'm afraid " my heart sank , what had happened now ?

" What is it Linda ?"

" Josh got bail , they charged him with ABH not attempted murder . Reckoned there was not enough evidence to prove he was trying to murder you ." she snorted with derision " He's got one hell of a good solicitor ...Tony Payne , criminal lawyer . expensive, but best in the business "

" Bloody hell! So he's out " I could see Val and Honeys astonished expressions

" 'fraid so. The good news is, I managed to get an injunction against him as regards to you. He is not to come within ten miles of your address in Cardiff, otherwise he will be arrested and bail revoked. Also, he has to agree a time and date with me when he vacates the surgery house for you to go there and collect your belongings and he will absent himself for two hours . The rest; finances and stuff, we try to negotiate with his solicitor.
You will have to testify in his court case probably.
Unless he pleads guilty ....but we'll go into that when we get a date "

" Well thanks Linda. I'm just disappointed he's not locked up "

" I know, but he's a bloody slippery bastard ...all these doctors are . "

" Yes, too true. Bye Linda "

" Bye Jodie, take care "

I put down the phone and Honey, wide eyed said
" They left the bastard out? "

" Yes, charged with actual bodily harm ...that's a bails or offense , and it's his first one"

" Umph.....there's no bloody justice "

" Just what I was thinking. "

We all moaned about Josh , the law and crafty solicitors . Then started talking about happier subjects .....I was fed up to the back teeth with Josh.
Val and Honey left in time to pick up the children from school , and my mother returned.

" Sorry to have missed the girls " she said " but Joyce kept me talking about Sharon and her new job in MacDonalds . According to Joyce, she's bloody running the place. "

" Aye she would say that ." I replied " I've had a call off Linda Meredith ....Josh is out on bail ! "

" Oh no! Surely not ....that's ...that's...ridiculous "

" Ridiculous or not...it's the truth . " I sighed

" Isn't there anything you can do? He'll be back here again "

" There's an injunction on him not to come within ten miles of me "

No Refuge

My Mother made a sound which meant " I bet " .

I telephoned Vince to tell him about Josh, but he already knew ....I should have known !

" I'm coming down tonight ....and staying. I don't care what you tell me " he said

" Ok ...that will make me feel safer anyhow . I'll tell my mother "

" Righto pretty lady see you later ....kiss kiss"
I laughed and put down my phone

" Mam, Vince is staying here tonight ...just in case "
I told her .

" Fine " she said . I'll get some blankets for the sofa.....unless you have other ideas ? " she gave me what used to be called ' an old fashioned look' .
" No, sofa will be good " I replied too embarrassed to say anything else.

Vince arrived late, around 10pm . " Very busy in the club " he explained .
I was thankful he was here now, he could have stayed until the club closed. People were still changing their routines for me.

Mam had gone out surprisingly , to Bingo with some of her friends. She had taken her car and arrived back just before Vince. " Any luck? "I asked " No, " she replied" but I had a good night "

We all had a bite to eat and a glass of wine . We chatted briefly about the Josh situation until everyone caught on that I was sick of talking about him. So we changed to other subjects .

I was surprised at the amount of travelling Vince had done and that our favourite countries for holidaying were the same . However,Vince had been to Madeira and fallen in love with it. I hadn't visited that particular country , but he made it sound lovely

" I will take you there pretty lady , you will have the most wonderful holiday of your life " he said, staring into my eyes

I smiled back at him, imagining us on a sun kissed beach.

Yawning , I announced that I was off to bed. My mother agreed it was time for sleep, and pulled out the blankets for Vince to lie on the sofa.

" Here you are Vince , I've put a little nightcap of whiskey, on the side table for you. , and moved it next to the sofa . " she said handing him the blankets . Vince's face fell, it nearly hit the floor.

" Thanks Betty" he said to her " I ' ll make myself really comfy and have a read whilst I'm sipping the whiskey "
He got up, took the blankets and made his way to the living room. Just as he got to the door my mother said " perhaps you'd prefer to bunk in with Jodie ...she's got a very comfortable bed ?"

Vince went pink ...I could tell by his earlobes and I was gobsmacked , my mouth wide open like some idiots. " You must think I came up the river in a banana boat " she said to me " I couldn't wait any longer for you two to tell me that you're an 'item,' as they call it nowadays. "

I laughed, and so did Vince . We both gave her a hug " Thanks mam " I said " for being so understanding"

" All I want is your happiness" she replied " You should know that by now . "

Vince and I made our way to bed. He helped me up the stairs, and gently took me in his arms when we reached the bedroom. He undressed me first, and helped me into the bed, checking that I was comfortable , with no pain.

No Refuge

Then he undressed and joined me. I enjoyed watching him take off his clothes and reveal his well toned body . I realised how attracted to him I was ...in all ways ....physically, mentally and emotionally ...that was quite a heady feeling.

However, I had once been attracted to Josh , I was still wary . Afraid of my own judgements and unsure of what I truly wanted from life.

He held me so gently, that I felt like crying....that anyone could be so considerate. He kissed me ...light feathery kisses over my face and body. I kissed him back with more intensity. I was aware we would have to be extremely careful if we made love, due to my injuries and condition. Softly, he caressed my breasts and touched my pubic area. " Does it hurt ? " he asked " No " I replied " if you're very gentle " I could feel his hard erection against my belly. The belly which held a child.

I touched him , slid my hand down the full length of his penis and ver, very, carefully guided him into me. We lay facing each other , on our sides. Vince started moving slowly inside me . Gently pushing in and drawing out. He was waiting for a command from me, as I held him tight and kissed and caressed, and tasted his musky skin. " A little faster " I said, and he started to move more quickly , but still carefully . " ohhhhhh " he whispered " are you ok? " " Yes " I replied, as he speeded up and I began to feel an orgasm building up in me . I was too nervous to move my pelvis, but I clenched my muscles around him , and he responded by making a low moan " Ohhhhh Jodie, Jodie " he cried " I felt the pleasure building...it was reaching bursting point " Ohhhh Vince " I moaned as I felt the utter, ecstatic release . He moved even faster as he felt me come , and gave a few strong thrusts, as he reached orgasm and shuddered with fulfilment.

" Oh my God , Jodie " said Vince " I never thought .....I wasn't going to ...but I love you so much ....so very much....it was wonderful ".

" Oh yes Vince truly, truly, fantastic. I have never felt like this before.... never. " I replied.

We still held each other, not wanting to part, enjoying the closeness of each others bodies.

" Oh damn " said Vince " I knew something was missing ......the glass of whiskey your mother left for me ". I laughed, then Vince joined in. We kissed deeply, and continued holding each other until we fell into a warm, contented sleep.

• • •

The following morning when I awoke, for a few moments I couldn't figure out who was with me , then Vince opened his midnight blue eyes. I smiled with relief and gladness.

We got up and took turns using the bathroom and dressing. Going downstairs to the kitchen I felt my embarrassment return at the idea of seeing my mother. We entered the kitchen, where she was already sitting with a fresh cup of tea.

" Want a cuppa both? " she asked cheerily

" Yes please" said Vince , as confident as ever. I slunk into the nearest chair, nodding my head and blushing.

" What's your plans for today then ? " asked my mam.

" I've got to go into work by 11am as there's a meeting with the consortium , about the rest of the renovations. It will probably be a busy day for me . Is it alright if I come back tonight , Betty? " asked Vince .

" Yes, of course love " she replied. I was still silent.
" I'll make us all a nice chicken dinner. " said Mam.

" Thanks " I finally muttered " I need to go shopping today . Will you drive me to Asda or do I need to book a taxi ? " I asked my mother.

No Refuge

" Don't worry love, I'll take you " she I replied.

We were finishing our breakfast when there was a knock on the door. My Mother answered it and returned with two police officers ...the same two as the other night . Sargent Phillips and Constable Delaney.

" Good morning " said the sergeant.

" Do you want some tea or coffee? Maybe some toast ?" Offered my mother .

" No thanks said Constable Delaney, the female officer. " Would you mind if we sat down? "

" Not at all ...take a seat " my mother indicated the empty chairs and an armchair in the corner. They sat at the table.

" Have you come to take my statement? " I asked them.

"No , Mrs Harrison " said Sergeant Phillips
" Afraid we've some unpleasant news for you. "

I was startled . What could they mean?

" What news ? " I asked, grabbing Vince's hand .

" I'm afraid your husband, Josh Harrison has been found dead "

" How? when ?where? " I gabbled

" He was found by his receptionist this morning when he failed to turn up for surgery . It appears, at first sight, that he died as a result of a sex game. Obviously, we can't be certain until the post mortem " I gasped with shock " Do you mean auto erotic asphyxiation ? " I asked

" Yes, Do you know if he had ever tried this before? "

" Yes'm I believe it was his latest thrill. I have photos of him doing it."

" Those would be very helpful Mrs Harrison "

" I'll get some for you " I got up in a daze. Walked across the room with my crutch and opened a drawer in the sideboard . I took out an envelope of photos and gave them to the male officer.

My mother and Vince hadn't spoken....they seemed just as shocked as me.

" I'm sorry, but you will have to identify the body later today " said the Sergeant

" Can't I do that? " offered Vince

" Sorry sir , it's got to be a close relative and Mrs Harrison seems to be the only one. "

" I'll do it . " I said " I'll be OK. When exactly did he die?

" Can't be absolutely certain at the moment , but looks like some time late last night or early hours of this morning "

" Oh, I see. What time do you want me for the identification and where? "

" In the hospital mortuary 2pm? "

" Alright , I'll be there "

" Anything else you'd like to ask me ? "

" Not at the moment . I'd like all the details after the PM "

No Refuge

" You can have them if you request them . There'll also have to be an inquest, but to be honest with you, it looks pretty straight forward "

My mother saw the police officers out, as Vince held me tightly as I sobbed.

I felt really strange, there was a sort of hole in my stomach and I felt sick. I was crying for the loss of a life, and the loss of the person I used to think he was . The dreams I had, a few short months ago when we married and the relationship I though we had for two years....I cried for those .
I also felt extremely guilty as I realised that the first emotion I felt, and still felt to some degree, was relief.

Vince sat me down, and kept holding me. My mother gave me tea. I started talking, trying to explain the mix of emotions swirling around inside me . I didn't lobe him, hadn't loved him since he knocked it out of me . But I still felt compassion for a needless death of a young man who , if he had wanted, could have changed and had a good life . A respectable life , even a successful one. Why did he throw it all away?

Obviously the police seemed to think it was a sex game gone wrong. I sincerely hoped this was the case. However, nudging at the back of my mind was the thought that it might have been suicide. That he didn't bite the orange, but allowed himself to die out of despair. Despair at what I had done to him? Vince and mam reassured me that it was not my fault. He chose his own path in life and if he did commit suicide, then it was his decision. Logically I accepted this ....but emotionally....? That's a hard thought to banish.....a thought which would occasionally haunt me in the depths of the night, for a long time to come.

Even deeper and darker in my thoughts was the possibility of murder. Did someone make it look like a sex game and deliberately kill him . Someone who he had made an enemy of, or hurt ? I didn't want to consider this . .... Who could it be ? One of the consortium who saw him as a loose cannon ; One of the girls he'd used and abused; ....Stan , on Honeys wishes ;.............or even.....Vince ?

I mustn't think like this . Could he have made love so gently to me last night after killing my husband? Oh dear God, I hoped not........but he had been in the military and they were trained to do all sorts of things. ....I knew I would never ask him , for fear of the answer , because I knew he wouldn't lie to me... he would tell me the truth.

We all sat in relative silence . Vince didn't go to work. I didn't go shopping. At 2 o' clock he took me to identify Josh's body.

●●●

The funeral was held in Llwydcoed Cremitorium two weeks later, on a sunny day in May . I was barely five months pregnant , hardly showing yet.

We were all there ....my gang. Vince, Stan, Honey, Val, Anita, my Mother Betty , Aunty Joyce and Sharon (who wouldn't miss a funeral for the world)

Even Lottie, two other girls and a representative from the consortium ......some Russian bloke , had turned up. There were very few from the community. One or two patients who had thought Josh was a top doctor , and the receptionists ;Sheila and Ivy. Not a large funeral for a doctor.

At the last moment , Josh's cousin and his wife turned up. I was surprised to say the least. Perhaps they hoped for some freebies, or a mention in the will. And of course, I was there.

The usual hymns were sung and a eulogy was read. Then the red curtain was drawn across his oak coffin...and he was gone...forever.

The post mortem showed that cause of death was from suffocation due to a rope which was tied around his neck.

The inquest found that Dr Harrison had died as a result of an auto erotic sex game which had gone wrong and the verdict was "DEATH BY MISADVENTURE . "

No Refuge

I was his sole beneficiary and had to decide what to do with the practice and house . He would never see the baby, if indeed it was his. I felt sad for a life wasted by cruelty and perversion, but all my tears had been spent.

I walked out of the Crematorium with Vince's arm around me . The garden of memorial was ablaze with the colours of Spring flowers, waving jauntily in the breeze.

This sight reminded me of life continuing, and of new life waiting to be born....just like the baby I carried in my womb. This child would hold promise for the future and be dearly loved by all it's family .....whether they were blood relatives or not, it didn't really matter.

What did matter was love....love and gentleness ....free from the control and cruelty of the past.

The End

Made in the USA
Charleston, SC
02 January 2014